FREE
SCOTLAND

To Janet

Saor Alba

Bill A.

The chorus of the Gerry Cinnamon song "Hope over Fear", page 73, is available at https://gerrycinnamon1.bandcamp.com/releases

Published under licence 2018 by Searching Finance Ltd.

ISBN: 978-1-907720-93-2

Front Page Graphic
This graphic, which I came across during Indyref1, belongs to Sookie Sooker. He has very kindly given permission to use the graphic. In a very considerable way, it was an inspiration for this book. You can find his fantastic work on:
https://sookiesooker.deviantart.com/
https://www.redbubble.com/people/sookiesooker

FREE
SCOTLAND

BILL AUSTIN

About the author

Bill served as a Higher Executive Officer with HM Customs & Excise (C&E) between 1977 and 2007 in the UK (including Northern Ireland), Republic of Ireland and France. Concurrently, he also served as a Territorial Army officer from commissioning at the Royal Military Academy Sandhurst in 1985. Between 1999 and 2007 the author served on continuous "Special Leave" for those eight years from HM C&E to the UK Regular Army, in the rank of major, serving in anti-smuggling roles on four Operational Tours; one United Nations tour in Sierra Leone, West Africa, and three NATO tours in the Balkans.

As a result of this extensive hands-on professional anti-smuggling experience the author crystallised this work in 2010-2011 with additional full-time primary research at the Department of War Studies, University of Glasgow resulting in a "Distinction" dissertation, titled "UK military involvement in anti-smuggling 1969-2010", gaining a Master of Letters (MLitt).

He worked on Customs reform projects as an international Customs consultant in Ethiopia, Djibouti, Democratic Republic of Congo, Sierra Leone and the Balkans.

Bill is also a Chartered Member of the Institute of Logistics and Transport (CMILT) and a Member of the International Network of Customs Universities (MINCU).

About Searching Finance

Searching Finance Ltd is a dynamic new voice in knowledge provision for the financial services and related professional sectors. For more information, please visit www.searchingfinance.com.

CONTENTS

Heartfelt thanks to Dr Colin Shaw, Queens University Belfast, who brought coherence to this project through his editing skills. To my very good friend, Dr Colin Fleming[1], whose discussions, over an occasional dram, on the strategic genius of Carl Phillip Gottfried von Clausewitz concluded much of the thinking behind a fictitious Scots rebellion. To an anonymous Scots ex-Royal Marine SNCO who gave up time to carry out credibility checks in order to spot, and therefore eliminate, self-inflicted military howlers (and keeping onside with the Official Secrets Act) my sincere appreciation. Finally, my grateful indebtedness to my wife, Lorraine, whose proof reading, pertinent thoughts and questions kept the story alive.

---

1   Dr Colin Fleming *Clausewitz's Timeless Trinity: A Framework For Modern War* (Ashgate, 2013)

This book is dedicated to every special, individual 16 year old who comes onto the Scots electoral register. Yesterday. Today. Tomorrow. These personalities will be eligible to vote in Indyref2. You are Scotland's future. Please save us all, soon. We can easily forgive a child who is afraid of the dark; the real tragedy of life is when men are afraid of the light.

This book is devoted to *my two fantastic, inspirational sons W.M. & C.J. Austin.*

INTRODUCTION

*"...not because we didn't like the British, but we love Freedom better.
I think all of us have the right to be free."* [1]

DAW AUNG SAN SUU KYI, a political prisoner of 15 years in her homeland of Myanmar, said these beautiful words to a very privileged audience of British Army Officer Cadets, and staff, at the Royal Military Academy Sandhurst (RMAS) on Friday 26th October 2013. This lady had been awarded the Nobel Peace Prize in 1991, "for her non-violent struggle for democracy and human rights". Her message was very well understood, and received.

She delivered an inspirational speech praising the concept of freedom which was eagerly heard by those present, who serve to lead, in a non-political army which defends the right to freedom. A noble cause, indeed. Many have, and will, serve in United Nations missions, under UN Charter which enshrines self-determination.

In the audience were many young Scots, some from our Universities Officer Training Corps based in Glasgow, Edinburgh, St Andrews, Dundee, Stirling and Aberdeen. The location and audience were at the very heart of the British Empire, and her opening words above, weren't lost on me during the months before Scotland's first Independence Referendum in 2014.

The thought percolated in my mind afterwards, "What if Scotland votes yes to freedom which London then rejects? Would this military audience enforce a political decision from their Westminster government to suppress freedom?" This book, of fiction, was born.

---

1   https://www.youtube.com/watch?v=s3ECulJ-fik, seen 26 July 2016.

1

In June 2017, extremely disturbingly, the UK government appointed the leader of the reactionary right-wing British nationalists in Scotland to a military role with the rank of colonel cancelling immediately the status of a non-political UK army which Daw Aung San Suu Kyi admired.

Aung San, father of Daw Aung San Suu Kyi, formed a revolutionary army in December 1941 to overthrow imperial British rule in their colony of Burma. His paymasters were the Imperial Japanese Army but in 1944,"...the British Government announced its intention to grant self-government to Burma within the British Commonwealth... [we discussed] the best method of throwing the Japanese out of the country as the next step toward self-government."[2]

Burma became independent on 4 January 1948, but not before the exploited Aung San was murdered by British weapons fired by Burmese collaborators, manipulated by the British, in July 1947 when it became apparent that he wanted full independence for his country, not merely dominion status. La perfide Albion. The inspiration for the fictitious Lieutenant Colonel Sean McAlpin in Free Scotland was found.

The ethnic cleansing currently taking place against Rohingyas (in former Burma, now Myanmar) is being carried out by Myanmar military. After 2016 elections parliamentarian, "Than Aung Soe opined: "We will try step by step to reduce the military percentage." Yet doing so will require either the military's consent or a true revolution. And no one should count on the former: ...military commander-in-chief Gen. Min Aung Hlaing emphasized the importance of the Tatmadaw [army] retaining its "leading role in national politics."[3] Are Rohingyans entitled to self-determination from military rule?

This book of fiction states all peoples are entitled to self-determination, especially, in the face of military dictatorship.

2 Field Marshal Sir William Slim, Defeat into Victory, Cassell & Company, 2nd edition, 1956

3 https://www.forbes.com/sites/dougbandow/2016/03/31/a-brighter-dawn-in-burma-myanmar-not-yet-a-democracy-but-no-longer-a-dictatorship/#39b888452f0f, 16 Nov 17.

The original UN Charter, written before the end of World War Two, had the intention of ending all militarism and Empires, including Britain's, by enshrining the Purpose "To develop friendly relations among nations based on respect for the principle of equal rights and self-determination of peoples." Over 80 decolonised countries, comprising some 750 million people across the world, have asserted their rights to self-determination since then. Interestingly, without any requirement to hold a Referendum. Scotland, hopefully, is now bonding with this exalted free assembly,

"...not because we didn't like the British, but we love Freedom better. I think all of us have the right to be free."

CHAPTER 1
SYRIA-JORDAN BORDER SEPTEMBER 2018

Syria-Jordan Border: September 2018

A PLATOON of heavily-armed Jocks are slumped exhausted in a windowless room, every eye staring at a huge screen. Behind the TV presenter is a huge, swaying crowd of Saltire and Lion Rampant flags filling Stirling Castle esplanade. Among the flags and hands and cameras, EU passports are being held aloft.

The CNN presenter, her voice straining over roars of the crowd, smiles and delivers her piece to camera: "Yesterday, on the 18th of September, Scotland voted in a referendum that, some say, will decide forever its relationship with the rest of the United Kingdom. A day on, and we know now that over 85% of the electorate cast their vote, that the referendum has been confirmed as, I quote, 'free, fair and democratic' by the monitoring OSCE or Organization for Security & Co-operation in Europe and the Scottish government has already called on both the UN and the EU to recognise its outcome. What question was put the Scottish people yesterday? They were asked, Yes or No, do you want to retain your European citizenship. 'What's that got to do with the UK?' you'll be asking. Well, if the Scottish government claims are true and it really has the green-light from Brussels to remain in the EU, then it is set on a collision course with London that many see as a requiem for the United Kingdom. Viewers will know that the UK is leaving the EU – that's BREXIT folks.

Now the Scottish people have said, with a resounding 61%, go right ahead mate, but you're leaving without us! It's independence without the word ever having been printed on the ballot paper. How is this playing out in London? Not very well, to say the least. The governing British National & Unionist Party, or BNUP, has already declared the referendum illegal and is refusing to even comment on its outcome. Millions of Scots, many of them behind me now, say otherwise. The focus now will be on how the EU and the other international bodies react to the choice of the Scottish people. The stakes couldn't be higher, nor could the mood here in Stirling – this is Angie MacDonald for CNN, from what everybody here is calling the new Republic of Scotland."

Sergeant Major Andy MacCreadie, slouches in an armchair, rusty springs and horsehair stuffing protruding from the pock-marked leather. Both have seen better days. He looks at his commander – Lieutenant Cammy MacAlpin – and taps the two flags on the arm of his sand-camouflaged desert shirt; a Union Jack above a blue and white Scots Regimental saltire flag. With his thick Glasgow accent making him sound like he's chewing a house-brick, he asks "W'ere does that leave us, Suur? Urr we Brits? Or Scots?"

The subaltern looks at him squarely, no doubt or hesitation in his voice. "You signed on as British soldiers! You're all Brits until you're told otherwise. We've got a job to do, so let's get to it!"

Cammy shoulders his rifle and makes for the door. Andy pushes himself up more awkwardly and signals for the other soldiers to follow their boss.

In the doorway, stands an odd, barely military figure, scruffy hair atop an officer's uniform. Cammy, laughing, extends his hand, "Rupert! You really have to stop combing your hair with a hand-grenade! What would His Majesty think of one of his officers looking like a buckshee Daesh?"

Rupert laughs brightly but replies earnestly, in a polished English public-school accent, "Now, you be careful out there, Cammy. The natives are on the war-path. Don't be taking any chances, my friend."

Cammy smiles at the concern and pushes past him. Rupert shouts to the soldiers' backs as they retreat into the night. "I don't know what you do to the enemy but, by God, you frighten me!"

They bimble quietly through the darkness towards dull engine noises that throb from several idling vehicles; four sand-coloured Brit Warrior infantry fighting vehicles (IFVs) lie in convoy in a moon-lit corner of a NATO Forward Operating Base. Small Scots flags are on the sides of the vehicles and fly from radio antennas. A helicopter thrums low overhead.

Climbing inside the dimly lit Command Warrior, Cammy straps in, glancing over his shoulder at his men in the dark cramped seated Section area. Tension and fear is now etched in the camo-painted faces of the young soldiers seated the length of the battlewagon, four to each side. "You know our arrest suspects group. We'll go in hard and fast. We pick the bastards up, then we're out of there. Questions?" Then each gives the thumbs-up in acknowledgment.

The night explodes with noise as the leading Warrior, followed by the Command Warrior then the final two IFVs, surge through the compound gates. After a bone-shuddering 20-minute dash, they cross a long urban unlit mud-house street at a T-junction. The first driver brakes hard lifting a cloud of enveloping dust. Partially hidden by a derelict building, this vanguard vehicle slowly brings its turret in line with a two-storey building silhouetted in the night sky, some 1000 meters away. For a second, there is silence. Then its 40mm cannon changes the night to noon as dazzling yellow-flashes announce intense red tracer rounds that scream towards the building sending bricks, dust and debris in all directions. The Warrior rocks on its suspension with the power of each delivery. On cue, the three remaining Warriors hurtle past, across the junction, smash through a low wall and hammer up another pitch-black street.

The Warriors pitch in a dust tempest manoeuvre up yet another street to a dilapidated wall surrounding the objective build-ing which the leading Command vehicle again crashes straight through. The following two Warriors slam to a halt, traverse their weapons onto their now visible goal and open fire. Three static fire-support Warriors now bring devastating, deafening fire from different directions onto the furiously burning build-ing. The Warriors spew bright red tracer rounds into their mark.

Sporadic small-arms firing emanates in return, including bright green tracer rounds which slam harmlessly against the armoured Warrior hulls before ricocheting spectacularly into the jet black sky. A Daesh Rocket Propelled Grenade whooshes dangerously close to an IFV.

The constantly moving Command Warrior tears across open ground using its own firepower. Tracer rounds continue to arc, in scarlet and emerald firefly-flashes, across the area whilst exploding flames light up the chaos of battle. The driver slews the Warrior to a halt, the guns still blazing against the battered building. At point blank range, the rounds smash massive chunks of debris from the rapidly deteriorating structure.

Inside the battle-wagon, infrared light gives Cammy a hellish glow. He peers through a laser viewfinder and talks into his throat mike, "200 metres! Switch fire left! Enemy infantry in open! Out!"

The supporting Warriors immediately traverse their turrets onto the western flank of the smashed building. Their combined fire-power slashes at a large group of heavily-armed turbaned Daesh fighters fleeing from the burning edifice.

Still in the Command Warrior, Cammy looks over his left shoulder and roars, "Move now!"

One soldier releases the rear door which clangs open then the four-man "Charlie" Fire-Team exit and run to the Warriors left front, followed by the next four-man "Delta" Fire-Team who exit around to the opposite side. Cammy, hefting a bulky radio, follows the first Team. They are all crawling on their bellies, searching whatever cover they can find, facing the inferno. As one, they fire at the buildings remaining doors and windows to add to the hammering. Rifle grenades, from Charlie and Delta, join the cacophony exploding onto their marks. Two Daesh fighters, only their arms showing, wave dirty white cloths from behind a doorway.

Cammy assesses the situation and calmly gives the radio-command to cease fire. His head is still throbbing after the final echoes of the fire-storm. His eyes never leave the target in the comparative quiet of crackling flames.

He shouts in Arabic, "Come out with your hands in the air!" Two badly wounded Daesh stumble out.

Cammy bellows "Delta - Give cover! Charlie - Secure the prisoners!"

Charlie Fire-Team dash forward. They scream and motion at the two Daesh to lie down. Cammy cautiously advances as his Charlie Team splits into two pairs. One soldier aims to a Daesh head while another soldier roughly pats down the prostrate fighter. They lie them on their fronts and fix each prisoners' wrists with plastic cuffs behind their backs. Then sand bags are shoved over their heads. One of the soldiers gives a gloved thumbs up to Cammy, who calmly speaks again into his radio-handset, "Hello Zulu-One-Zero. This is Sierra-Three-Zero-Alpha. Prisoners secure, over."

A Black Hawk helicopter whumps low overhead. The US pilot acknowledges, "Roger, Sierra-Three-Zero-Alpha, Target prisoners secure. I'm inbound now, out."

The Black Hawk swoops out of the darkness, landing in a dust-storm near the Command Warrior. Cammy exchanges a thumbs-up with the pilot. Charlie Team rag-doll their prisoners into the chopper. Crew members haul the Daesh on board, followed immediately by the Jocks - as Scottish soldiers are universally known. They just manage to strap themselves in before the aircraft lifts, accelerating away from the sand storm it leaves behind.

Cammy and the other Jocks dive into their Warrior. Strapped in, he taps his driver's shoulder, "Job done, wee man, now get us home." The young commander adjusts his radio head-set, his words patched through to the other three Warrior vehicles, "Return to Zero now! Out!"

He sets his radio frequency to HQ to pass on the Mission "success" password and smiles broadly, pleased with himself. "Hullo Zero! This is Sierra-Three-Zero-Alpha. Claymore! Claymore! I say again! Claymore! Returning to Zero now! Out!"

The Command Warrior spins on one track and hurtles back through the gap in the crumbling wall, past the three fire-support Warriors heading to the pre-planned waypoint.

The other vehicles quickly bunch up, zipping along a deserted road closely paralleling a disused canal.

Cammy says into his head-set, "Well done lads. Best speed back to base. We're home fr...."

A massive explosion hits the Command Warrior broadside, throwing it clear across the road, the following Warriors swerving violently. As it lands sideways, it skids dangerously close to the canal edge... a second's pause and it begins to list slowly as the sand banking gives way. A second later and it rolls over, its roof hitting the black water. Then it sinks, only its front protruding above the bubbling water like a stricken prehistoric metal beast.

The following Warriors slam to a halt, the rear doors crashing open. Automatically, the turret weapons are scanning potential enemy positions. A few Jocks dash from their vehicles to the canal edge as others set up a defensive ring of weapons around the immediate area.

Inside his Warrior, Andy frantically jabs at his Global Positioning System for a location. The unit shows blank. He smashes it with his gloved fist, shouting into his head-mike as he frantically reaches for his personal GPS from a jacket pocket.

"Hullo Zero! This is Sierra-Three-Zero-Bravo! CONTACT! My Zero-Alpha severely damaged by I.E.D! Casualties not yet known! Request immediate support with CASEVAC! Grid! Foxtrot-Yankee! Five-two! Niner-Niner! Three-One! Sitrep to follow! Wait Out!"

The two driver seats in the ambushed Warrior, now upside down, are the only part of the interior not submerged. Water swirls and splashes inside. Two figures surface into this air-pocket. Cammy, gulping and gasping, has an arm supporting an unconscious soldier, his hand keeping the youths face above water. Of the other soldiers, there is no sign.

Cammy looks up on hearing clanging metal upon metal above them and muffled shouts, "Wee Man! Wee Man! Can you hear the other Jocks? They'll soon have us out! Don't give up Wee Man!"

Blood bubbles from the nose and mouth of the unconscious young soldier. Cammy desperately pulls them both up into the diminishing air pocket. Their upper shoulders are being rapidly immersed. Cammy is panic stricken. He screams, "We're in here! Hurry! We're flooding! For fucks sake, hurry!"

Above, the soldiers are frenetically hammering their rifle-butts at a damaged but unmoving hatch on the belly of the Warrior, shouting obscenely.

Inside, water is rising. Cammy's head is squeezed against the bulwark and is desperately holding his comrades head above the dark, swirling, stinking canal water. They choke as the water forces its way into their mouths. Cammy whispers to his unconscious companion, "It's OK, Wee Man. It'll no' be long, the Jocks'll save us. They'll no' let us doon..."

UK Army HQ, Amman Jordan: Dawn

Rupert sits in front of a lap-top screen and closely scans the detail:

19 SEP 2018: CASUALTY REPORT
HQ JSAF TO HQ LONDON.
9 DEAD: ROYAL SCOTLAND REGIMENT.
WARRIOR MINE-STRIKE.
PERSONNEL DETAILS – ANNEX A.
NEXT OF KIN TO BE INFORMED IMMEDIATELY.

He places the cursor over "Send". He pauses and hangs his head. He covers his mouth with his hand as if to be sick. He sighs deeply, looks up and clicks the screen instruction conveying the dreadful news to unsuspecting homes.

10 Downing St, London

Prime Minister, "Bomber" Harris, listens intently to a brief from a senior army officer.

"Sir, I refer to the nine Scottish soldiers killed today in Southern Syria. Your press office and close advisers, ehm, are suggesting that, ehm, you may not wish to give a statement of condolence to the Nation. May I have clarification please?"

Harris looks down, "You are aware, General Wilson, Scotland has illegally voted for Independence. It is my opinion, and that of my Government, we must carefully consider the implications on

Scottish public opinion if it is announced nine of their country-men have just been killed fighting on London's orders in what they, ironically, see as an illegal war. A media D Notice has been issued instructing a complete media blackout on this matter for the moment."

The General stares at the Prime Minister in astonishment as the PM continues, "I understand these men were killed when a roadside bomb caused their Warrior to overturn into a canal. We are considering that this matter is treated as an unfortunate Road Traffic Accident, not Killed in Action. We leave out the I.E.D. It is not in the interests of my Government to give that bloody shower in Scotland a propaganda coup!"

The General struggles to control his voice, "Sir! On behalf of these men, I must protest! They deserve every military and state honour befitting their sacrifice. Politics cannot come into this!"

With cold malevolence, the PM leans forward, his eyes lifting to meet the General's. "You will do as you are bloody told! And you will ensure that the Army complies with my direction. These Scottish soldiers will not provide fuel for Scotland's fire. You will issue a statement saying the remains of these men.... after this tragic accident... will be buried at a Military Cemetery in Cyprus. Do you understand me, General? They will not be brought home!"

General Wilson stands up slowly. He adjusts his Service Dress jacket, staring at the PM. He makes to speak but is interrupted by an effete gentleman languishing on an antique leather chair, "If you have any more questions, General, I suggest you put them through my, sorry, the PM's Press Office."

The outraged senior officer turns on his heel and storms from the office. The press secretary turns to the PM," I thought you handled that jolly well, sir. I shall see to it that the lid is firmly kept on this little issue. Now, to the main business. How do we stop these morons in Scotland from turning off the supply of North Sea oil money to our Government?"

"Indeed, Harry", mused the PM. "The first thing we must do is rubbish their independence result and then instigate a delaying mechanism for as long as possible. Until, ideally, we have had all of their black gold! Scots manpower is a bigger problem, though."

"I don't understand, sir?"

The PM continues, "Unfortunately, like these nine dead Scots, we need them for our Armed Forces to carry out our foreign policies. We can't sustain British Forces in places like Syria, Iraq, Afghanistan or anywhere else for that matter without the damned Scots! They might be only 8% of the UK population but they supply around 20% of our Forces manpower."

Harry laughs, "You mean a sort of Scottish Blood Tax, Prime Minister?"

Harry and the PM bellow with laughter.

"Jolly good, Harry. Yes, quite...plus we need them as a base for our nuclear submarines. Scotland is much more suitable for that than our green and pleasant land! No nuclear weapons, no seat at the UN Security Council for London. We play for much higher stakes than just their oil, my boy."

Military Operations Room, Brigade HQ, Stirling

Two soldiers are studying a military operational map. Stirling Castle can be seen through a rain-streaked window. One reaches to pick up a ringing telephone.

"Good Afternoon! Sergeant Wallace, 52nd Highland Brigade Ops Room, Sir!" He listens and scribbles a note. His face becomes very grave. "Nightmare, Sir. OK, Sir."

He looks at the other soldier and grimaces, "Fetch the Duty Officer, Major Findlay! A signal is arriving from HQ London about a Road Traffic Accident in Syria with nine Jock fatalities."

The soldier hurries from the room and returns with a young officer as a printer regurgitates paper. Major Findlay silently reads each sheet as it prints off, "OK, Sergeant. Let's get cracking with finding out who's available to visit these poor bastards' families. I'll inform Colonel McCloy. There is to be zero publicity on this matter, understood?"

Findlay strides along a corridor and knocks on a door-sign: LT COL McCLOY 2 LINCS. He enters. McCloy is busy at his computer.

He looks up at Findlay's grim face and sneers superciliously, "Not more Jock death-o-grams Findlay? I've more important things to do!" His nasty tone is exacerbated by a posh-Jock public school whine.

Findlay says nothing and puts the folder on his desk. He waits. McCloy continues to type and eventually, impatiently, thrusts himself away from his computer. He grabs the folder and reads, "Did you know, Findlay, that in the First World War we staggered the release of Scottish casualty figures in order to suppress the true extent of battle fatalities?"

Findlay remains silent but his eyes can't betray his distaste. McCloy enjoys provoking the young officer, "Indeed, General Wolfe at the 18th century Battle of Quebec said of the casualties from his Scottish Regiments "No great harm, if they fall!" Excellent sentiment, don't you think?"

Findlay composes himself before replying, "I think then, as now, their countrymen, wives and children would disagree with you and General Wolfe, sir."

McCloy laughs caustically and puts the folder down. He waves Findlay away whilst instructing him to find teams of Casualty Notification Officers to disperse throughout Scotland to visit tragedy upon the unfortunate families.

The dead soldiers are no longer the only victims as families, friends, colleagues and the CNO's themselves join the mounting toll of heart-breaking, devastating anguish across the country. Many will need welfare and mental health support for the rest of their heartrending lives. Some will find solace in the bottle and drugs. Brutally, some will end their own lives.

Major Findlay mutters angrily to himself as he walks along the corridor, "We're all being fucking exploited. Totally and completely fucking exploited."

CHAPTER 2
SOUTH CAROLINA
SEPTEMBER 2018

South Carolina: September 2018

THE SOUTHERN STATE basked in the heat of the setting September sun. Two young men, Tyson and Will, laze on the green graveyard hillside on the fringe of the diminutive town of Calhoun. The cicadas distinctive buzz-saw whirring is everywhere, with no other sounds all around.

This remote corner of the state has always been known as the Upcountry for good reason. The wooded, steep hills of the State Parks shimmer in a blue haze to the north on the line of their sister state, North Carolina, with captivating names like Table Rock, Caesars' Head and Gorges.

Many, many seasons ago this was Cherokee country. Effective ethnic cleansing had ensured the Native Americans were removed from the surrounding regions during the time known as "The Trail of Tears" in spite of the best efforts of Chief John Ross, a Scottish Cherokee mixed-blood. Since the 17th century, Scots had settled in large numbers, willingly or not, in these wild, remote valleys.

The two friends chatted quietly amongst the gravestones. This rural area was never particularly populated which was reflected in the sparse, random manner that the headstones sprouted from the wild grass.

They were discussing a particular weather beaten grey-stone grave. To a visitor, it would be unremarkable amongst the tens of

14

similar style around it. It read, "PVT JAMES McKENZIE, CO. E, 4th REGT SC INF, C.S.A. 1843 – 1861" The proportion of headstones to the then population was appallingly excessive.

The uniformed youngster spoke softly with the distinctive drawl of South Carolina. He explained, "Jim was my pa's grandfather's youngest brother. Great Grandpa Michael passed in the early 1920's. Young Jim was killed at First Manassas with some of the other fella's right here from Pickens County. Company E were mostly from here and remembered as Calhouns' Mountaineers, or sometimes Guards. Their regiment served in Colonel Jubal Early's brigade at Manassas."

"My dad would love all of this, "laughed his friend, quietly, in an equally distinctive West of Scotland accent. He lay face down in his white track-suit with the initials "SPU SOCCER" emblazoned in bold blue letters on the back. As a talented pro-youth footballer in Scotland he had won a Sports Scholarship to play "Soccer" at a top American university as a student-athlete.

"Your dad's still serving in the Brit army along with your older brother, Cammy, right?" asked the Southerner.

"Yeah... Dad's somewhere in West Africa on an UN tour right now and Cammy's in Syria with his regiment, "replied the Scots youth. An almost imperceptible glimpse of pain and concern appeared briefly on his face. "How long do you still have to serve with your army, Tyson?"

Tyson aims his camouflaged cap at the youth, "I've told you before, man, I'm not army!" he laughed in exasperation. "I'm United States Marine Corps! Guys from this part of the world don't join the blue-belly army and haven't done since the time of great-grand Uncle Jim's Company E! We join the Marines!" He leant across, grabbed his cap back and pointed at the globe and anchor Marine Corps badge. "Marine!" he hooted.

"Don't gimme that!" teased Will. "Calhoun is inland at least 250 miles from the nearest navy base at Charleston! Where did you tie up your boat?"

"I told you already, dude!", said Tyson making a dumb face. "When I came back from Afghanistan as an enlisted NCO, the

Corps funded me to go through the Reserves Officer programme at SPU. That means I have to spend at least one weekend per month carrying out Reserve Officer Training Corps instruction while I study for my degree. Get it?"

"OK, yeah." Will smiled. "It's good you have a Marine Corps career to fall back on as you're shit in our football team!"

"Muthafucka!" exclaimed Tyson as he re-launched his cap at Will who held up a single finger to his lips indicating quiet whilst comically hinting at the surrounding boneyard gravestones.

Tyson immediately understood, paused and whispered, "Sorry ol' Uncle Jim, "causing them both a fit of giggles. Eventually, Tyson laughed out, "Let's go, dude. We gotta get back on Campus, eat and then get some sleep before socca training at Oh-My-God-O'Clock tomorrow mo'nin'" placing great emphasis on drawling out the word "socca".

"I don't think I'll ever get used to these military-type sparrow-fart morning training sessions," bemoaned Will.

They both sauntered, bantering, towards the nearby dirt road where a large, sparkling green pick-up truck was parked. Will, once again, started to climb into the "wrong" side of the vehicle resulting in more good-natured abuse from Tyson who pushed passed him to climb behind the wheel of his good-ol'-boys truck. They sped off in a dust cloud towards the campus.

CHAPTER 3

LIBERIA, WEST AFRICA
OCTOBER 2018

Liberia, West Africa: October 2018

SOLID VERDANT FOREST stretches to the horizon in every direction. The terrain is featureless apart from an occasional small brown river. An old white ex-Soviet helicopter, flying fast and low, stands out sharply against the green background. UN, in large bold black letters, are apparent on the fuselage. Suddenly, a plume of blue smoke pours from the engine causing it to rapidly loose height. As it dives, it auto-rotates violently, side-slips and plunges savagely onto a riverbank. The rotors thrash the undergrowth then stop. Blue smoke continues to billow.

A Scots soldier, in jungle combats, drags a screaming companion from the wreckage. The Scot, incredibly still wearing a distinctive Glengarry bonnet rammed onto his close-shaven head, is in his late forties, tanned and athletic. On his sleeve are two small flags identical to the Jocks' in Syria: the British national emblem and his Scottish Regiment's. His comrade's sleeve has a distinctive red and white chequered shield with HRVATSKA (Croatia) in gold letters. He leaves the badly wounded man and staggers back to the chopper, climbs inside, and comes out with an unconscious figure clad in a green flying suit. The exhausted Scot strains to pull the heavy lifeless man to where the screaming Croat lies. The chopper is now engulfed in the smoke which rises skyward in a thick pillar. Other than the wounded man's screams, the forest is eerily silent.

17

In spite of his own injuries, the Scot uses all his resolve to attend to the two guys. Regretfully, he notices the pilot's two unseeing eyes which he closes. He kneels beside the Croat, pulls open a pouch on his own belt, extracts a medical field-dressing and firmly applies it to a gaping wound on the Croat's thigh. He ties it off quickly and tightly. The Scot slumps down beside him to reassure him.

"Tomislav? Tom, we'll be picked up in no time. This smoke will be seen for miles. Old Soviet helo's can't fly for shit but they do make excellent smoke-signals."

Tom tries to laugh through his pain but only succeeds in inducing a coughing fit. The Scot wipes the blood-flecked phlegm from his friend's mouth and chin and puts his arm around his shoulders. Both men drop into drained unconsciousness.

UN HOSPITAL, LIBERIA

The Scot and Croat are sleeping peacefully in a spotless infirmary room. A British officer, with a generals red-tabs on his combat shirt collar, enters with a doctor who speaks gently, wakening the Scot who grimaces. "Sean! Colonel MacAlpin?"

The general waits patiently as he comes around. When Sean is groggily awake the General says, "Sean, I hear you are improving every day. That's fantastic news. The Croat government is also delighted that you saved Major Stanic's life. Is there anything I can do for you?"

A drowsy Sean responds, "Thanks, Sir. I'll be OK."

"We'll casevac you soon, Sean." The general's demeanour changes and his voice becomes very grave..." But first I have some very bad news...I'm truly sorry...It's your son, Cammy. He was killed in Southern Syria a few days ago when his Warrior was written off in an RTA. Your ex-wife has already been informed."

Sean is stunned. He lets out an animal-like howl of "No!" which causes Tom to stir and look over to witness his friend's terrible grief. The doctor prepares a syringe as the general puts a hand on Sean's shoulder, "Young Cammy is being flown to Cyprus for burial in the British military cemetery there, along with eight of his men who were killed alongside him. The prime minister's office has directed that they are buried there because of the political situation at home in Scotland. You must understand Sean. The government wants to avoid inflaming Scottish opinion. London doesn't want public funerals for these young men. You understand, don't you?"

Sean stares incredulously at the general and screams, "My son is dead and you bastards are playing at bloody politics? Are you insane, man? I want to see him! Where is he?"

Calmly the general attempts to reassure him, "We're arranging to fly you to Cyprus as soon as possible, Sean. I'm so very sorry for your loss. No man should have to bury his own child. But you are a very fine officer and I'm sure that the pain you're feeling now will be replaced in time with your clear duty to our Government to do what is right for them. In spite of what must seem an appalling choice. We'll let you know as soon as possible when we have flights arranged for you."

The general nods at the doctor who administers the injection to the grief-stricken Scot. Sean lapses into tortured unconsciousness as his Croat friend stares at him in horror.

Southern Presbyterian University (SPU), Calhoun S.C.

SPU football team are on the campus practice pitch. The air is full of shouts and groans from the players as the coaching staff bellow both approval and opprobrium. Unusually, for the game of football, the staff are not swearing or using foul-mouthed expressions; this is bible-belt South Carolina, after all.

Team-mates Tyson and Will are still totally unaware of the tragic family event in Syria.

The boys in their SPU white strips, or uniforms, depending on how you interpret the divide of our common language, are at full tilt as they successfully pull off a neat 1-2 interplay on the edge of the opposition penalty box sending two leaden footed defenders sprawling. The final pass from Will sets up Tyson beautifully for a clear strike at goal. Tyson takes a single touch bringing the ball artfully under control and then lashes the ball as hard as he can. The kick fires the ball 10 feet over the bar and into the trees behind the pitch. The goalkeeper jeers at Tyson's amateur attempt as Will roars unintelligible Scots foul-mouthed insults. He doesn't do bible-belt.

Tyson is beside himself with laughter as Will jogs over giggling, "Mate, that's gotta be one of the worst strikes I've ever seen!" Tyson can't speak for shoulder-shaking mirth and is saved from further football embarrassment when the Coach blows the full-time whistle and calls in the players for a hot-debrief.

The briefing finished the players amble and joke their way to the changing rooms to collect their kit-bags then head up the tree-lined walkway to their student accommodation in the tranquil, warm Southern evening. The beautiful campus is filled with grand 19th and 20th century buildings set amidst broad avenues and gorgeously maintained gardens. It's a dream location for this and any other young Scot to graduate from whilst building on their sporting dreams.

Will and Tyson's small apartment, in one of many modern student-blocks, rapidly fills up with hot steam as they throw their soiled football kit into the washing machine and take turns to shower.

Soon, they are glowing and refreshed. Will is outside on their small veranda which is almost filled by a book-strewn table. The view is glorious, green countryside topped with a cloudless blue sky.

In the kitchen area Tyson poaches some eggs and toasts some brown bread which he then brings outside to share, "Can't get enough egg protein immediately after exercise to aid quick recovery, dude!"

"Nice one," mumbles Will as he unceremoniously horses the food. "How is your history presentation coming on for Friday?"

Tyson wipes his lips with a paper napkin and ponders for a moment. "It's finished but it's sure gonna cause a whole heap of controversy..."

"How so?" asks Will smiling and intrigued.

"This is difficult. Real difficult, "as Tyson summons, with an effort, the willingness to continue. "Do you recall our visit up to the churchyard when I showed you my Great-great grand Uncle Jim Mckenzies' grave?"

Will nods.

"It's gonna be about Jim and his Company E buddies. Why they enlisted and fought for the Confederate Army, "and paused for Will to respond.

Will merely raises an eyebrow in anticipation and said, "So?"

Tyson sighs and looks down. "Dude. The "so" is gonna be beyond controversial. There might even be a riot."

Will laughs, "How can it be? It's local history. It's gotta be interesting to everyone there in the classroom."

Tyson explains, "We don't talk about the subject. The war finished nearly two hundred and fifty years ago but is still being fought today. Slavery dominates the way we look at everything. African-American rights today is the prism through which we see the Confederacy. Coy E and the rest of the Confederate army has been Nazified. Folks get riled up real quick on this which oftentimes leads to punches and people getting hurt real bad. Sometimes killed. Redneck savagery versus Blacks."

Will shrugs expansively, "OK. I can see it's an emotive subject but don't really get how it can be any more contentious as a history subject, than say, racist Nazi Germany?"

"In Scotland, that might be true. But here in the good old US of A, and particularly here in the State that was the first to secede from the Union and so gave birth to the Confederacy? Big issues, dude. Bad issues. Like today's White Power Nazism."

Will, looking into Tyson's African-American features begins to detect real worry in his friend and queries, "But you're right to call out the Confederate slave state army, aren't you?"

Tyson leans back, rolls his large wide-open eyes and whispers, "I support and understand the majority of Coy E's reasons for fighting for Independence." He sits forward and pinches up his black skin on the back of one hand. He pauses for dramatic effect to which Will responds, deadpan, with, "Ah." They both giggle.

Eventually, Will says, "Right. It's a bit like an Israeli Jew saying he understands why his Jewish German ancestors fought for Nazi Germany. My country right or wrong? Yeah. I can see that being a bit...eh...unbelievably improbable. Yeah. You'd definitely struggle to win support for that wee concept."

21

Tyson smiles as he digests Will's response and nods his head in agreement. "Very accurate. Except for one evidenced distinction. Black people did fight for the Confederacy. Not many I agree. Plus today's White Power apologists use the argument to defend the indefensibility of the pro-slavery policy of Southern States government. Thing is. Ol' Jim McKenzie was white."

Will is visibly perplexed and dubious, "You've lost me, Tyson."

Tyson is now enjoying himself, "Dude. You can't be that young that you haven't heard of shocked, appalled and astonished same-colour parents, black or white, giving birth to babies of the opposite colour? Google it!" and laughed.

"OK...," "cringes Will , "I'm not sure I like where this is heading as I've got pictures in my head I could do without, mate..."

Tyson winks conspiratorially, "It's Scotland's fault."

"Ah, get tae Fuck!" shouts Will leaping to his feet, "I was listening politely and noo ye'r talking complete ba's... ya bawbag!"

Tyson understood enough Scots invective from the football pitch to recognise yet another Scots tongue-in-cheek putdown. He immediately recalled his delight when, during yet another long night on campaign in Afghanistan, Will's brother Cammy explained that the deadpan piss-taking Scots phrase, "Aye. Right" means the irreverent opposite of agreement. He had immediately incorporated it into his own growing Scots invective vocabulary to add to, "Ya bawbag! Jobby! That's keech!" Flippant hands across the sea, indeed.

Tysons good natured laughter subsided "It's true, man. Listen up." To which, slowly, Will sat down with a wry grin, responding, "No bother. Go for it..." He then adopted a faux cross-legged listening pose with a mocking middle-finger of one hand below one eye, "You have my full attention!"

Tyson smiles "Our family can trace our ancestors back to 18th Century Scotland. We are McKenzie. Normally, a black guy in America with a Scottish surname has one of three likely sources of origin. His surname might have come from a slave plantation owner or slave overseer, it might have come from the name of an American town or county where they had lived or," he paused, "like our family we can prove our Scottish roots." Will listened intently now.

Tyson continued with a smile, "Like many God-fearing Southern families we have a bible passed down through the generations with the names, place and dates of birth recorded in the cover. We have one. It's very carefully preserved in a waxed leather satchel at our grandpa's home. The first name is Neil McKenzie, born in Elgin, Scotland in May 1720. Our family have been able to prove this. We can also prove he enlisted as a private soldier at the first muster of a Scottish infantry regiment in Aberfeldy, Scotland in May 1740. His regiment is now known as...The Black Watch."

"See!" cried Will as he leaped to his feet, "I actually listen to you then you go and rip the pish again! I wish I had a Yankee dollar for every bloody Yank that claims descent from a bastard Hielan' Chieftan!"

The US Marine joined Will in paroxysms of laughter. It took a good few moments until they could both speak normally yet again.

Eventually, Tyson continued with an effort but with a huge smile, "It's true, dude. On our family bible, it's true. Neil McKenzie existed and became a British red-coat soldier." The smile began to fade as he spoke, "The next trace we hear of him was on a military nominal roll of about 100 names in 1743. They were Black Watch who'd mutinied in England, then been convicted and exiled to British West Indies colonies either into slavery or other regiments. These guys enlisted to serve at home in Scotland – not to fight for the Crown in their colonies. So they mutinied and tried to get home. When they were all captured three Scots soldiers were executed *pour décourager les autres*. Neil was one of those sent into slavery in Barbados." Will listened now in captivated silence.

"Our family have done a lot of historical research to back up what I'm saying. It would make a great book. But what happened to Neil subsequently in order to continue his incredible journey landed him in South Carolina...to begin a family which continued to live, and fight, in these parts through our Revolutionary War of Independence and then onto the War of Southern Independence. The story would make an awesome six-part trilogy," he joked.

"You're not kidding," mused Will, "the movie screenplays from the six-part trilogy would also be worth reading...and probably the non-fiction historical documentaries. Have you thought of pulling this together?"

Tyson replied, "Sure I have. There are McKenzie adventures in the 20th Century too. But I must finish my History degree here first. But you can't make this shit up, dude. Neil's brother had remained loyal to the Black Watch and was wounded with the British Army, at their battle of Fontenoy, in Belgium in May 1745. Then he was driven from his home a few years later during the Highland Clearances after Culloden ending up, along with his brother, in South Carolina," he blurted excitedly.

"Couple that with the lies and treachery of the day that saw Clan McKenzie fight on the losing side at Culloden in April 1746 whilst the Black Watch were purposely held out of the action back in Flanders. Do you know who commanded the Brits and Black Watch at Fontenoy?"

"Haven't a Scooby," said a curious Will.

"The Duke of Cumberland, dude! Stinking Billy, the Butcher of Culloden! That's who! Join up the dots, man! "Stinking Billy" had the mutinous Black Watch decimated at Fontenoy to prevent the Regiment from potentially going over to the Jacobite rebels!" enthused Tyson, now in full passionate flow. "Murder having been done in Flanders, Cumberland returned to Scotland to finish the job at Culloden."

Excitedly, in a passionate manner only historians have for history, Tyson rattled on at speed, "So, Neil was in Barbados, right? Who does he meet in December 1751? Major George Washington! The George Washington! In Barbados with his convalescent brother! But not the President-Good-Guy we all know from our history! This was the British-Officer-and-Slaver-George, he who bought, sold, flogged and owned slaves himself in his Virginia tobacco plantations. Read George's Barbados diary, dude! Neil's family then get fully involved with old George's Revolutionary performance right here in South Carolina. Are you following this, Will?"

"Defo, mate. Defo," he responds with mock seriousness, "Whose side though and what's all of this fascinating gibbering got to do with your Confederate chums?" he asks mischievously.

"For American Independence, of course...oh wait...some of the family stayed loyal to the King and fought against Washington... and had to flee to Canada after the War," and laughed, "As you would expect! And I'll get to the Civil War!"

"Sweet Jesus," whistles Will, "I had absolutely no idea that Scottish-American history was so complicated... or so intriguing. Honestly! But would anyone be convinced by a modern black guy saying he understood the guys who fought for the slave-Confederacy?" quizzed a serious Will.

"I see where you're coming from and, yeah, this'll give me a lot of grief from the Brothers. But everything I've read about says that the average Confederate foot soldier believed the Cotton-Aristocracy propaganda. They were taken advantage of. Soldiers have always been exploited by governments. This will never change. The misinformation of the day told them it was all about their Southern Independence and States Rights while the plantation owners and Richmond government knew it was all about slavery.

"Damn few of the soldiers ever owned slaves but the Cotton-Aristocrats, the 1% of their day if you like, ensured secession from the Union by encouraging racism to bring it about. No question many soldiers and officers fought to protect the institution of slavery and its expansion into the new Western States...but I believe the majority of Company E trusted that they fought for self-determination, as we know it today. The reality was the Confederacy was established by men who organised a system of government to maintain a system of slavery and to destroy the United States.

"And anyway. You Brits are doing exactly the same right now as the jack-bastard Confederate government did back then! You are seceding from the Union in Europe by exploiting racist votes whilst your 1% gets even richer than they are now!" Will doesn't manage to utter a word from his stunned wide-eyed face at this blindingly obvious comparison made by his laughing black friend, who dumbfounds him still further by stating, "By the way, have I mentioned Neil brought his beautiful, black Barbadian woman with him?"

Will's mouth now opened in genuine astonishment. Then delighted enlightened realisation concerning the offspring of such a relationship. This, followed by potential real-time drama in subsequent generations, demonstrated by the smiling McKenzie in front of him with grinning Afro-American features.

"For fuck's sake, mate! I can only guess at how a white guy with a black woman must've been appreciated way back in the day. "Controversial" doesn't even begin to cover it!"

"Tell me about it, dude. My first step to book and movie-screenplay stardom begins with this presentation to let my rebel, redneck good-old boys know that my McKenzie family fought for Southern Freedom! Yeeeeehaaaawwwww!" which immediately convulsed the pair of them in laughter once more "This isn't a distinctly black and white issue!" Tyson spluttered causing further hysterical hilarity.

They were still laughing when they heard a knock at their apartment door "Your turn," Tyson insisted, "The whole McKenzie history has left us all with a love of Independence and fighting for Freedom!"

"Aye, right," Will responds laconically as he opens the door with a grin. His warm, "Hello!" was cruelly and immediately dissipated by the sight of his grim-faced, University Principal who was accompanied by the equally austere University Doctor. Gently, the Doctor asked, "May we come in, Will?"

Non-plussed and sensing something was wrong he said, "Sure. Please," then more hopefully, "Is it Tyson you want to speak to?"

"We're here to see you, Will. Please stay" the Principal replied as he entered the untidy, clothing-strewn room, "You'll need to sit down."

Tyson looked over his shoulder from the veranda and saw the consternation on their faces. He joined them in the living area and sat down beside Will.

The Principal hesitated before continuing, "Will, I have some terrible news. Your mother has just contacted me. She couldn't reach you on your phone." He was wringing his hands in anguish, "She asked me to prepare you for a call she'll be making at one o'clock by bringing some support from our University." The room seemed colder.

Will sat ashen faced as the Principal mumbled, "Your brother, Cammy ...who was also such a great student here... was killed on Active Service in Syria. We are truly, truly sorry son."

Will said nothing but stared straight at the man. His chest began to heave as his breathing quickened. He began to swallow and gulp furiously as the shock took effect followed by huge tears escaping from his reddening eyes. Tyson leaned across and placed his arm around his young friend's shoulders and pulled him towards himself. Will broke. Sobbing. Unable to speak. Tyson, appalled, nodded to the two opposite.

The doctor knelt next to them and put her hand gently on Will's knee, "Will, we are so sorry. We will do everything we can to help you through this. I can stay with you or I can give Tyson my cellphone number. I want you to call whenever you need to," whilst handing over a slip of paper wrapping a small box of sedatives to which Tyson could again only nod as he silently swept his own tears from his own cheeks with the back of his hands. He waved goodbye to them.

The door closed quietly behind them. Will and Tyson sat and rocked together for what seemed an age. Will's phone eventually rang. He didn't appear to register what his mother was saying.

The call ended, the boys sat. Hours later, the sun set and they remained motionless, utterly broken.

CHAPTER 4

10 DOWNING ST, LONDON
OCTOBER 2018

10 Downing St, London: October 2018

THE PRIME MINISTER and his Press Officer, Harry Slessor, are watching CNN. The announcer is toiling to be heard against a backdrop of a massive, angry, noisy, demonstration on Edinburgh's Princes Street. The Imperial statue of the mounted Royal Scots Grey looked down on the scenes. Few in the crowd knew of the irony that this renowned Regiment was formed in the late 1670's in a pre-1707 independent Scotland.

The CNN announcer states, "In a prepared response the London government has announced that they are unilaterally suspending the results of the Scottish Independence election result for a minimum period of five years. London claims this will allow the Scottish people time to consider the implications of breaking up the United Kingdom. At the same time, the government will explore the possibility of agreeing to an Independent Scotland, but only after a 2nd referendum. Predictably, this has caused uproar among Scots at what they see as the illegal withdrawal of their democratic right to decide their own political destiny. British security forces in Scotland have been placed on full alert to combat growing unrest and London is sending English troops into Scotland to ensure that order is restored in what is seen by many Scots as a provocative measure.'"

The PM, smiling, switches the screen off and turns to Harry, "If those bloody Scots think that they can just waltz off with their troops and to make themselves one of the most oil-wealthy countries in the world just because oil has tipped $110 a barrel then they had better think again. Their bloody renewable energy industries are also worth a bloody fortune but more importantly we need it exported from them to us for free or the bloody lights in London go out! Not to mention their endless supply of fresh water that we need. Now. What's the progress on the House of Lords Constitution Committee and their new Act of Union? It's essential that it includes a no-Referendum clause without our permission." Harry purposely left the Prime Minister's office on his task.

Scottish Parliament, Edinburgh: 1 November

Members of Scotland's devolved regional government are in turmoil. The Press Area is jammed with cameras and jostling reporters from the world media.

In the debating chamber a parliamentarian is making an impassioned speech, "We cannot allow a repeat of the 1707 annexation of Scotland by England! We stand here in a state legislature controlled and now imprisoned by London. But no more! The Community of Scots, of all colours and religions, overwhelmingly reject London rule! We totally reject London's claim to our most important asset – not our oil, but our people! We have broken the chains that held our country to allow London warmongers to exploit our sons and daughters. No more shall Scotland house London's nuclear weapons of mass destruction! No more will London mis-use Scotland's wealth at the expense of our young, our old and our infirm!"

Roars of approval greet this defiance. Most members are on their feet. The ovation dies down as the First Minister, Margo McCrindle, rises to speak. Her head is bowed in deep thought then rises slowly.

"Ladies and Gentlemen. This Parliament awarded me the greatest of honours when you elected me First Minister. I accepted this privilege, humbly, on behalf of the Scots electorate but also as a great believer in the world-renowned sense of fair-play that are by-words for Great Britain.

"Today, I stand before all of you that you witness my utter devastation at London's betrayal of every democratic principle that I, and all of you, hold dear. We held a free, fair, and democratic referendum on continued EU membership with every notice that a majority vote, on our self-determination, would bring about exactly that.

"London rejected our call for an open and democratic Yes or No Referendum because they knew the pro-Independence parties would achieve a "Yes" majority.

"We lost the 2014 Referendum. But we overwhelmingly won the 2015 and 2017 Scots vote in the UK General Elections and again our Holyrood vote in 2016 along with our overwhelming rejection of Brexit. London's answer is to foist a proscriptive new Act of Union on us. We reject this imprisonment!

"Our servicemen and women are currently in harm's way in Afghanistan, Nigeria, Liberia, Iraq, Libya and Northern Ireland. These conflict zones do not include NATO'S illegal war in Syria. London's aggressive military foreign policies are antagonising peoples across the world instead of seeking diplomatic, regional solutions to their challenges. I now assert this militarism is against the stated will of our electorate and parliamentarians.

"Illegal Trident weapons of mass destruction are now being renewed in Scotland against our wishes," which brought parliamentarians to their feet in cries of protest.

As the outburst subsided she continued, "As the price of North Sea oil has recovered to record levels, London is now raiding our oil reservoirs with outrageous speed, with no heed for conservation. This is unashamed fiscal piracy.

"I am not surprised therefore, that in such circumstances, Scotland voted for independence within Europe and I accept their judgement - as should London. Brexit, Trident renewal and war in Syria has been crucial in that decision.

"Scotland has already paid its dues to London in blood after 50 years of continuous bloody wars in Aden. Ireland. Dhofar. The Falkland Islands. Bosnia. Kosovo. Sierra Leone. Iraq and Afghanistan. These are the conflicts the public know about... Hundreds of Scots lives have been lost in those British conflicts in addition to those 5,000 plus who were wounded, physically and mentally, and are now reliving their pain every day within our Communities with little or no London government support. This disgraceful behaviour stops now!"

She allows the cheers of approval to subside before continuing, "We mourn for those hundreds of pour souls who, having come home as veterans, sought an end to their torments in suicide.

"And what of the anguish and grief of their fathers, mothers, sons and daughters who share their continued sorrow? I am very, very conscious that Syria is a war-too-far for the Scots public. We are left mourning for nine more of Scotland's sons a few weeks ago as a result of their tragic road accident.

"But Scotland has spoken. Enough is enough!" she paused to allow yet more spontaneous applause subside.

"Now London, in an appalling, authoritarian edict has refused to accept the stated will of our people. We cannot accept this! I firmly accept our, and any other peoples, right to self-government. I swear before you that I shall do everything in my power to ensure that Scotland's right to determine our own future is upheld!"

Loud defiant cheers echoed around the Chamber in addition to ecstatic applause from Members and the mobbed public galleries which greeted this statement. Outside the Scottish parliament buildings crowds also waved flags and cheered as they watched their First Minister's speech on large screens.

McCrindle flushes and raises her hand to quell the collective defiance.

She holds up a UN headed sheet and reads aloud, "UN CHARTER, Chapter 1 Purposes & Principles. This Charter was raised in 1945 to bring an end to Empires and Reichs. I quote: "Article 1 The Purposes of the United Nations are:

1. To maintain international peace and security, and to that end: to take effective collective measures for the prevention and removal of threats to the peace, and for the suppression of acts of aggression or other breaches of the peace, and to bring about by peaceful means, and in conformity with the principles of justice and international

law, adjustment or settlement of international disputes or situations which might lead to a breach of the peace;

2. To develop friendly relations among nations based on respect for the principle of equal rights and self-determination of peoples," Margo repeats this second Purpose with great emphasis continuing, "and to take other appropriate measures to strengthen universal peace."

3. To achieve international co-operation in solving international problems of an economic, social, cultural, or humanitarian character, and in promoting and encouraging respect for human rights and for fundamental freedoms for all without distinction as to race, sex, language, or religion."

"Today, this Government of Scotland will brief emissaries to be sent immediately to the United Nations, the European Union and Commonwealth capitals with our legitimate claim to self-determination and to seek our democratic human right to join the independent, peace-loving brotherhood of nations! Concurrently, we shall take steps to form a Provisional Government which will assume control over fiscal policy, diplomacy and defence."

Tear-filled, joyful pandemonium erupts. Some are heard shouting, "Freedom!" A few hard core pro-Union members storm from the Parliament berated by the ecstatic democrats.

10 Downing St, London

Harry and the PM angrily watch the live scenes from the Edinburgh Parliament . The PM points to the screen, "The traitorous bitch! I want her removed."

Harry lifts the phone and makes a series of demands.

CHAPTER 5

EDINBURGH, NOVEMBER 2018

Press Conference, Edinburgh: 9 November

HARRY SLESSOR sits in an adjoining room listening on a monitor, on which a Canadian journalist questions Sir Geoffrey Cuthbert, a London Minister.

"Malcolm MacIntosh, sir, CBC. Can I just confirm, Sir Geoffrey, that your unelected London governmental Constitution Committee have just suspended Scotland's democratically elected First Minster and her parliament?"

Sir Geoffrey, immaculate, replies in clipped tones, "While I resent the language of the question, I shall point out that the suspension is only for five years, my dear chap. The Prime Minister has decreed that McCrindle has exceeded the powers devolved from London and has been suspended for taking action that negatively affects the strength and stability of the United Kingdom."

The Canadian sits down and is replaced by another reporter.

"Gus MacGregor, Australian NBC. The rest of the world may see your actions as wholly undemocratic and force Scotland into rebellion, given that London has just removed the ballot box as the normal, peaceful option for such decision-making. Would you judge such potential rebels as terrorists...or freedom fighters?"

Flashes flood the room and talking-heads chatter excitedly to camera, as all attention focuses on the chuckling Sir Geoffrey, "I believe your question to be rather fanciful, old chap. Any Scot would be absolutely insane to step outside the law and take up arms. Besides, the British Army has over 50 years' experience in successfully dealing with terrorists worldwide.... Now, if you'll excuse me, I have work to do."

Sir Geoffrey smiles at the cameras and begins to leave the conference as a barrage of questions is ignored by him. He suddenly turns back to the cameras, "Oh... did I forget to mention...Scotland's little parliament is not allowed to vote for separation. Only London can allow such a vote."

He looks condescendingly at the cameras, then leaves.

George Square, Glasgow City Centre, St Andrews Day: 30 November

Overlooked by grand buildings, a massive throng fills every inch of the Victorian heart of the city. In spite of the grey skies, they listen and cheer a stage filled with public speakers, mounted in front of the City Chambers, the town hall. A massive banner "SCOTLAND UNITED" is draped above the rostrum.

A popular grey-haired firebrand called Tam Muir is rousing the Glasgow public with his rhetoric, his raised right fist clenched in defiance. "Don't be intimidated by London's defiling of democracy! Every small country in the world has been told at some stage you are too wee, too stupid and too incapable of looking after your own affairs or making your own decisions! Well, now we are showing every wee country in the world, of any ethnicity or creed, that we all have the right to stand on our own two feet! It's our democratic right to choose self-determination!"

Huge roars of approval and applause rise from the Square. Muir laughs ironically, "This from our pretendy wee Edinburgh parliament, the White Blether Club which was set up to stop self-government from taking place at all. It wasn't set up to bring about new possibilities but merely to strangle them at birth! This pretendy wee parly was like an impresario that establishes the most expensive nightclub complex in the toon but then refuses to sell swally in it or permit the dancin'!"

The crowd roars with laughter then spontaneously sing "Flower of Scotland", a popular folk song.

In a narrow back-lane off George Square "Flower of Scotland" can be clearly heard. Harry remonstrates with the police commander.

The two are alone, but watchful policemen at the end of the lane eye the pair discreetly. Harry, furious with rage, finger-jabs the senior policeman, "Clear that bloody square! Those separatists, those fucking lefty extremists, are preaching the break-up of the United Kingdom, man! I'll have your head if you don't!"

The senior Glaswegian policeman has extremely short, grey stubble hair and sports a long-broken purple nose brought about by his love of football and expensive malt whiskies. He casually removes his uniform hat, with the distinctive black-and-white chequered band, then suddenly administers a savage blow with his forehead onto the bridge of Harry's nose, colloquially known as a "Glesca Kiss." Harry's nose instantly bursts in gushing blood. The policeman pokes his hand-held radio into Harry's chest, forcing him to crash back, sprawling into garbage bags against the wall. Harry barely recovers his balance.

The policeman growls, "Son, if ye ever prod your finger in ma face again ah'll fuckin' bite it aff. Noo, I might be mistaken, but peaceful political demos were OK up to this moment, or are we working for Adolf fuckin' Hitler!? My city gave tens of thousands of lives to fight wee fascist keech like you!"

The policeman's bloodshot yellowing eyes burn out from his lived-in face, inches from the petrified face of the distraught Englishman who desperately tries to staunch the flow of blood with the back of his hand whilst audibly whimpering.

"Noo...fuck off oot of ma city and if ah see your face, or your like, we'll send ye homeward to think again!"

The big policeman stands back to let the dishevelled, bloodied adviser scurry to the end of the lane. A by-standing constable winks slowly at Harry and whispers, deadpan, "Haste ye back, sir."

British Military Hospital, Cyprus: 14 December

Sean, strained, listens with closed eyes on a mobile phone to a hysterical, screaming woman – Cammy's mother, "What did our son die for – Syrian democracy or America's oil corporations? You and your bloody army got him killed! What price your stupid officer and gentleman ideals when we can't even bury our own son at home? His funeral is for what? You have let our own son be cynically exploited by those bastards in London, you stupid fool! How many other mothers and families have paid this price? Are you listening to me? Answer me!" a long painful silence ensues. She finished in a hate-filled menacing declaration, "Go to your bloody Brit funeral. I would never, ever sanctify its stinking hypocrisy with my presence. Bring my son home or I'll make you regret it!"

Sean swallows guiltily and wipes away tears. He hangs up without talking. A military driver approaches and coughs politely, embarrassed at the tears, "Sir, I'm here to take you to your son's funeral."

British Military Cemetery, Cyprus

They arrive at the sun-drenched burial ground, overlooking a beautiful bay. Hundreds of white crosses row-on-row stand mute in the sun. They are silent witness to many British wars. A British flag, the Union Jack, is draped on each coffin which lie at the side of nine graves.

A small group of kilted comrades, friends and relatives stand under makeshift awnings to protect them from the baking sun.

Sean advances on the coffins and with one hand scoops up his sons' medals and Glengarry which bedeck his coffin whilst his other hand rips off the Union Jack and throws it to the ground, as the shocked mourners look on.

One by one, the relatives of the other Scots soldiers follow his example but more respectfully remove the British flags and carefully replace the bonnet and medals. A wee lassie steps forward and takes a small Scots flag-handkerchief from her handbag and places it silently on her father's coffin.

The young officer in command of the burial party recovers and barks out commands to seven soldiers standing at ease nearby. The subaltern was chosen as a close friend of Cammy's as are the ashen faced young soldiers who were comrades of the dead.

They fire three volleys over the graves. In one practised movement, they bring their rifles down, and reverse arms, heads bowed. A piper plays the ancient haunting lament, "Flo'ers of the Forest".

No-one speaks or moves. Sean, shaking with emotion, whispers quietly to himself, "No parent should have to bury his child...especially for a lie. I trusted London with your life, Cammy. They will pay a heavy price for our betrayal, I promise you, Son. As my word is my bond, blood will burn."

Graithnock Community Centre, Ayrshire: 22 January 2019

A few weeks later Sean is laughing heartily in the middle of a group of chatting, seated men and women. Glasses of beer and spirits cover the tables in front of them. They appear delighted to be in each other's noisy, animated company. The bar door has a temporary hand-written sign, fixed with huge lumps of Blu-Tack, stating, "B Coy, 3 RSF, Old Comrades Association."

Sean's phone beeps as it receives a text message which he quickly reads. He stands up whilst making his smiling apology and heads outside.

He strides towards a Range-Rover with tinted windows which sits at the discrete rear door of the Centre. As he approaches the rear passenger window slides open to reveal Scotland's First Minister, Margo McCrindle.

Sean opens her door and offers his hand, which she accepts as she steps out, "Great to see you, again, Margo. There is no media to bother us and the lads have been briefed they have a special visitor so no media contact to be generated from them." He kisses her lightly on the cheek.

"Thanks Sean," she smiled as they walk together into the Centre, "It's been a long time since we were at school together in Graithnock, the cultural capital of Ayrshire," she joked.

They both giggled indulgently together as they stopped alone in the entrance corridor. Sean shuffled like an embarrassed tongue-tied schoolboy belying his professional military background, "I'm delighted you could make this, Margo. Thanks. The boys will be well chuffed that you've taken the time to be here this afternoon and I know how busy you are with all that's going on in the country."

Margo smiled politely in return but her unsmiling eyes were dark, hard, unfathomable and soulless like those of a great white shark. "I've made my afternoon available to you, Sean, because I know it's important to you and your veterans. We go back together to our schooldays and I'm very conscious since all that time you've never asked me for anything until now. That, intrigues me. I wouldn't want to serve in the British Army. But I was proud, as we all are from wee Graithnock that you'd done so well in your career. I'm very, very sorry, however, for the loss of your son, Sean," and touched his arm. He smiled silently.

"I don't know enough about our Veterans' community but would like to learn from this trip particularly with our stream of casualties returning from Syria. I'm all ears, Sean."

"Excellent, I may have had a military career but that pales into insignificance to a Graithnock lassie who made First Minister," he said and waved her into the meeting area, "Ladies and gentleman, may I introduce a very dear friend, Margo McCrindle."

Natural warm applause greeted the popular First Minister. Margo sat with them and quietly explained her genuine wish to understand any issues the former Jocks and their partners wished to discuss.

Initial reticence gave way to sincere and pertinent conversation and not a little banter. Margo being a keen observer however, was drawn to a silent, staring grey-haired man in his fifties at the edge of the group. As soon as she had answered a question on military pensions she smilingly asked the man, "...and what about you? Do you want to ask me anything?" The question manifested itself as a showstopper. The only sound that could now be heard from the previously semi-raucous company was the shuffling of feet and polite coughs.

Sean filled the void by quietly stating, "This is former Colour Sergeant Gary McIlvrae. He can't say much really as he has some, er, health issues. The community tries to help him – when he lets them. Countless tours of Northern Ireland followed by the first Gulf War effectively...well...snapped him. There but for the Grace of God go all of us. He used to chat but only blamed the drugs cocktails the army forced them all to take, like anti-malarial's", murmured agreement emanated from the now sombre group.

Sean continued, "He was one of the reasons we invited you here. Gary was a regular army soldier but has been pretty much left to his own devices in our Community. The army is no longer directly responsible for any of these guys or girls. Aye, they get some pension but any medical care is born by us, through our NHS. His regimental association does what it can but they are no more mental health carers than I am. So what? Guys like Gary are out of sight out of mind, so to speak, to the London government. We, and other groups like us throughout Scotland, need more support. Urgently. With your permission, I'll shortly drive you down to a facility just outside Ayr, called Combat Anxiety. Gary lives there and we can drop him off. Is that OK?"

"Of course," she said, "we should really go as soon possible though."

A very sallow, tall, frail but distinguished looking veteran stood up and opened a box revealing a regimental crest. He asked for the attention of the group, "Ma'am, Sir...I used to be their Sergeant Major. Bobby Hagg's ma name", which generated good natured mockery from his former soldiers and not a few wee smirks from some piratical types, "On behalf of the B Company lads and lassies we'd like to present you with this memento of your visit. Very sincerely, we'd like to thank you very much for taking the time to listen to us and we know that Colonel McAlpin will follow up, and let us ken aboot whit we've discussed."

Applause, followed by the obligatory selfies, prevented an immediate reply from an engaged, but somehow humbled, Margo.

Eventually, she managed to thank them with a predictable response about proud service yada yada yada, which caused a wee old woman to grip her sleeve. This alarmed Margo but provoked barely concealed amusement within the company. The wee woman hissed, "Listen you tae me, hen. You're the country's heid-banana. See tae it that nae mair Scottish sojdgers ever again fights London's bloody wars. I mean it! I'm bloody sick of it. We all are!"

Margo winced from her whisky breath as the wee woman's grip tightened and pulled her face closer to hers. Bobby attempted to intervene, "For God's sake, Aggie, leave the heid-ban...sorry, First Minister alone."

Ignoring his remonstration, Aggie insisted, "Ma faithers faither came back fae the First War a broken man. Nae work. A pittance of a pension. Ma faither came back, barely alive, fae the Second World War fae the stinkin' Jap prison camps. Tae whit? A Land fit for Heroes? Ma bloody arse! Enough is enough ah tell ye! Look at these boys here noo. Look at them! Proud enough tae serve wae their pals but ignored and forgotten by their country. Anything they get is fae charities and local communities. London disnae gie a flyin' shite aboot them. Nae mair! Nae mair ahm tellin' ye!"

Margo placed a hand on Aggies and softly said, "The Scottish people have said as much when they voted. I hear them. And I hear you, Aggie. No more London wars for our children."

"Aggie! Yer trying to fling wur First Minister aboot like an empty tracksuit. You'll be shoutin' "Aloha Snackbar!" next like they mental Taliban ragheids that we fought," said a huge laughing Jock who was unceremoniously unhanding Aggie at the same time as clutching his bagpipes. Margo laughed in relief taking the opportunity to escape from wee Aggies grasp who stood her ground, wizened eyes narrowed in unconvinced malevolence.

Fergie, the grinning piper, cranked up his pipes and blasted out their old regimental March, "Hieland Laddie." Sean took the cue to hug and kiss farewell to as many of the boisterous group as he could whilst ushering Margo to his car. Gary, completely oblivious to the throng, was gently led by the arm to the back seat by his ex-Sergeant Major Hagg. The crowd thirstily returned to their beers.

Margo quickly told her minders to meet her back at the Centre in the evening as Sean made sure Gary was buckled in. As soon as Margo was in the vehicle Sean sped out of the car park and made great haste on the short journey down to the Ayrshire Coast.

A sombre discussion en-route confirmed the salient issues focussing on the care in the community many of the discarded and forgotten ex-servicemen and women received. Gary said nothing.

They pulled off the main road into the long gravel drive at the former country mansion now converted to a residential and day care centre for veterans with mental health issues.

Sean changed the subject by talking about the fantastic support given to former servicemen by a dedicated, motivated staff. Margo was aware of its existence and was quick to point out the support provided by the Scottish Government, both agreeing a lot more could be done.

Gary climbed silently out of the car unaided and headed into the reception area where he was warmly welcomed back and checked in. He was escorted by Margo and Sean who hugged his former comrade farewell. As they left the foyer he delayed Margo at a large elaborate noticeboard of a type common in most military establishments which lists names of regimental battles, dates and campaigns or former Commanding Officers. Every war zone the patients had served in had been carefully painted on by hand.

"I heard your recent speech in parliament when you listed the campaigns our lads have served in over the last fifty years." He slowly pointed at a list of names she had not mentioned, "There are lads and lassies who receive care in here and elsewhere who served in these places. Palestine. Korea. Indonesia. Malaya...all of these former colonies during "Retreat from Empire" etcetera, etcetera. Does the public know or care about these guys? Many were conscripts." He looks directly at her.

"Fortunately, that no longer applies" she said.

They drove silently from the place as they headed North on the Ayrshire coast road. To the West the setting sun was providing a spectacular deep, warm reddish sunset which embraced the skyline of the Isle of Arran a few miles offshore.

In the middle-distance they could see the 14th Century Portencross castle sitting majestically on the shoreline. It was a marvellous sight as it stood sentinel overlooking the Firth of Clyde with the Isles of Bute and Cumbrae as beautiful backdrops behind it to the North and stately Arran opposite in the West.

"Can you spare five minutes here? I've got something I want to show you," asked Sean. "Sure," was the reply. "Do you mind leaving your mobile phone in the car please, with mine?" he requested firmly. She did not ask why but complied uneasily.

Sean pulled off the main road and parked up at a small churchyard overlooked by the imposing high, square walls of the stone castle. They could both smell and taste the salt on the wind which drifted in on a cool breeze from the Firth of Clyde.

"My mum and dad used to bring me and my brothers down here in the summer for picnics when we were wee," reminisced Sean, almost to himself. "The castle and the coastline just here are almost like one of Ayrshire's best kept secrets. I love it, "and smiled broadly.

Margo did not smile in return as they stopped at the stone dyke which lined the footpath to the castle. She knew Sean had not stopped here to discuss childhood memories or the scenery. They were alone without witnesses and no chance of their phones being used as listening devices by any government agencies.

"Let's hear it, Sean", she said.

He looked at her intently and saw her as the highly intelligent, committed, capable professional that she had become. No warmth, only an extremely business-like woman yet he could not bring himself to his subject immediately.

"Robert the Bruce gave this land to the Boyd's of Kilmarnock immediately after Bannockburn. Robert Boyd built a Hall-House initially and it became, over time, the Tower-House we see now. Bannockburn," he repeated. "As a wee boy that battle and everything that surrounded those legends fascinated me and my pals. I mentally compartmentalised the Independence malarkey when I was commissioned at Sandhurst as you would expect of a newly minted young officer from the "Chap Factory." I swore my Oath of Allegiance to the former Jelly Bean and then to her heir and successor, King Billy."

Margo looked askance at Sean's irreverent references to the reigning monarch and the recently departed Queen. It was not what she expected but she remained silent.

He continued earnestly now, "As well as compartmentalising any thoughts of Scotland's independence, I'd done the same with my favourite uncle's talk of politics. It wouldn't have been a great career move in the army to mention he was a dyed-in-the-wool Red Clydeside Communist Shop-Steward. "Monarchy sanctifies the inheritance of privilege" he would say. School visits at Graithnock Town Hall to see the brilliant productions of the old 7:84 Theatre Company carved a socialist love of Scotland in my head and heart forever. Remember them?"

Margo nodded in agreement. He pointed over the stone wall at some gravestones, "Notice anything unusual about those three there?" Margo could make out each one had the same carved army regimental crest which she did not recognise. She scrutinised the letters and said each had the same "R.S.F." initials on them but a different number preceding them. After a short pause she identified, "Gallipoli, Loos and Somme" separately from each.

"Anything else?" he asked which she replied negatively to.

"You'll be suffering from battle and campaign overkill today, I reckon," but continued, "The Royal Scots Fusiliers were our county infantry regiment from Ayrshire, R.S.F. Each number in front represents the number of the respective battalion each of those Jocks served in. Nineteen R.S.F. battalions, of approximately a thousand Jocks each, served wherever the King & Empire sent them during World War One. Most local war memorials will show the wars end as 1918 or 1919.

"These Jocks are not on the local war memorial. I've checked. Look again at the dates they died: 1922, 1924 and 1925". They clearly served in the R.S.F. and their families were probably compelled by these poor bastards to record where they had served in the Kaisers War. I know, because I've checked that too, they died of their wounds received, including mental breakdown. Because they died well after the Armistice, London decided they didn't count.

"I challenge you to visit any graveyard in Scotland and you will find the same story. Forgotten Gordons, Argylls, Seaforths, H.L.I. etc and on and on the disgraceful list goes. As well as not being listed on local memorials you won't find them listed in the Scottish National War Memorials nominal role of the Fallen, in Edinburgh. They stopped recording war deaths at 1921 only two years after the war finished. That is, the official list. How many were not included? No one actually knows. Add in those killed between the World Wars. Shamefully. The clear fact is London suppressed the true number of Scotland's war dead...along with the rest of Britain's. London has form for supressing casualties. Does anyone give a monkey's fuck into a flying donut other than their regiments, military-anoraks and surviving relatives?" he angrily demanded. "Do you know what that generation gave their lives for in France? Miles and miles of shit-coloured fuck all! A hundred years later and London intends to do the same all over again and again! They always talk about "The Fallen." A nice clean sanitised phrase, eh? But it conceals filth, ugly horrendous wounds, screaming pain and agony, mental breakdown. A lifetime of nightmares and the abject emptiness of loss... and then what... relying on charity like a tramp? Are you aware London supplied one-way tickets to the Jocks for Canada after the bloody "Great" war? Because it was a pragmatic option to remove hundreds of thousands of pissed off soldiers with no work who might be thinking of continuing the 1919 Glasgow riots ?"

Margo was astounded by this "new" Sean that she had not known existed. "Please go on, "she said hesitantly.

He paused as he considered his high-risk course of action, then, "When I was at my son's burial in Cyprus, two fucking thousand miles from Scotland, I couldn't help but think, "Why?" Why war? Why did he die? These are leftie-type questions I've always ignored because he and I were volunteer professional soldiers. We know that the public would say if we were looking for sympathy we would find it in the dictionary between shit and syphilis. But this was different," as he paused between gasps.

"Why should it be different?" Margo asked softly, recognising his pent-up agony.

Sean uttered, "Why? Why vote for Independence? All of these questions are intrinsically linked. I was so proud when he commissioned into the army. Into my regiment. The professional risks and the realpolitik of serving in a profession that is actually run by dysfunctional Alpha Male public school bullies was by the by. To be ignored - and to focus on the comradeship, the arduous challenges, the spellbinding sense of service that no fucking raspberry Mivvy could ever understand etc etc...and then... to be confronted that it was all a shameless lie. A con. My career was devoted to a fucking lying system that recruits and trains Good Guys then exploits them for the fucking Yankee Dollar...and has cost me my beautiful, lovely son's life." In spite of himself his eyes welled up.

Heartlessly this time, an impatient Margo replied, "You couldn't honestly have expected any less. Military service has always meant carrying out government policy – whatever that may be."

Sean glared back, "Fucking naïve, is it? Naïve to expect government can be run by the Good Guys? To have policies of principle that can make us proud to serve? To know that having carried out any such policy our soldiers will be properly looked after and not have to rely on charity handouts as homeless beggars in the street? Do you have any fucking idea how many of our guys have committed suicide, been sectioned in mental institutions, are in jail or homeless because of serving their fucking country?" he shouted.

Both were furious now. Margo stabbed back, "You volunteered. You all did. Tell me something new about London and soldiering! Even auld Aggie understood all of this better than you!" she shouted. "And don't you dare swear at me, Sean McAlpin!"

Sean was visibly shaking with rage, "Don't fucking swear? The politician that you are! How much do you want Independence? Enough to die for it? Enough to stop sending our kids and those of our future generations to fight London's fucking illegal wars? You know that London is bringing back conscription, don't you, and what are you doing to stop it? Is that fucking enough material change for you?"

"What did you say? Conscription? Did you just say that, Sean?" she asked, aghast.

Sean visibly composed himself. It took a long few moments to calm down. Margo's questions hung in the air. She stepped forward and took his hand, "Sean. Conscription?"

"I apologise for my temper, Margo. My mental health has been in smithereens during the last few Ops, what with the stresses plus Christ knows the effect of fucking drugs like anti-malarials. Cammy's death has left me staring into the abyss" he said as he looked intently at the nearby graves.

"Sean! Conscription?" she insisted.

"I saw Top Secret papers in MoD Main Building in London last week during my Liberia debrief. UK military involvement in the Middle East must increase because of Washington Pentagon demands. We don't have enough soldiers. We've been haemorrhaging hundreds every month from the Army. They're leaving because of the constant Operational Tours and the effect on the soldiers and their families. Not enough young people are stepping forward to join up. Those leaving and those not joining aren't stupid – they know the Iraq war and the Syria wars were illegal and they know if they lose the plot over there, on the ground, by malleting a fucking raghead they can end up prosecuted and in jail. Some Scottish councils have already banned recruiting in their areas. Conscription is the only answer to the army's severe manpower shortage in the face of government deployments and they are doing something about it."

Margo seemed stunned but Sean continued, "But that's not all", hesitating, "London refused us a second independence Referendum because they knew you would win. Your unofficial referendum victory called for UDI".

He held up his hand to stop Margo's attempted protest, "Or whatever label you want to put on it. It's heightened their contingency plans for military occupation of Scotland."

Margo spluttered, "Military occupation! You're not serious?"

"Absolutely", Sean asserted. "What do you think the Joint Operational Planning Centre in Northwood does with its time? It's your turn to be naïve," he smiled briefly.

"They do contingencies, which they update continuously. Then if something kicks off anywhere on the planet where there is British-related interest the Crisis Planning Team reach out for the relevant file. Currently, the "Scotland File" categorises the aim, objectives and end-state as military occupation of the Unionist border counties, the City of Aberdeen and the Shetland Isles in order to fragment the newly formed self-governing Scotland and, concurrently, to undermine its ability to generate income through oil revenues which will therefore continue to London. The military planning has been done to translate the political intent on the specific authority of the Cabinet Office. The Prime Minister is discussing further action with Washington right now. They have just to say, "Go" and it will take place. I predict within a few weeks. Currently, they estimate oil is the hub of all of our power therefore our centre of gravity. Westminster will nullify this."

"I'll stop it," fizzed Margo furiously. "They can't do this to us."

"You won't", stated Sean very determinedly, "because you'll immediately cause my arrest. You must give me time. The Brits are already sectioning soldiers under the Mental Health Acts. They'd take one look at my Med. File and have enough evidence to bang me up and throw away the key. You are going to give me until the end of June and you and your government are going to remain extremely focussed on the strategic big prize – Independence. At every opportunity you will use the very real genius you have, Margo, to break the chains from the Unicorn!" in a popularly understood reference to the national British coat-of-arms which displays Scotland's unicorn in chains.

It was Margo's turn to be visibly horrified, "What are you going to do Sean?"

He paused before replying, "It's important you don't know in order that you can truthfully deny all knowledge. I repeat, focus on our strategy of Independence...politically. And get a hold of a translation of the master strategist, Von Clausewitz's book, 'On War'" he laughed, "Especially the bit where he says, and I quote, 'that War is not merely a political act, but also a real political instrument, a continuation of political commerce, a carrying out of the same by other means.' You must also understand how he explains such events can be utterly chaotic. Clausewitz describes this as 'the fog of war' but when you understand and anticipate this whilst remaining focused on the strategic aim you can better react to unfolding episodes faster and more effectively than London does."

"For God's sake, Sean. Please, please tell me you aren't going to start a war?" she whispered wide-eyed.

"No, Margo. I'm not going to start a war. London is. But tell me this. London has seized the ballot box from the hands of the Scottish people by trashing the conclusive result of an open, free, fair and democratic vote, removed you from office and fucked off our parliament! Beg for a second Referendum? Hope the nice people in Brussels and the UN ride to our rescue? Roll over and continue to take it up the fucking arse and then lie in our own fucking pish like the kiltie in 'Outlander'? Not any more, Margo," smiling crazily he then laughed in a mock Australian exaggerated accent, "They make take our lives etcetera etcetera...Etcetera!"

After a short pause Sean turned to Margo with a different, more earnest manner, "Cammy and his men weren't killed in an RTA. They were killed-in-action by a roadside Daesh IED."

"What?" she gasped. "That's not what we were told! How do you know?"

Quietly, he stated, "His Company Sergeant Major told me. He was there. I guess the public will find out eventually but the soldiers are all employed under the Official Secrets Act plus the Westminster government issued a D Notice on the incident. You and the public were only told what London wanted you to know."

"That's totally unacceptable. I'll contact the Prime Minister immediately!" she shouted.

"No you won't" replied Sean evenly, "You don't know because you haven't been told. Any of this! I'm still sworn to the Secrets Act as well, remember. I can't afford to spend any time in jail. You'll wait and, by the way, remember you've been deposed by those you would seek to warn," he concluded brutally. Margo turned and walked away with her head in both hands.

Sean stared out, gazing towards the last rays of the spectacular setting sun over the Western Isles. He lifted a hand to shade the sunset glow. Unwittingly his gaze fixed on a jet-black silhouette cruising slowly and silently southwards on the surface of the sea between him and the "Sleeping Giant" mountain peaks of Arran; a backdrop of ancient Scotland against London's 21st Century weapon of mass destruction. It was the unmistakable outline of a British nuclear submarine slinking from its Faslane lair.

Southern Presbyterian University (SPU): January 2019

Will and Tyson are sitting in their student apartment. Will's red-raw eyes and tear stained cheeks a statement to his sorrow and loss. Tyson is no different. Their decent into depression and isolation is unchecked; they care neither for themselves nor each other. Football and study have been long ignored.

The news of Cammy's death in Syria has gutted them. Each sips at massive drams of straight malt whisky. They can't look at one another. A TV can be heard faintly from an adjoining student apartment but that is the only sound. The curtains are drawn whilst light barely seeps in around the edges.

Will begins to moan again. Massive waves of uncontrolled rib-hurting sobs rack his already exhausted body. Tyson gets up and crosses the room to hug his team-mate but is rejected by an outstretched palm. He heads to the bathroom, nausea filling his body.

CHAPTER 6

DUBLIN, JANUARY 2019

Dublin Airport: 4 January

Sean walks out of the Customs area to be met by a beautiful Irish woman. They embrace each other hungrily, silently and walk to a waiting taxi.

In the taxi Sean buries his head in her shoulder and whispers her name, Sinead. She holds him gently and murmurs quietly to him as she would a small boy.

Sinead's Dublin Home

Sean lies naked in bed, sleeping in Sinead's arms. She lies awake gazing down at his scarred, wracked body. She strokes his profusely sweating back lovingly as if to ease away the pain.

He sits up violently. A fierce twitch is apparent at the corner of his eyes. He stares unseeingly around him, completely disorientated, screaming "Where is my rifle? Where is my fucking rifle? Cammy! Cammy! Where is your fucking rifle?"

Sinead, terrified, seizes him by the shoulders and holds him tightly, whispering, "It's OK Sean. You're safe. It's OK."

His sweat soaked body half-heartedly attempts to twist free. Sean's panic-attack nightmare drains him as he begins to weep as he sleeps. Sinead, still frightened, holds him until his terror subsides. In only a few moments he returns to his tormented slumber. Sinead lies blinking in terrified confusion until she too eventually falls into uneasy sleep.

Aer Lingus Airbus

Sean looks out of the window down onto the Croatian city of Dubrovnik. The sparkling blue waters of the Adriatic contrast spectacularly against the cities' yellow stone walls and brick red roofs. Sinead is beside him.

Dubrovnik Airport, Croatia Friday: 19 April

The Aer Lingus flight lands at Dubrovnik airport. Sean and Sinead walk from the aircraft into the terminal.

Dubrovnik Saturday: 20 April

A beautiful coastal mansion overlooks the gorgeous blue Adriatic and Dubrovnik. Some people are gathered on a large terraced area drinking orange juice and coffees. The owner is the Croat, Tom Stanic. He warmly welcomes the two new arrivals to his home, Sean and Sinead, "It's fantastic to see you again Sean. I believe you know everyone else?"

Sean smiles, he puts down the laptop case he is carrying and strides confidently into the group and introduces Sinead to them, "Sinead, I'd like you to meet your new comrades-in-arms. We are the founding members of the SLA, the Scottish Liberation Army."

In an open hand he holds a rectangular cloth badge. The badge is a blue and white Scots St Andrews flag with a forward-facing golden rampant lion superimposed on it. "This is how we shall be identified."

Sinead returns Sean's comments with a hard stare. Sean continues, "Tom has bitter experience of fighting for Croatia's independence against Serbia. Croatia is now investing in friends for the future... isn't that right my friend?"

Tom smiles enigmatically.

Andy sits easily in a large chair, looking every inch the professional soldier, "Sergeant Major Andy MacCreadie was with Cammy when he died. We both have a score to settle. Andy is now my second-in-command. He is one of the most capable Senior NCOs it has been my pleasure to have served with. He also speaks his mind, which is essential for what we have planned."

Andy doesn't flicker.

Sean walks over to an attractive young woman with a huge, likeable grin. She sits holding a large chocolate cream cake. He crouches in front of her and returns her broad smile.

"And this is Jill, our secret weapon. She works for the UK Border Force Intelligence Service."

Jill catches the glare from Sinead which bores into her head. Her lovely smile fades abruptly.

Sean, aware of the static between the two women, stands up and unhurriedly moves opposite a young black man with a haircut that can only be described as "Jarhead". Their gaze meets and exchange mutual pain. Sean speaks softly, "I think you'd better introduce yourself, Tyson."

Tyson speaks with the pronounced drawl of the deep Southern States of America. "How y'all doin', sir? I'm so truly sorry about Cammy. You know how close we were. I still haven't gotten over his......". His head lowers as he composes himself. He looks up at Sinead and at the others, as if to explain, "Sean's sons, Cammy and Will, went to University in South Carolina on sports scholarships. I am...", he hesitated, "was...in the same team as Will. They called it football...we call it soccer...", and smiled at the memory, "Cammy had already graduated and went home. He joined a Scottish Regiment at the same time as I was already a US Marine Corps Sergeant in Afghanistan."

Again, Tyson looks down and continues the memory with unease, "I met him in the 'Stan. My unit was in-country too. We talked a lot, coming to the same conclusion that the only reason the good ol' USA was in Afghanistan was to set up gas and oil pipe lines whilst ignoring the billions made from heroin production and London was helping us do it. Democracy? Horseshit! It's all about oil and gas and how the USA is producing less and less and why we need to take other peoples, pure and simple. Syria and Iraq are the same.

"When I finished my tour, I left Cammy still serving in Afghanistan. I enrolled in our Reserve Officer Training Corps programme in my hometown university at Southern Presbyterian in South Carolina.

Cammy's younger brother, Will, arrived last summer to play soccer. It was awesome to meet him too. We've since heard the truth of Cammy's death – and his men. Unbelievable," he whispered, "Will has gone home to be with his mom. I've resigned from the ROTC programme. I believe you want to make London pay for Cammy's life. I would like to help you, sir."

His face lit up as he smiles suddenly with his zeal, "After all, I'm an ethnic Scot named McKenzie," and laughed.

Sean joked at the young guy's passion, "Thanks Johnny Reb! I know both my sons loved your friendship. I'm glad Will is with his mum. Tyson's Scots-American family and friends have, very generously, agreed to financially back the SLA, everyone. We're going to need all the strong help we can get."

"So, what can I tell you about Sinead?" Sean looks directly at her, "Sinead was hard core IRA, an organiser, a specialist in funding, money laundering and smuggling. The brains behind the guns. A passionate hater of London. I commanded the team that arrested her."

Everyone glances at Sinead who laughs loudly at the last comment, "I was one of the fastest runners in the IRA. It took 70 million Brits eight years to catch me." She continues to chuckle for a moment, then returns everyone's look, "...and Lieutenant Colonel Sean MacAlpin, Royal Scotland Regiment...passionate Scot but loyal to his Queen, King and country. Until they suppressed his son's death...and a democratic Referendum."

She looks sympathetically at Sean, "It took you a long time, Sean, to realise that London only ever looks after London. They have never cared about Ireland or Wales or any of their other colonies, including Scotland. They exploit and belittle. I'm glad that you have recognised that now. I can't think of a better leader to set his country free."

Her soft features harden and she addresses them all, "But if any of you think that you are involved in a romantic, heroic, struggle against the Forces of Darkness leave this terrace now."

She eyeballs every individual and looks into their souls, "London will brand you as terrorists, not freedom fighters. They will hunt you, your families and your loved ones as if you are animals. They are experts. They have been invading and conquering lands and peoples that don't belong to them for centuries. They enjoy it. They have the corporate knowledge to achieve it and the Eton and Marlborough system to dispense that knowhow to ensure retention of power within their elite. They will continue to deceive, rob and manipulate as they have persisted in doing for hundreds of years."

Sean acknowledges Sinead's words with a slow nod. He looks focused and walks into a lounge off the terrace, followed by Tom and his other guests. Tom picks up a remote which brings a large wall-TV to life as Sean opens his laptop switches it on. It produces an image of a North Sea oil rig on the screen. He beckons everyone to be seated in the lounge. They sit in a horse-shoe around the screen.

Sean explains, "Sinead is right. What we discuss right now is considered terrorism... but London can call us whatever they like. We have a country to liberate. I hope you have prepared as I requested. I also remind you the plan is nothing, but planning is everything. Tackle risks before they escalate."

He looks around the room and receives positive nods. Sean points at the screen. "Scotland – my daft wee country – is going to light a beacon of hope for down-trodden people everywhere."

Sean continues in a crisp, professional manner. He brings up another slide on the screen. It has only one phrase: FREE SCOTLAND. "We are going to fight London's forces in our land in order to bring about Scotland's independence. I believe we will be massively aided by what Dr Jung called 'synchronicity'".

Andy interrupts, "Synchronicity? Officer-speak. What's that in my language?" Tyson replies, "Synchronicity means an unlikely convergence of events at a specific time."

Andy gives him a suspicious stare.

Sean continues, "Thanks Tyson. Absolutely right. The specific time is 23rd June. The date's the anniversary of the Battle of Bannockburn."

Tom gets up and pours himself some orange juice and interjects, "The battle at the end of the movie Braveheart? When Scotland won its Independence? Are we going to take some oil-rigs?"

Laughing, Sean agrees, "Correct on Bannockburn in Braveheart. But take some oil rigs? No. Have you any idea how much experience the Royal Marines have in dealing with attacks on the rigs? No. We'll fight on ground of our choosing...."

Leaning forward, Andy is interested now, "So what are the other events?"

Sean responds "The political state of unrest in Scotland, the release of the Conscription plan and English occupation of Scotland's border counties, our formation of the SLA, the UK forces over-stretch and... the Scotland v England football match in Glasgow on 22nd June. Serendipity."

Andy is bemused, "Serenity-now? You've lost me again. I was with you up until you mentioned football and that word."

Smiling, Sean replies, "Serendipity can be explained as unexpected good luck. You know the English hooligan "Soccer Crews". They'll be arriving in Scotland in their thousands to Sock-a-Jock and make a wee statement about our blank firing election result. Those animals will be like throwing a naked flame into a summerdry forest. We are going to take advantage of the conflagration that'll surely follow."

Andy leans back weighing Sean up, "I just hope we are not consumed in the conflagration...."

Sean continues by bringing up another slide which shows an ancient black and white photo of an old Victorian building. It is destroyed and badly burned. It's headlined: GENERAL POST OFFICE, DUBLIN, EASTER RISING 1916.

Sean explains, "Our recent Independence vote has been ripped from us. History repeats itself. Ireland had an unsuccessful rebellion in Easter 1916 as a result of conscription being imposed on them. Subsequently, Ireland voted overwhelmingly for independence in the 1919 UK General Election having been promised if their manpower fought for King and Empire in the war to protect small nations, such as Belgium and Serbia, then they as a small nation themselves, would be given self-government. London reneged on that promise. Clearly, London has form for lying to its own peoples. So, the Irish were forced by London to fight for their self-determination between

1919 and 1921... today, incredibly, Scotland is also left with no choice but coerced to do the same. Or do nothing?"

Andy looks at Sinead, anticipating a response from the IRA volunteer. It doesn't come.

Andy muses, "The 1916 Easter Rising in Dublin was an utter military disaster for the Irish at the same time. Approximately 450 civilians were killed in the fighting – including 40 children. Are you suggesting we slaughter ourselves as they did, in some sort of blood sacrifice?"

Sinead runs a hand through her hair as she decides how to answer, "It was a military disaster because there was virtually no military experience amongst the Command of Connolly's Citizen Army and the Volunteers. Unlike us. But they held out against the Brits for a week, against all the odds. It was that which ultimately touched the hearts of every Irishman and woman, giving them the strength and resolve to see the struggle through to Independence."

Andy points a finger at Sinead, "You missed the best bit. Connolly was a Scot from Edinburgh and like the rest of the Irish Command was taken prisoner by the Brits and executed. You want that for us? High Treason in the UK is the only offence which holds the Death Penalty."

Sean interjects, "I don't intend to be taken prisoner, or executed, but the Irish analogy is intentional. Right now, London's critical vulnerability is Brexit. Negotiations with Brussels will be hard enough for Westminster without international opprobrium coming down on their heads from EU, UN and the Commonwealth. The SLA will exploit London's weakness by asserting our Edinburgh government and UN mandated right to self-determination. Our critical requirements are to protect not our oil, as they see as our centre of gravity, but our fundamental right to democratic self-government. We must influence our centre of gravity decisively. Some might call it Freedom...."

He brings up a fourth slide, STIRLING CASTLE, "It's a natural defensive position fortified over many centuries. It's also recognisable as a world-famous Scots landmark. We take it, we hold it and we let the world know we've done it until our democratic vote is recognised and acknowledged internationally...and by London."

The atmosphere is now electric. Then the fifth slide appears.

OPERATION ST ANDREW: SUNDAY 23 JUNE

Sean barks, "Our Situation! Scotland has a choice. Subserviently accept London's actions with no effective political response ... or fight to bring the support of the European Union, the United Nations and the Commonwealth to bear on London in recognition of our democratic referendum for self-determination".

Jill accepts the handheld laptop pointer from Sean, who sits. She is confident and composed. She brings up a map of Scotland.

"I'll now give you an Intelligence Brief. Enemy Forces! All of the UK's armed forces are severely overstretched because of their commitments across the world not least the current campaign in Syria."

She clicks the pointer and RM CONDOR MILITARY BASE appears on the map on the east coast of Scotland, near Dundee. She continues, "Firstly, Royal Marines and Navy. Condor is a Royal Marine base. They have an under-strength Commando Unit of approximately 200 men, consisting of one Close Combat Company (X-Ray Company) plus support troops (Whisky Company) whose primary task is provide security to the UK Oil Rigs in the North Sea."

She clicks again and FASLANE appears on the map in the west, near Glasgow. "Faslane is the Royal Navy's nuclear submarine base. Security is provided by 43 Commando Royal Marines and Navy Special Forces."

Click: EDINBURGH appears, "Edinburgh Barracks holds 1st and 3rd Battalions, The Westminster Regiment, known as 1 and 3 WESTMINSTER. They are both English Infantry Battalions. They're administrative Rear Party's, each of approximately 100 men who are based in Scotland whilst the rest of the Battalions serve on Operations. Neither have armoured capability."

Click: INVERNESS appears, "2nd Battalion, The Lincolnshire Regiment is located at Fort George, known as 2 LINCS. They are also only approximately 100 soldiers of a Rear Party."

Click: RAF LOSSIEMOUTH and LEUCHARS STATION appear in the North East & East, "An RAF base is at Lossiemouth and Scots Dragoon Guards, known as SCOTS DG are at Leuchars. The RAF have no current strike capability as the majority of their aircraft are in Cyprus and Syria. They also have extremely limited helicopter capability. RAF have a small scale operation at Leuchars."

Click: KINLOSS. "Kinloss holds a Royal Engineer unit."

She pauses for questions and continues when she receives none, "Friendly Forces! Other than those sitting here the Scots Liberation Army exists only on paper."

Andy snorts loudly and gets a reproving look from Sean in response.

Coolly, Jill fixes Andy with her determined gaze, "We have identified many good men and women who are extremely concerned at the way their country is being treated...like yourself Andy." He remains silent.

She continues, "Tomislav will support us with Croat ex-Soviet arms. Sinead with IRA know-how. USA, and now Mexico, continues to be extremely easy to obtain military grade weapons from. The professional UK Customs & Excise no longer exist. UKBF focus 90% on immigration therefore are no effective counter to weapons smuggling. Tyson represents ethnic Scots from North America who want to help with military logistics and finance."

Tom, Sinead and Tyson nod grimly in acknowledgement. She brings up a slide of a plan view of Stirling Castle, "As you can see the castle is a number of concentric inner circles, designed specifically for defence. It is perfect for us."

Sean stands again, "The Aim of Op St ANDREW is to occupy and hold Stirling Castle, for as long as possible, in order to compel London to accept the legitimacy of Scotland's Independence.

Execution of the plan in outline! Before 23rd June, we shall orchestrate civil disobedience incidents across Scotland to stretch and confuse the UKs limited security forces as a deception plan to cover our occupation of Stirling Castle."

Sean moves into the centre of them in order to dominate the space, "We must ensure London fires the first military shots. We must also ensure that we have our communications systems in place to let the world know. Andy...."

Menacingly, Andy stands up, "Operational security is paramount. If we allow these matters to be known out-with this circle we are writing our own death certificates. You are all aware the death-penalty has been restored for High Treason. Brit intelligence would take us out in a heartbeat. I will let you know how, when and where our next briefing is to carry out the operational phase of Op St ANDREW. I will brief you later on how we communicate between ourselves in order to manage and minimise Brit, or other countries intelligence operations, identifying our plans."

As the leader Sean again takes the floor in order to summarise. "Our staff planning must be the science of analytical, methodical and logical preparation. From that we can balance the military command art of experience, intuition and manoeuverist action. We have the initiative and surprise on our side, team. Questions? OK. If we end up in a fair fight we haven't planned our mission properly!"

No questions forthcoming amongst the laughter he repeats the salient points of the plan but brings up a final slide which appears in quartiles. He says nothing, allowing his audience to read the information:

Top left quartile:
1988
Operation FLAVIUS
GIBRALTAR
3 IRA Volunteers Active Service Unit (ASU) Executed by SAS
No option to surrender given

Top right:
1980
Operation NIMROD
LONDON
5 Iranian Arab nationalists

Executed by SAS
No option to surrender given
Bottom left:
2011
Operation HERRICK
AFGHANISTAN
Wounded Taliban prisoner
Executed by Royal Marine Senior NCO
Bottom right:
1987
Operation JUDY
LOUGHALL, North of Ireland
8 IRA Volunteers ASU
Executed by SAS
No option to surrender given
(1 Civilian passer-by killed & 1 wounded in error by SAS)

Sean looks into the faces of his listeners. He sees the horrified effect his penultimate slide has achieved. He clicks the remote a final time and the screen is covered by one final slide:

1985
Glenmoriston, Scotland
Willie MacRae
Scottish Independence Activist
Executed by British Secret Service

He allows time for the shock of British state-killing in Scotland to fully sink in. He concludes, "This is London shoot-to-kill policy, Ladies and Gentlemen. These executions are from Open Sources. Closed Source execution slides would take hours to set out. Be in absolutely no doubt, my friends. London will do all it can to ensure that the same fate awaits us all."

CHAPTER 7

SCOTLAND, MAY 2019

Army Headquarters, Scotland: 29 May

A GROUP OF MILITARY OFFICERS and civilians sit at a long table. It is chaired by a senior English army officer, "...therefore, although politically, Scotland demands independence there is no evidence for this Intelligence Committee to believe that there is any nationalist paramilitary or terrorist activity. As the Iron Lady, Baroness Thatcher, said on more than one occasion, "The Scots have no balls for independence." He got up from the table indicating he was satisfied with the day's work. Some laughed dutifully. The majority laughed uproariously, amongst them a young, beautiful female army colonel who sniggered nastily. She followed the senior officer out of the meeting room to his office along the corridor.

Jill is present at the briefing opposite McCloy. On the table in front of her is a tag "UK Border Force (UKBF)" McCloy's tag reads "SO1 J2, Military Intelligence, 52nd HIGHLAND BRIGADE." Along with the others she gets up and leaves. In the corridor, as the others disperse, McCloy hangs back and waits for her. He puts his left hand, with wedding ring, on her arm and kisses her lightly on the cheek, "My wife is taking the kids to the cinema tomorrow night. I can meet you in your flat at 8, if you want?"

"Perfect! Tomorrow night, then..." and she smiles.

In the senior officer's office the slim, attractive colonel Margaret Ross sits opposite her boss. She crosses her legs causing her shapely thighs to accentuate her beautiful curves through her tight-fitting army skirt. This caused her boss to momentarily pause as carnal thoughts flashed through his mind but almost as instantaneously reminded himself of his subordinate's rumoured sexual preference for other women.

"What do you make of all of this, Margaret?" he asked, "from your Scottish viewpoint."

Margaret paused to gather her thoughts, "We need to be more proactive in infiltrating the separatist political parties. My specialist political department would benefit from more resources in the form of Intelligence officers, regionally based throughout the country. It would help if they were highly motivated British patriots, by which I mean, not pressed men. And I would prefer to interview them myself, with your approval, Sir."

"From the police?" he asked.

"Yes, sir, but also from the army. I have some dedicated men and women in mind," she responded.

"OK, I approve. The bean-counters will push back on the financial resource implications of your new team but we both agree that Britain needs to assert itself as strongly as we can in order to ensure we can target subversive separatists. I'm deducing that with your own political BNUP background that you'll be selecting the...shall we say...the right sort of chap?" his eyes sparkled with revolting inference.

"Leave it to me, sir," she acquiesced, "We'll soon have some prisoners and we'll have the bastards squealing in no time. If there's anything happening in Scotland we'll know quickly enough. Queensberry rules don't apply to these scum," she coldly avowed.

"Indeed, Margaret, indeed. Strong British national action is essential. Don't worry about causing any...collateral damage. The Prime Minister wants us to go hard because he insists British national interests must be aggressively asserted", he crossed his office to shake her hand and confide, "you know, your excellent suggestion to combine your political office with a military internal security role is extremely timely and of considerable benefit to the British nation. Don't let London down."

"I won't sir and nor will my network of British loyalists", she icily replied.

Stirling Castle

Tyson, wearing a colourful Hawaiian shirt, tartan trousers and open sandals with cameras hanging from his neck, happily saunters up the broad castle esplanade towards the main gate. He is every inch the stereotypical American tourist: invisible in plain sight. He snaps and camcorders the Castle and its approaches from every angle. He collects updated plans of the layout of the Castle from the friendly tourist office and later leaves the castle with a broad smile having completed a successful reconnaissance.

Fogbank, North Minch

A large seagoing vessel noses out of the fogbank. Its engines pulsate across the calm water. Ambient moonlight illuminates the scene. A dim eerie green glow in the wheel room of the boat reveals two people, Tomislav and Sinead.

Sinead turns to Tom, "We are just off the West coast of Scotland. We should be able to see our contact's signal light soon."

Tom and Sinead stare intently forward. They are suddenly stunned by a powerful searchlight that completely bathes them and the vessel in ultra-white daylight. A sleek warship-grey patrol vessel cuts through the water towards them keeping its searchlight on its prey.

Tom grimaces, "We're fucked! We can't outrun that craft! If they board us they'll find the weapons and ammunition."

Tom and Sinead are expressionless as instructions are fired at them from the other vessels loud-hailer system.

"This is UK Border Force Cutter 'Swan.' Cut your engines and standby for boarding!"

Tom cuts the engines and they begin to drift.

The cutter cruises alongside and uniformed UKBF officers throw ropes which are used to bring the vessels together.

In the wheelhouse, Tom reaches into his jacket and starts to pull out a pistol. Sinead gently puts her hand on his and shakes her head.

Hooded in a heavy sea-jacket and thick woollen muffler across the face a Border Force officer boards from Swan then clambers up into the wheelhouse. Tom and Sinead turn to face the official who suddenly pulls back the muffler revealing a huge chubby grin. Jill laughs delightedly at the look of consternation on their faces which immediately turns to laughter with Tom and one of undisguised fury with Sinead, who shakes her fist at her.

Sinead screams, "You bloody idiot! Do you know how petrified you made us? I should punch you."

Laughing heartily, Jill responds, "Sorry...Not! What better way to escort you into a safe haven unmolested? All my lads are up for the Cause! I trust my life to them, so you can rest easy. Now, Tom, cast off, please follow *Swan*."

She starts to laugh again, principally at the passionate anger she had provoked in Sinead. Tom orders his crew to cast off and then sets the vessel in motion, following in Swan's wake.

Jill, still grinning, continues, "We've identified a cove which is guarded by a team of Sean's men. They'll help unload the cargo into our vehicles and get you away as soon as possible."

Sinead baulks at this and launches her retaliation, "We're here for the duration. I'm staying and so is Tom."

It is Jill's turn to look astonished and then furious, "That's not part of the plan! Sean won't like it!"

"That's why we didn't ask him. It's a lovely surprise isn't it?" smirks Sinead.

Jill glowers and Tom sighs heavily.

A busy scene is taking place on a remote West Highland jetty. UKBF Swan stands off in dark silence guarding the mouth of the cove. The smuggling vessel is alongside the jetty. Figures labour with heavy boxes moving from the vessel to three British Army trucks. There is no light or sound, only purposeful movement. Summer mist floats eerily on the surface of the water.

After a few hours, Tom summons his crew to the wheelhouse of his vessel. He shakes hands with the crew members and speaks in Croatian, "Thank you and good luck. One of Sinead's IRA teams will re-supply you at the rendezvous near Cork before you head back to Croatia. Signal: *Swan*."

A crew member flashes a beam briefly at *Swan*. Both vessels start their motors and the smuggler casts off and heads off to the open sea disappearing into the fogbank, away from *Swan*.

On the dark hillside road, near the jetty, the smugglers bolt the rear of the trucks to secure them. Tom stands beside Sinead in dark shadow. No sounds are heard and only moonlight illuminates the scene. A young, athletic Scot, wearing a distinctive military Tam O'Shanter hat complete with a red-over-white feather hackle at the left side, camouflaged face, combat-jacket, and a kilt advances on the pair. Tom grimaces in undisguised contempt at the Scots mode of dress. She smiles in response.

The soldier speaks in Gaelic to Sinead, "Sinead? A hundred thousand welcomes to Scotland. Please board the rear truck. We've prepared sleeping bags, hot drinks and food for you. We'll be driving a few hours to a safe location to secure the arms. A car will be there to take you to Colonel MacAlpin, who has been told of your arrival. I want to thank you both for helping my country."

The soldier runs to the front truck and climbs into the cab. Camouflaged sentries emerge from hidden positions and run back to board the trucks which move slowly off up the steep hill road.

After clambering into the truck, Tom and Sinead make space for themselves among the huge crates, zip themselves into sleeping bags, open a small haversack and bring out flasks of coffee and a very large bottle of Johnnie Walker Red Label whisky. They grin with pleasure. Tom pours hot coffee into two mugs, doing his best to avoid spilling the liquid as the truck bounces along. Sinead, with a very broad smile, pours a large amount of whisky into each steaming mug. Tom, "I make toast! Živjeli! Skotland!"

Sinead, suppressing a giggle, responds, "I like toast! Sláinte! Alba gu brath!"

The sun appears over the top of a purple heather-clad mountain. In a stunningly beautiful glen, beside a roaring mountain stream, the three army trucks eventually stop and are unloaded into farm buildings in the early dawn light. A car approaches and Tom with Sinead are escorted to it by their kilted host. They shake hands briefly and get into the car. Sinead rolls down her window.

Their host speaks again in Gaelic, "Friends are good on the day of battle. Until we meet again, may God hold you both in the palm of His hand." She smiles and replies in thanks in the ancient tongue. The car accelerates down the glen.

Glasgow Reserve Army HQ: 30 May

A police car and a USA military staff car drive up to the entrance of an Army Reserve Centre in one of Scotland's greatest cities.

Magnificent, traditional, Glasgow red sandstone tenements overlook the staid military building. An immaculate, kilted Regimental Sergeant Major (RSM) signals to a bored piper, resplendent in full uniform, in the doorway of the Centre. Fergie the piper, with attitude, nips a lit cigarette tucked in the palm of his hand and throws it into a gorgeous rose-bush in the well-tended entrance garden. The RSM, gives the piper an evil look, then crashes to attention saluting the parking car. The piper plays a spirited tune.

A British senior officer hurries out from the Centre to greet the American emerging from his car. They hail each other warmly and head into a vast well-lit training hall. Dotted in groups around the hall are Scots soldiers in combat suits, Tam O'Shanters with red-over-white hackles.

The two senior officers observe the soldiers being instructed in former Soviet weapon-systems: distinctive AK-47 rifles, light and heavy machine guns, mortars, shoulder launched anti-tank and anti-aircraft systems. A Corporal blows a whistle and checks a clipboard sheet with timings. The groups rotate briskly to the next Stand nearest them.

A Recruiting Stand, instructed by a sergeant with Indian subcontinent hue and features, captures the attention of the two officers. The sergeant, with a very broad Glasgow accent, shows an AK-47 to a group of very interested soldiers.

The US senior officer drawls in a quiet, amused voice to his host, "You guys recruit muh-jah-had-een? We teach our guys that the only good Muslim is a dead 'un... I guess he's the only potential terrorist within miles of here?"

The American sniggers at his own joke and provokes a grin from the Brit, "I couldn't agree more, old chum. Wouldn't have them anywhere near a uniform, never mind giving them weapons. Unfortunately, we must have a handful to keep the Race Relations people happy. I'm jolly sure in spite of this Independence bally-hoo Scotland will stay loyal to His Majesty. Scots terrorists?...Hah, Hah!"

Andy MacCreadie enters the hall and marches across to the visitors, halts and salutes. He barks an introduction.

"Sirs, my name is Sergeant Major MacCreadie. What you see is my Rifle Company receiving interest lessons on ex-Soviet kit in use by insurgents world-wide. If you have any questions, fire away. Sah!"

The two officers motion Andy away to a quiet spot. The Brit confides quietly, "Very good, Sergeant Major. Perhaps you could tell us about the Asian chap."

"Aye, Sir. That's Sergeant Naveed Hussein. Born in Glasgow to Pakistani parents. Dual nationality – joined the Pakistani army first when he was 16. He was at Mogadishu helping his Pakistani battalion pull Yank "Black Hawk Down" asses out of their self-inflicted hellhole. I believe he is still asked to take wee occasional holidays on the Pakistani/Afghan border to help out UK & US Special Forces, if you understand me...sir...."

Andy is pokerfaced as he watches the two senior officers visibly swallow their prejudices, "Will that be all, sirs?"

The Brit nods and takes his visitor to the exit. They ignore the salute from Andy, in a show of poor military manners, who moves on to the group being taken by Sgt. Hussein.

"Make sure you listen to Sgt. Hussein, lads," insists Andy, "He knows what it is to use these excellent weapons on the two-way range. You can look forward to live-firing all of these weapon systems in the next few weeks." Andy nods at Sgt. Hussein, "Thanks, pal."

"Nae bother, Sarnt Major, that pair were just twa cheeks o' the same erse..." Everyone laughed, "Noo, listen-in lads, this weapon has a range of...."... Andy winks conspiratorially and moves away.

Weapon Ranges, Highlands

A few days later the same groups of Scots soldiers are firing every manner of ex-Soviet weapon systems. The highland hills echo to the sounds of war.

Sean's Glasgow Appartment: 20 June

Sean, Sinead and Tom watch TV. The Irish Nationalist Sinn Fein leader Gerry O'Neill talks in his soft Belfast brogue to an interviewer, "The people of Scotland have democratically expressed their will for self-government. It is inconceivable that London can deny them that right. We, in Sinn Fein, support the democratic process and are appalled at the totalitarian behaviour of the Harris government. Our talks with the Scots Nationalist parties lead us to believe that a free Scotland would withdraw any Scots troops from Northern Ireland. Indeed, we firmly believe that a United Ireland and an independent Scotland will have a very close, productive future."

Sean turns to Sinead, "We'll done for arranging that, Sinead. That was word perfect. I'm glad you decided to stay with us after your surprise appearance!"

Sinead basks in Sean's compliment. He looks up as Andy, in uniform, enters the room. He sits down opposite the three.

Andy briefs them, "The lads are all set, their training complete. We'll move to final positions tomorrow night. Our kit is in place ready for use including a few surprises."

Sean gets up and pours everyone a dram of ostentatiously expensive malt whisky, "Well done, Andy. Operation St Andrew is on schedule. We've prepared everyone as well as we can. Providence will decide whether we succeed. Let's free Scotland!"

Police HQ, Glasgow: 0100hrs 22 June 2019

A large van and a motor bike draws up outside the city centre building in the night-time pouring rain. The van driver, wearing a motorcycle helmet, with visor down to protect his identity, cuts the engine and lights. He gets out, locks the vehicle and climbs onto the vacant pillion. The bike roars off into the city.

Glasgow, River Clyde: 22 June

The motorbike is parked on a pavement in a dark lane, the rider still astride. The pillion passenger stands alone on a deserted foot bridge overlooking the river Clyde which flows through the city. The wet Glasgow *smirr* clouds the helmet visor, which he lifts – Sean, speaking in a credible Belfast accent, says into a mobile phone, "BBC?... OK... There's a bomb outside Glasgow Police HQ. You have 10 minutes to evacuate the building. More bombs will be planted. Our code-phrase, to prove these warnings are no hoax, is "Scotch on the Rocks."

Sean, replaces his visor, launches the mobile into the river then strolls to the bike. They speed off into the damp glistening empty city streets.

Military Operations Room, HQ Scotland

A phone rings. A heavy-eyed soldier, wearing t-shirt and shorts, slips out of his sleeping bag on his military cot, picks up a notepad and pen, crosses the room to the phone and picks it up, "Duty Ops Room, Corporal MacPherson speaking, sir."

His tired face turns to one of huge amusement as he scribbles the message, "OK, I'll do that, sir."

He puts the phone down and begins to laugh as he looks through a phone record, muttering offensive oaths about Glasgow Police. He finds the number and dials.

Colonel McCloys Quarter

A sleeping McCloy eventually reacts to his mobile phone ring-tone, Rule Britannia, "Hello?"

"Duty Ops Room, Corporal MacPherson here. Sir, there's been a Category 1 event. I've been ordered to instruct you to come in immediately and take charge of our side of the incident."

McCloy acknowledges then puts the phone down. He turns to face the young woman stirring beside him. He puts his hand under the sheets to touch her. She protests. This arouses him and he raises himself on one elbow and forces his mouth onto hers. She pushes him off. Jill pulls her hair back from her face. He laughs and gets up to dress, "There's been a Cat 1 incident. I'll have to go to HQ."

"Can you tell me what it is?" asks a tired Jill.

McCloy finishes dressing and moves to the door and looks down at the naked girl, "Nothing for you to worry your wee Scotch head about. You'll receive a call, from the J2 Committee I suspect."

Jill hears him leave. When the door closes she looks at her watch. She smiles fleetingly, then gets up and walks to her bathroom. She switches on the shower and gets in. She is sobbing now, scrubbing herself furiously between her thighs.

Army Headquarters, Scotland: 0500hrs 22 June

A sign on a door, "J2 Intelligence Committee" identifies a briefing room. Tired looking civilians and military mill around a coffee machine pouring coffees.

McCloy grabs their attention, "If we could take our seats, ladies and gentlemen, please."

Committee members shuffle wearily into their seats. He continues, "I've called this meeting for two reasons. Firstly, to inform you that an Irish terrorist bomb threat was carried out at 0100hrs this morning at Glasgow Police HQ. Secondly, to request any intelligence on this incident as soon as possible from your own resources."

A civilian questions McCloy, "Why do you assume it's from Ireland, Colonel? It's very rare here that we have such incidents."

"An Irishman left a coded warning, which is normal IRA practice. After Sinn Fein's TV appearance this evening supporting Scottish separatists it would appear this is a spin-off. Do any of you have any intelligence to contradict my working assumption?"

No-one responds.

"OK, this group will re-convene at 1700hrs, here, today. I must stress that we have to nip this Irish thing in the bud. Things are bad enough politically here in Scotland without this additional bollocks. This Committee will be reporting direct to the Prime Minister, through me. Is this clear?" All nod.

"Good, I'm expecting an aide from the Prime Ministers team any moment now flying up from London".

The sound of a helicopter surrounds the building. McCloy and the rest of the Committee leave the room, ignoring Jill. She waits to be last then takes out her mobile phone from her hand bag. She dials a number and hears a voice say "OK". Leaving the mobile on, she takes out a roll of tape, kneels at the top end of the table and secures the phone under the table edge. Satisfied with her conceal-ment, she leaves and enters a Ladies toilet in the corridor.

HQ Scotland, Playing Fields

McCloy waits as Harry, resplendent with a sticking plaster across his broken nose, which accompanies his two black-eyes, leaves a military helicopter then waves him towards the building behind him. They walk to the briefing room he had just left.

In the room they sit down at the top of the table unaware of the concealed mobile. He opens a folder as Harry helps himself to coffee.

"OK, Harry. We've got sod all to go on with this. It's known in the trade as an Intelligence Desert. We have a tenuous link between a Sinn Fein TV appearance and a phone call using Irish modus operandi. The Irish would love to take advantage of UK mili-tary overstretch to bring about withdrawal of Scots troops from Northern Ireland...."

"Not Scots nationalists then?" asks Harry.

"The Scots? They don't have the cojones," laughs McCloy.

Seans Appartment

Sean, Tom, Sinead and Andy sit grinning around Sean's Ansaphone. The sound of Harry and McCloy laughing can clearly be heard.

Briefing Room

"So what do I tell the Prime Minister?" asks Harry.

McCloy rubs his chin in thought, "Tell him I've put all the resources I can into this, but we'll cope."

"OK, Justin. Keep me informed. I'm staying in Scotland this week-end, "as Harry produces a football ticket, "I'm off to the Scotland v. England football match today at Hampden Park. England will stuff the Jock tossers and I want to be there to savour it."

Justin McCloy joins Harry's smirking and they leave the room together.

71

Ladies Toilet

Jill listens to the two men joking their way up the corridor. She waits for silence then leaves the toilet, enters the briefing room and retrieves her mobile. She watches from a window and sees them drive away in a car. She leaves the building.

Sean's Appartment

Sean, focused, looks at his watch, "Superb. Our plan is working so far. Andy, you've got a meeting with some Tartan Army foot-soldiers at 1200hrs and I've got to be in Edinburgh to meet Sinead".

Tom looks at Andy confusedly, "Tartan Army? I thought you said the Scottish Liberation Army would be the only military organisation?"

Sean grins in response. Andy, as ever, just looks menacing.

Sean explains "The Tartan Army call themselves foot-soldiers, known internationally as the world's friendliest football fans. But, not today. They are going to acquire as many handy bastards as Andy can muster from Scotland's football hooligan fraternity."

Andy contrives to grin forebodingly, "Some Scots fans love nothing better than to kick the shit out of each other. Today they have the opportunity to do so for their country and give the Scots police forces the run-around, as they also love to do. England fans will turn up to fight just because of the scumbags that they are..."

Tom intercedes, "...and provoke English soldiers based in Scotland to react and tie-up police resources to help further reduce the security agencies from our paths?"

Sean and Andy give each other the thumbs-up. Tom grins.

Edinburgh Folk Club: 1100hrs 22 June

A group of off-duty English soldiers wearing England football tops are behaving obnoxiously. They abuse a small band of intimidated folk musicians on a stage. The soldiers rant out "Rule Britannia", some stand giving fascist salutes. The bearded Folkies sit, intimidated, as Sean walks in.

Immediately, Sean senses the fear and provocation in the room and strides to the band. Sinead sees him across the club.

"Play 'Hope over Fear'!⁴ Play it!" commands Sean to the band which they immediately play at a high tempo with Sean singing. The folkies instantly join in belting the song out, most rising to their feet in passion, as Sinead looks adoringly at Sean. The cowed audience now find their voices and join in lustily.

The English increase their volume and stridency with Rule Britannia but are drowned out by the fervency of the Scots and eventually give up sullenly. The chorus of the Scots song triumphs as it fills the room with passion and defiance:

Hope over fear – Don't be afraid
Tell Westminster Tories that Scotland's no longer yer slave
Carpe Diem – Will you seize the day?
Rip the chains from the unicorn – Show them that Scotland is brave.

The last words merge with the ecstatic cheers of the folkies who fervently mob Sean. A random French tourist is present who shouts, "Vive la liberté!"

Heavily outnumbered by the now aroused Scots folkies the English thugs knock over some tables and push through the crowd. One of them snarls at the club manager, "That guy", indicating Sean, "is trouble. We'll be back but he better not be here!"

The thugs leave to cheers of the Folkies as Sean, being back-slapped by many, joins a beaming Sinead at the table.

"Sometimes you just have an aura, a' around," she teases in a mock Scots accent.

"Aye, very good..." says an embarrassed Sean, "...are you just going to sit there or are you getting me a Guinness?"

Glasgow City Centre Pub: 1200hrs 22 June

Shortly after Sean's *stramash* in Scotland's rival city, Edinburgh, Andy enters a packed Glasgow pub. He wears a dark-blue Scotland football top, kilt and sporran, white kilt socks at his ankles over Timberland working-boots. Everyone else is dressed in virtually the same manner but with kilts of every available varying tartan and variation of decades of Scotland football tops. They are all very

---

4   https://gerrycinnamon1.bandcamp.com/releases

drunk. He winces at the volume of the chanting throng and more particularly the song they are belting out.

They are known as an Army because, invariably, they gather in groups of like-minded football fans from the same villages, towns and cities throughout Scotland and beyond. Some call themselves battalions and divisions. Often they include small groups of friends from previous football trips at home and abroad known to themselves as "campaigns." However, they are not hooligans. More lovers than fighters, mostly.

When tens of thousands of these men, women, boys and girls of every shape and age congregate in city squares around the world they always catch the eye. Unvaryingly, they march noisily and colourfully with flags and banners, as one, to the football stadium led by pipers. The epithet "Army" becomes self-evident. There the military analogies end. There is neither rank-structure nor established organisation within this irreverent, ribald mix. They are truly anarchist with one aim – getting to the game wherever it may be by plane, train and taxi or whatever transport mode is available. Helicopters and horse-driven carts are known to have been employed by panic-stricken fans fearing they may miss the match Kick-Off. It is bad form to miss that, or their flight home, no matter how outrageously drunk they may be.

Incongruously, the crowd in Andy's pub are raucously singing, a theme-tune from the early 1960's 'Sound of Music' Rogers and Hammerstein movie, 'Do-A deer' complete with synchronised hand actions.

Andy forces his way to a corner of the pub where a group of fans sit at a table. They are dressed like the others but are sober, straight-faced and only have Cokes on the table. Andy shakes hands with them all. He cups his hand and presses his mouth against the ear of a young very fit, evil looking skull-faced man. Andy shouts, "Are we all set Skull?"

"Skull" nods. He looks at his military issue G10 watch then holds up five fingers and indicates the door. They nod and seem as oblivious of the boisterous chaos surrounding them as the drunk Tartan Army foot-soldiers are of them.

After five minutes, Andy's small group pops out of the noisy pub. A row of bare arses are simultaneously slapped and pressed against the bar window from the inside. The group laugh and give the pub obscene hand-gestures, leave the street and enter an adjoining lane where Skull posts lookouts at either end. He and Andy push themselves into a door-way out of sight.

"Right, Skull. What's the plan?" Andy asks furtively.

Skull holds up his hand as his mobile rings and answers after a moment, "Aye. OK. Aye. No change. Smashin'...it's the Full Bhoona then? Nae bother. Have a nice day."

Skull turns to speak but his phone rings again, "Aye, no probs. It's the Full Bhoona. Have a nice day."

Skull glances cautiously both ways up the lane, removes the phone battery then speaks, "We've got three crews on the ground, as Sean requested. The English soldiers in Inverness and Edinburgh have taken the bait as we knew they would. 2 LINCS in Inverness are notoriously nasty bastards. We've got a crew for each of them and I've got my own crew here for the England Firms heading into Glasgow."

"Brilliant, Skull", grins Andy, "How many guys are in the crews and have they managed to avoid the usual Police spotters?"

Skull guffaws contemptuously at the last question, "The polis? Thick bastards. When have you and me ever had a problem out-witting those twats? It's really not fair entering into a battle of wits with unarmed men." They both cackle. "We've got a full turn-out. Easily a hundred in each crew. Our lads RV at the Royal Infirmary and then batter fuck out of the Sassunach scum. "Full Bhoona" was the code-words for our other two crews to crack on so let's get moving."

Skull called in his look-outs and then together, marched purposefully, merging into the tens of thousands of Tartan Army in the main pedestrian Glasgow thoroughfare.

Sean's Appartment

Sinead and Tyson work at a laptop. The screen shows bank transfers taking place. The amounts are in millions of dollars. The banks

75

involved are Chase-Manhattan and Bank of Geneva. They stop tapping the keyboard as the transactions cease. Tyson smiles with satisfaction, "That should be enough to pay for Tom's weapons... and then some!"

"What about the American weapons systems?" Sinead asks.

He replies, "They are already across the border in Mexico. No problems. They are being containerised now for shipping to our exchange point in Barbados. A container ship is already waiting at Bridgetown to receive them." He laughed.

"What's so funny?" asked Sinead.

"Scotland kept the Confederacy going by Blockade Running. This is just my way of saying thank you by reverse Blockade Running," and grinned.

"By the way, did I mention my Specialism in the Marine Corps?" he continued to grin. Sinead shook her head.

"Sniper," he replied. "I just love my Tennessee made .50 Model 82A1 Barrett. A 10-round magazine with accuracy out to 6,800 meters. One shot, one kill." His smile was betrayed by the steel in his eyes.

Glasgow Royal Infirmary

Small groups of Tartan Army foot-soldiers congregate innocuously in the area of the Victorian hospital building. They arrive discreetly in twos and threes from taxis, city busses, delivery vans and on foot. Skull and Andy nod to those they recognise. A large van specialising in ice-cream sales pulls up. Its back-door opens and disgorges more determined looking foot-soldiers. Skulls phone rings. He listens but doesn't speak then puts it away.

He whistles loudly and everyone looks at him and closes in. Assertively he says, "The main English firms have avoided the cops by coming into the city on one of the local blue-line trains. One of my girls is on the train with the English. She reckons they're getting off at Duke Street. It's very near here so we better get cracking to get the ambush in place."

Andy gives a thumbs up and grins, "Fair one! Happy Days!"

The group jogs steadily and purposefully from the area of the hospital towards a nearby local inner-city commuter station.

Duke Street Railway Station, Glasgow: 1300hrs 22 June

A blue train pulls into the platform and empties a huge horde of menacing, short-haired, silent, expensively dressed men of all ages. None wear football colours. They swarm up the steps and onto the street. A young girl remains on the train lying on the floor, badly beaten. Shocked passengers rush to help her. The horde marches straight on, occupying the middle of the street. Cars and buses screech to a halt. Passers-bye scurry away. Terrified bus passengers stare out of the windows.

Andy stands with a small group of Tartan Army foot-soldiers on a street corner. They run towards the mob shouting obscenities, throwing bricks and beer cans, which spew beer as they fly. The missiles find their marks causing horrendous injuries and screams. The English mob surges forward with a roar after their attackers who sprint away up a side street. The side-street is a narrow canyon of glowering red-sandstone tenement buildings.

As the foot-soldiers reach the end of the side-street they are met by another group, led by Skull, who frantically drag large numbers of massive heavy metal trash-bins across the road blocking it very effectively – they are armed with a variety of swords, machetes and large knives. Skull is holding two vicious looking Gurkha kukri blades. He lobs one to Andy as the group throw more missiles into the face of Andy's pursuers. The mob viciously storms the bin-barricade whilst the large ice-cream van, which had earlier dropped off foot-soldiers, blocks off the opposite end of the side-street. The driver leaps out and runs around to the petrol cap, unscrewing it. In his hand is a small rag which he stuffs into the petrol cap. He then takes out a cigarette lighter and ignites the rag. He screams at passers-bye to get away as he escapes.

A vicious street battle rages. The English smash doors and windows the length of both sides of the street as they discover them locked and barricaded. Andy and Skull slash and hack at their enemies. Horrendous wounds are inflicted. Bottles smash. Police sirens wail.

Then the ice-cream van explodes with a roar, sending sheets of flame and metal into the screaming horde. It's the cue for foot-soldiers to open the windows, high in the tenements, the entire length of the street. Molotov cocktails, bricks, metal bars and even a large white fridge shower the screaming, terrified English hooligans. Foot-soldiers howl victorious obscenities.

Multiple police sirens are heard rapidly approaching in the distance. The barrage finishes as quickly as it began. Scots fly down internal stairs of the tenements, spilling out in every direction. At the barricade, Skull and Andy continue to rip and scythe frenzied English hooligans. Police cars and vans surge into the surrounding streets with flashing lights and blaring sirens. Andy grabs Skulls arm, "C'mon! Time to GTF! Let's get to your car!"

They both sprint away up another side-street, their kukris blood-red.

A lone, very young policeman arrives on the battle scene on foot. He is at the end of the street with the trash-bin barricade. Bins lie on their side, strewn across the road. Screaming, savagely injured English hooligans slither and stumble blindly and loudly. The cop gags. Dark smoke billows into the city air as police vehicles, ambulances and fire-engines screech into the area.

Skull drives sedately in a top-of-the-range BMW. Andy wipes blood from his face with his sleeve. The car-radio reports massive chaos in Glasgow, Edinburgh and Inverness as police contain serious disorder. Skull and Andy break into wide grins. Skull punches the air, "Job well done! We'll change at my place."

The BMW soon drives into an expensive, tree-lined Glasgow south side suburb. It cruises into the drive of an elegant house and straight into an integral double-garage, which is already open. They wait until the electric door loses behind them, then get out and Andy removes a hold-all. They are both filthy, sweat-covered and bloodstained. Skull locks the garage door with his car-key and motions Andy into a utility-room. They silently strip off putting their clothes into a bin-bag, including the kukris. Skull produces two towels and throws Andy one and gives him a military hold-all. Skull ties the bin-bag and puts it in his car boot, "Use the downstairs shower-room. Be ready in 10 minutes."

After showering Andy puts on his Regiments camouflaged uniform from his hold-all and joins Skull in the living room which is littered with children's toys including a baby-walker. Skull is already there in uniform but clutches the fawn beret with winged badge of the SAS, a royal-blue waist stable-belt and captains rank insignia. Andy is un-surprised. He turns on the TV. A reporter is interviewing a police officer in a city street who is saying, unconvincingly, that they believe the rioting is under control. Devastation forms the back-drop.

Andy observes, "The cop is bluffing for Scotland. Look at him... he's lying."

Skull switches the TV off and turns to Andy, "You're right... now, the kit I need is at our Reserve Army Centre. Where's yours?"

"Same," says Andy, "I'll get a taxi across town."

Andy and Skull embrace warmly and shake hands, "All the Best, Skull," grins Andy, "See you at the Independence Parade in Edinburgh."

"Aye, you too, my friend. Stay safe," Skull replies rather too seriously.

Andy is inquisitive, "What task has Sean given you?"

"You should know better than asking questions like that, pal... let's just say I'll be waiting for High Value Opportunity Targets...."

Andy laughs and calls a taxi from Skull's land-line phone as a bare-headed Skull is already cruising from his drive.

SAS Army Reserve Centre, Lanarkshire, Scotland

Skull gets out of his BMW at a locked security gate. He looks up, smiles and waves into a security camera. He punches in a security code on the gate which slides open. He parks in a space which says "Officer Commanding." He smiles as he approaches a large sign, on the outside of the building, with SAS insignia:-

"B SQUADRON, 24 SAS Regiment, Army Reserve, Scotland"

He enters and walks along a corridor which resounds to the voice of a TV announcer. He stops at an office-sign saying "PERMANENT STAFF INSTRUCTOR." He pops his head in, "How's it going, Shagger?"

Shagger, a mean looking regular army Special Forces Senior NCO, has his feet on the desk, laughs and points at the TV, "I put the telly on to watch the fitba and instead I seemed to have tuned into 1970's Belfast. Have you seen this, Boss?"

Skull stares at the riots on the TV screen, "Aye. I heard it on the radio. Mad business... Anyway, I'll be taking a sniper rifle and ammo up to the ranges at Stirling this afternoon for a shoot. I'll overnight at the Camp, practice tomorrow, and be back in the afternoon."

Without taking his eyes off the TV screen Shagger gives a thumbs up over his shoulder to Skull, "Nae bother, Boss. Enjoy yourself."

Skull walks to the armoury door, keys in the combination code into the security panel and opens the door. He unlocks the cage inside the armoury and then signs out a sniper rifle, boxes of ammunition, sniper telescope and camouflaged carrying bag. He places the weapon in the bag and then carries it all to his nearby office. He returns to secure the armoury and then proceeds back to his office. He retrieves his personal equipment from his locker. Carrying his equipment, weapon and ancillaries he loads up a Land Rover. He recovers the bin-bag containing his bloody gear from this morning's riot from his BMW and places this in the Rover. Satisfied, he drives the wagon from the Centre.

Visitor Centre, Grangemouth Oil Terminal: 1500hrs 22 June

Sean and Sinead listen to a guide explain how millions of barrels of oil, worth billions of petro-dollars every year, is processed through Grangemouth direct from North Sea pipelines. Sinead discreetly taps Sean on the hand and walks towards the Ladies. She has a girlie multi-coloured rucksack on her back.

In the Ladies, Sinead coolly takes off the rucksack in a cubicle and extracts a large plastic box. Wires, batteries, an alarm clock and a small plastic-type lump can just be seen through the lid. She lifts a cistern cover from the toilet, pushes the box in and replaces the cover. She hooks the empty rucksack over her shoulder and leaves.

Sinead re-joins Sean who puts his arm around her as the guide finishes the presentation. The visitors applaud politely and disperse to the car park.

The two leave and drive to a remote public call box they had previously identified in a nearby village.

Sinead, with gloved hands, calls the BBC HQ in Scotland, "It that the BBC? Scotch on the Rocks... There is a bomb in Grangemouth oil terminal."

Sinead hangs up, finds Sean in the car and they drive off.

BBC HQ, Scotland

A flustered telephonist picks up her note-pad, rushes to her manager and quickly explains the message that she has just taken. Her manager immediately lifts the phone and calls the police.

Grangemouth Oil Terminal

Flashing lights and loud-hailer commands are seen and heard from a nearby suburb where the Blue Light teams are mustered as police clear the oil terminal. Large numbers of Emergency vehicles are also parked up on high ground overlooking the terminal in the distance.

A police officer, wearing a luminous jacket, with "Incident Commander", stands next to an Incident Control truck and tells a posse of media that they are at a safe distance until an Army Bomb Control Team clears the terminal.

An explosion suddenly erupts from within the Visitor Centre. Emergency vehicles rush to the scene. The media cameras click and whirr at the belching flames and smoke in the distance.

Faslane Nuclear Base

A massive student protest is taking place, led by pipe-bands, with banners from Scots Universities, Colleges and European Universities. Many carry placards with slogans calling for Freedom, Independence and the banning of nuclear weapons. The protest is peaceful but with a heavy police presence. To the 60's sonorous civil rights protest song "We Shall Overcome" they are singing "Scotland Shall Be Free":

Scotland shall be Free,
Scotland shall be Free,
Scotland shall be Free someday,
Oh, Deep in my Heart,
I do believe,
Scotland shall be Free someday.

Military Operations Room, HQ Scotland: 22 June

McCloy, stressed, stands in front of the Intelligence Committee. A clock shows 1700hrs. "Quickly, around the table, indicate if you have anything?" he barks.

Only Jill raises her hand.

"OK, Border Force, what do you have?" he demands.

Jill states, "I have just received e-mails from my opposite-number in Belfast. They state the IRA are smuggling explosives into Scotland from Ireland."

McCloy nods, "Excellent, well done. That confirms the Irish connection. Anyone else?"

The meeting is interrupted by an Army officer who knocks and enters. She places a sheet of paper on the desk in front of McCloy, who quickly reads it, "Ladies and gentlemen. An explosive device has detonated at Grangemouth Oil Terminal destroying the Visitors Centre. A telephone-call gave a coded warning from a female with an Irish accent. Emergency Services are securing the main Terminal against any further outbreak of fire and further risk of explosion."

McCloy looks up at a police superintendent, "How are your resources coping, Jamie?"

"We are absolutely stretched to the limit, across the whole country. All police leave is cancelled," repied the cop.

"OK, thank you for that, Jamie. So, no need for panic at the moment then. Now, onto our Intelligence Acquisition Plan...."

McCloy brings up a power-point slide and begins to describe priority areas of interest.

Stirling Castle

Tyson stands on the castle ramparts on this beautiful summer evening. He wears a flamboyant Mickey Mouse t-shirt and an oversized Pluto rucksack. Far in the distance, he can see the orange flares from an oil terminal. Flashing blue lights can be seen winking in the area. A young couple are standing hand-in-hand nearby. Tyson points, "Excuse me sir, what's over there?"

"That's Grangemouth. I was looking there too, it looks as though there's been some sort of incident", replies the local man. The couple look amusedly at Tyson's attire and move to the edge of the rampart-stairs and climb down. He glances at his watch, which shows 1750hrs. A sign on a wall says: 1800hrs Closing. He lifts his rucksack and climbs up into a stone tower. He gets to the top, breathless, and conceals himself. He sits and gazes out at the stunning views.

Stirling Castle Tourist Office

An old lady locks the door. She greets an old man wearing a security uniform wandering up a cobbled lane inside the castle. The man has both hands in his pocket and wears a huge grin. The lady laughs, "You look very happy, Sandy. Just because you're finished for the day?"

"Aye, for sure...but have ye no' heard the football score?" the old man punches the air and does a little highland-fling causing the old lady to giggle, "Scotland beat England 4-Nil this afternoon!" he claps and shouts, "Fantastic, is it no'? I'll be having a few drams the night!"

They chatter and laugh, sauntering down towards the main gate to leave. Tyson watches them, unobserved from his tower. He gazes as the outgoing security guy jokes with his equally elderly rotund replacement who arrives at the drawbridge gate.

Forthbank University

A few miles away from the castle lies a modern university. In the Principal's study a gathering of determined like-minded people began to take their seats around a mahogany table. Fifty-something, well heeled, middle aged men and women stand around the room, most have helped themselves to the generous array of malt whiskies and expensive gins provided by their host who sits below a portrait of the King, flanked by two massive British Union Jack flags. The exception to this rally of lawyers, financiers, industrialists and trades union leaders was the focussed, determined-looking leader of the BNUP in Scotland, Margaret Ross - she sat with only a small glass of water in front of her.

The Principal stood up and firmly declared, "Ladies and Gentlemen. I give you warm welcome. Please be upstanding as I propose a toast to His Majesty, the King!"

They immediately rose, as one, and loudly declared in unison, "The King!"

As they shuffled back into their chairs the Principal remained on his feet, "Ladies and Gentlemen, you know why we are assembled here. British Nationalists must organise and smash these bloody traitorous, separatists once and for all!"

This declaration produced immediate roars of approval, clapping and thunderous banging and slapping of palms of hands on the long table surface.

The Principal continued, "We are very honoured, this evening, to have as our guest speaker, Margaret Ross, leader of our very own British National & Unionist Party, who will give us direction and guidance to our noble cause!" Rapturous cheering and applause fill the wood-panelled room as he returns to his chair and Margaret rose, sullen-faced.

She allowed the room to quieten. She consciously delayed speaking for a long few moments which produced an eerie, electrical, expectant atmosphere. Eventually, she spoke, quietly at first, "British comrades. We have campaigned politically, long and hard, to preserve our beloved Union. Some, in the background, have provided essential financial and moral support in order to safeguard our British way of life. I thank them. We have done this within the liberal democratic process. But, you know, we live in a time when that might not be enough. What do I mean by that? Democracy is not the only answer as it brings us to the edge of the break-up of Great Britain...we know of the immigrant problem we face and we know the answer to this is to ensure we take back our borders from those bloody Brussels bastards!" at which, deafening endorsement forced her to pause. Subconsciously she extended her right arm in salute and acknowledgement with approval of their accord. "Our Free Trade Empire will ensure there are no restrictions or bureaucracy on our imports and exports. None! No Tariffs! No delays! Unrestricted movement of goods but total control on immigrants!"

Slowly, she lowered her arm as the volume reduced, "I need you to find me every scrap of information from every part of this region that may identify and assist in crushing the saboteurs. Who do I mean by saboteurs? You know exactly who I mean... those immigrants who brought about this illegal referendum and their bloody EU passports, those gypsy travellers who infest our countryside with so many bringing their disgusting Irish republicanism with them, those socialists and liberals who bring down our history of Empire and denigrate our wonderful armed forces", again she had to pause as the assembly of British nationalists and fascists reverberated their shouts and exclamations around the hall, "But, my fellow Britons! We have had enough of them all and their sons of Abraham bed-fellows! We need a killer instinct! We must show no mercy! We'll send all niggers back to their slum shitholes! Join our compatriots who serve in our gallant army and our brave police force! Death to traitors, freedom for Britain!"

The throng leaped to their feet in thunderous, rolling adulation as spontaneously they joined the few who immediately gave the fascist salute and, together, began to sing, "Rule Britannia" which seamlessly flowed into the British national anthem, "God Save the King" as some pulled on Orange sashes over their shoulders.

Eventually, the tumult subsided as Ross remained on her feet. This time her extended right arm was not retracted. Again, she controlled her audience by imposing silence on them. When she eventually spoke it was in contrived fury, "Our white national-ist brothers and sisters in the United States are showing the path which we must follow! Alt-right is good! We must aspire to our desired society worldwide! We must dominate the lower races and those who oppose our ideals! Make Britain Great again!"

Again, the assembled fascists boomed their admiration and support She took control of the ecstatic neo-Nazis eventually by banging the solid base of an available crystal whisky glass on the gorgeous mahogany table until they regained their seats and settled down as best as they could. Their rapt beaming faces and shining eyes turned towards her as the stench of rampant insanity filled the room.

"I have some more good news, ladies and gentlemen," she began, "Last night, in our Westminster parliament, the English mother of parliaments, handed all power to the BNUP executive!"

Disbelieving gasps of astonishment and incredulity rippled amongst the authoritarian racists. One was heard to acclaim, "It can't be true? This is wonderful!"

"I can confirm that it is true," glowed the exultant fascist, "Our BNUP which extols love of monarchy, strong central authority and British military power passed the Brexit Bill which simultaneously promises to keep foreigners out of Britain and remove centuries of checks on executive power! We can ensure Britain awakes!"

This time she laughed at the exultations of her anti-European companions. Ross indulged them their winning cup-final type celebrations. Eventually, she continued but held both hands out, palms up, in anticipation of further interruption of her message, "We need the Brexit negotiations to fail!" She failed spectacularly to contain them. She was well aware she had ramped up racism, but knew her audience. She produced a slip of paper, as the furore finally began to calm down, and read: "*Regulations under this section may make any provision that could be made by an Act of Parliament (including amending this Act).*

"This fantastic clause that our MPs voted for last night ensured the surrender of the entire legislative power Parliament gained over 600 years, to our BNUP Executive. If the Act is held to limit the scope of that executive legislative power in any way, we can simply make a provision to amend the Act to remove that limitation. Finally, we shall remove the legislative competence of the Scottish Parliament". Delighted laughter greeted this introduction of authoritarian power across Scotland and the UK which morphed into rapturous cheering and ovation.

Once more she was forced to wait until their euphoria subsided. Shining with the passion of someone who knows her moment has come she gushed, "We can stop the niggers from coming here and I include those white niggers from Eastern Europe! With the help of our British Trades Union leaders, here tonight, we ensured that British workers will be protected from wage competition! Please rise to accept our thanks!"

A coven of thirteen Trades Union leaders rose in unison as they radiated and shone their appreciation on their fellow racists who commended and praised their companions.

After a few moments of indulgence the BNUP spearhead persisted, "Our Trades Union leaders, and their political party in Westminster, have evidenced their true British Nationalist concern for our British working class! Our yeoman British working class that provided our military might in days of Empire and in two World Wars against our natural enemies of Germany have shown their true worth again and again in rejecting Europe to protect our blood and soil white racial purity and heritage! We also thank those Trades Unions for supporting retention of British nuclear weapon capability at the Scottish naval base in Faslane!"

The dark hypocrisy of their British Nationalist concern for the working class of one nation only, with denial of the opportunity for working class people from other countries to advance themselves was oblivious to them. This fascist congregation was displaying a peculiar kind of socialism that objects to wage levels being raised in countries where they are lower, a socialism which values the working class in one country only.

The disgustingly wealthy, through BNUP and Brexit, had now successfully, and profitably, promoted reactionary populism, through ownership of the mainstream mass media, which, extremely effectively, diverted the responsibility away from the 1% who siphon Britain's wealth, and on to impoverished immigrants.

Those devious manipulators representing the 1%, within this assembly, laughed inwardly at the gullibility of much of the population that they keep in deprivation and propaganda-fed ignorance. "The ideal subject of totalitarian rule is not the convinced Nazi or the dedicated communist, but people for whom the distinction between fact and fiction, true and false, no longer exists," historically stated by Arendt. And so this Brit Nationalist fake-news audience evidenced.

She continued, "Our national socialism goes hand in hand with last night's vote to remove all caps on executive power! In truth, we must continue to exploit our popular racism which underlies our election successes. Additionally, our Home Office document on how to implement a hardline anti-immigrant policy worked superbly for us. Our core support is more important to us than the Brexit negotiations!" which provoked pandemonium.

"Here we are, about to be protected from the EU, free to make our profits without a Vestager, Competition Commission and a Customs & Excise just twenty miles from France! Twenty miles! It's nothing! Just one small step, looking for a man, or a determined woman," she laughed as her eyes shone, "who wants to be an effective Prime Minister of Great Britain, with the cash to make it possible. What I am saying is, we have now what we have always needed, real partnership with the government. Tax exemptions, no import duties and few labour laws. What's not to like?" The shameless applauded, laughed and cheered.

The fascist tumult continued as Ross took the opportunity to strut, unsmiling but satisfied, from the room followed by the beaming University Principal.

CHAPTER 8

STIRLING, JUNE 2019

Stirling, Army Ranges: 1800hrs 22 June

TOTALLY FOCUSED, Skull lies behind his L511A3 British Army sniper rifle on the firing point. He looks through a tripod-mounted telescope at his side and checks the accuracy of his shots on his soldier-shaped target boards in the far distance. He makes one adjustment on the rifle telescopic-sight, then prepares to fire. With the rifle-butt in his shoulder he controls his breathing then, very gently, he squeezes off one round and checks the telescope again. He sees the round has struck in the centre of the body in keeping with his honed first-round hit skills at 600m. Satisfied that he has zeroed his rifle, he ensures the weapon is unloaded and then walks up to the Range butts to remove the target. His attention is distracted by an Army Bomb Disposal truck arriving at some huts, but continues with his task.

Army Range Office

Sean, wearing Bomb Disposal insignia, speaks to the Range Officer, "Sorry we haven't been able to give you any notice but HQ Scotland has ordered my team to locate here in readiness to cover central Scotland. I'd be obliged if you could allocate us some accommodation. There are six of us."

"No problem, sir," answers the Range Officer. "I heard on the radio there's an incident at Grangemouth. Are we expecting more?"

"Aye, that's it. G3 Ops have put us on stand-by. The whole country seems to be on fire. It's prudent to have us on the ground now," confirmed Sean.

The Range Officer takes a bunch of keys from a key-cabinet and invites Sean to follow him. They open an old wooden accommodation hut and Sean signals to his team to leave their vehicle and join him.

Range Car Park

A few hours later a small group of noisy, excited young boys and girls dressed in Scottish Army Cadet uniforms spill out from a couple of minibuses. Two harassed adult sergeants try to direct them to some of the old accommodation huts nearby.

Sean and his men are unloading their vehicle and heading in the same direction, "You've got your hands full with that gang of pirates!"

"You're not kidding, sir," re-joins one of them. "It's like trying to herd cats. The good news is that we've only got them for this bank-holiday range-weekend".

Sean chuckles "All the best! I don't envy you."

Army Accomodation Hut

Sean and his team, composed and relaxed, sit and lie on beds. The sound of school children squealing with laughter is heard from adjoining huts.

Military Operations Room, HQ Scotland: 2000hrs 22 June

McCloy is alone in the room pouring over a map of Scotland, which is covered with coloured pins. A whiteboard at the side lists incidents which are colour-coded with the map. GREEN – RIOTS, RED - BOMB THREATS, BLUE – DEMONSTRATIONS. He jots into a note-book then strides to a phone, "Pull all the Army Reserve training programmes for the last two months and bring them into me ASAP", he suddenly shouts, "I don't bloody care if it's Saturday night! Get it done!"

He slams the phone down and goes back to the map boards. He turns as a furious looking Harry enters the room, "Scotland annihilated us at football! It's bad enough the bastard Australians demolished us at cricket a couple of months ago but this is just unbearable."

McCloy snorted, "That's the least of our bloody problems. Scotland is on the verge of anarchy. I'm positive all of these incidents are co-ordinated, I can smell it. And I don't know why! Some-one is pulling the strings. Every policeman in Scotland is on the ground. All three infantry battalions & RM Condor are virtually either under arrest or nursing their wounds in barracks... and I don't think it's finished. Incidents are coming in all the time. London and Washington are furious about the disruption to North Sea Oil through the Grangemouth bombing!"

Harry stares open-mouthed at the mass of coloured pins, "Do we have anyone left?"

McCloy rubs his tired face, "I've already sent reports to Army HQ London asking for reinforcements. I've asked for Reserve Army training programmes for the last few months in order to identify who can be brought to a higher Readiness State to aid the Civil Community. We are only being re-active. Whoever is organising these events has us on the back foot. London may have to declare a State of Emergency. What about the Scottish Government?"

"What about those oxygen-thieves?" Harry retorted, "We sacked them, remember! We are the bloody power here," and makes for the phone.

A Prestiguous Edinburgh University: 2100hrs 22 June

A steady stream of laughing students filed towards the Principal's Manse at the heart of the august institution. All were dressed, as had been requested, in black and white striped pyjamas – the "entry-fee" to this surprise party organised by the University Officer Training Corps (UOTC).

The prestige of the venue added to their buoyant mood as the main hall filled with happy guests, mainly from the Students' Union and other left-leaning political groups. They seemed delighted to attend this "pyjama-party", with their Officer Cadet hosts, as it was seen as an olive-branch offered by the university Military Education Committee to reduce friction between the recruiters of the UOTC and the anti-militarist free-spirits of the student community. It therefore made sense to have a "thank-you" party for them as a peace-offering before the beginning of the Freshers events in September, which would again include UOTC recruiting.

The evening flowed with great music, dancing, high-spirited games and copious amounts of alcohol.

Later in the evening, with an unseen command the Officer Cadets faded discreetly into an adjoining ante-room. There, black shirts, skirts and trousers, were pulled on by the silent, grinning cadets.

The unsuspecting, merry and pyjamaed students had not yet noticed and continued their enjoyable partying at the bar.

In the ante-room there was now an excited frisson of whispers, "She's here! She's here!" Nazi Swastika arm-bands were hastily produced from black-shirt pockets and pulled onto left upper arms. The command, "Attention!" was given by the Senior Under Officer as Margaret Ross strode into the centre of the room. "Are those pinko scumbags here?" she rasped. The cadets responded in rapturous union, "Yes!" with glowing excitement at the presence, amongst them, of the leader of the BNUP and at the promised "sport" which would conclude their evening.

"I've just arrived from a fantastic evening at Tayforth University. Let's continue our British National momentum here, tonight! The future is ours!" and marched towards the double doors of the adjoining ante-room swinging them wide open on first contact. Her Nazi acolytes followed immediately behind.

Clued-in bar staff immediately moved to lock the other bar doors as another flicked the music to a deafening version of "Rule Britannia" as the Nazis marched in.

Some students immediately grasped the significance of their striped pyjamas in the presence of the black-shirted fascists. They had been suckered into wearing Concentration Camp prison gear. The fascists knew exactly who their prisoners were and in twos and threes grabbed their victims and slapped Velcro triangles on the screaming, shouting, crying dupes. Pink triangle for gays. Red triangle for socialists. Six pointed triangles for Jews.

Punches, slaps and kicks immediately rained down on their defenceless quarry, accompanied by obscene oaths. Margaret Ross, hands on hips, looked on approvingly at the carnage. A simpering university principal stood by her holding prepared letters thanking them for attending the party and pointing out any false reports about high-spirits which got out of hand, to police, parents or media, would result in their instant dismissal from university.

On a barked word of command, the fascists immediately withdrew, leaving their shocked, injured and bloodied sobbing victims. The principal unlocked the main door to the bar and then ushered the injured from his manse as he pushed a copy of his letter into the hands of the staggering and stunned unfortunates.

Ross, her message clearly imparted to the student opposition leadership, smiled and shook hands with the principal. A job well done.

Army Accomodation Hut

Sean receives a call on his mobile. He listens intently then switches it off. He wears a conspiratorial smile, "Pack your kit. We move in 10 minutes."

Security Office, Stirling Castle: 2200hrs 22 June

The aged security guard sits petrified in the corner, tied up and gagged. He stares at a large plastic container on his desk. The lid is slightly opened; enough to reveal wires, batteries and a clock. Tyson, now dressed in combat uniform with an SLA badge on one arm, points a Soviet airborne AK-47 at him, "Thanks for making that call to the UXB Team. Jes' sit tight and everything'll be OK." He slickly unfolds the stock on the weapon to its full length.

Range Car Park

A police car pulls up where Sean stands waiting beside the bomb-disposal truck. His team are already in the vehicle as it sits in the evening mirk. An exhausted policeman gets out of his car, walks up to Sean and they salute, "I'm your escort, sir. We'll take you to the bomb incident in the Castle."

"You look knackered. Are you OK?" sympathised Sean.

"Ma neebour and I are in tatters, sir. We've been on since six last night and no sign of being stood down," he grimaced.

Sean kind-heartedly puts his hand on the cops shoulder.

Skull sits in his darkened land-rover in the car park, unobserved, watching the scene. He has no insignia, his face is covered in cam-cream. He waits until the red tail lights of the vehicles leave, switches his engine on, and then slowly drives out of the camp.

Stirling Castle

The police car and the Bomb Disposal Truck park at the imposing main gate on the esplanade. Sean waves away the cop car which immediately leaves. Two soldiers, in bomb disposal gear, leave the truck and enter the castle. They make for the security guards office.

Castle Security Office

Tyson looks at surveillance system screens and sees the approach of the 2 spacemen-like soldiers who have helmet visors down. He sits on the edge of the desk, AK-47 across his lap, one hand resting on the bomb container. The security guard is frantic with fear.

The two bomb disposal soldiers enter the room. They stand silent, taking in the scene. Tyson gingerly removes his hand from the box, stands up and backs up to a wall. One of the soldiers walks around the table and crouches down behind the container, examining it carefully and deliberately at eye-level. He stands up and places his hands on the lid. The tension is palpable. He tentatively lifts the lid and places it, gently, on the table. He inserts both thumbs into the rim of the container and lifts out a tray full of wires, batteries and clock and places it next to the lid. His hand, now holding a pair of pliers, hovers above the container and then reaches in to remove something. The security guard faints with a loud groan and slumps sideways off his chair.

The soldier slowly extracts the pliers to reveal a ham and lettuce white-bread sandwich. He speaks with a heavy foreign accent,

94

"Dobro. It still looks quite fresh. I wondered where my sandwich box had gone to, Tyson."

They laugh as the soldiers lift their visors and step forward, with Tyson, to pull out sandwiches from the "bomb" and begin munching. Tom is the soldier with the pliers and a military radio, "Hullo, Zero Alpha. Situation contained, mopping up now. Out."

The soldiers and Tyson guffaw as they finish the sandwiches. Tyson glances at the unconscious body of the guard, bends down and unties him.

Outside Sean receives the radio message, looks at his driver and jerks his thumb at the castle, "Get the vehicle into the castle then I want one of you on this gate as sentry. Make sure you contact Army HQ Scotland and the local police to tell them we'll maintain security tonight and check for any other devices. Make sure they acknowledge. Keep them happy, eh?" The soldiers salute in rejoinder.

Sean walks over a drawbridge to the castle as the vehicle enters. He stops at a statue of Sir William Wallace. He leans on a wall and whispers, "You're a hard act to follow, Mel, but I promise we'll do our utmost for you." Sean looks around sheepishly.

A car, driven by Sinead, drives up the esplanade to him. He gets in and they drive off.

A Remote Hillside Car Park

Skull finishes applying branches to the camouflage net over his barely visible Land-Rover. He shoulders his rucksack, lifts the sniper rifle and places it over his shoulder and stalks off into the night. On his shoulder is an SLA badge.

Ochil Hills: 2300hrs 22 June

An army truck with no lights, towing a trailer, pulls in to a dark deserted car park. Camouflaged SLA soldiers, with blackened hands and faces, silently disgorge pulling on Bergans and their weapons. Two take kneeling positions as sentries at the entrance to the car park while the rest unload the trailer of dark large tubes. The truck leaves, still blacked out.

Skull steps out of the darkness and joins a soldier who is kneeling on their own, taking a compass bearing. He kneels beside the soldier and takes out his compass, too. They agree on a direction, pointing at a large clump of trees silhouetted on the dark horizon.

Skull snaps his fingers and the sentries return to the group. The soldiers help each other hoist the heavy tubes onto each other's backs. Skull and the other soldier lead the heavily-laden group on an uphill march, toward the distant clump of trees under a cloud-less sky.

Hillside

The groups of soldiers are working in pairs. They dig trenches along a ridge line. Each pair also has three tubes. They work fiercely with a purpose.

Skull and his companion lie under a camouflaged poncho, in the trees, their faces illuminated by a tiny red torch. Skull whispers over a map,"...your lads have to be dug in before first light. Make sure their Surface to Air Missiles interlock their arcs of fire, cover-ing 360 degrees of your position. We believe the area in front of you will be used as a Form-Up Point for any heli-borne assault on Stirling Castle because the hills here would mask them off from the Castle on the other side. OK?"

The other soldier nods her head. She is very blonde but has the hard features only a Glasgow lassie could have. Then, she points to Skull questioningly. He shrugs his shoulders as though clueless. She laughs. The torch light goes off and they both emerge from under the poncho. She heads to her soldiers and Skull lopes back downhill.

Hotel Suite, Stirling: Sunday, 23 June

Sinead and Sean make love passionately. Once satiated, they sleep. Later Sinead, naked, rolls over and looks at an alarm clock: 0030. She hears Sean crying softly in another room and pulls a sheet round her, moving toward the sound. She stands silently in a door-way as she sees his head bowed, naked shoulders heaving.

Sean sits holding a head-and-shoulders photo of two lovely smiling young boys. Huge tear drops fall from him onto the photo and run down the glass. The boys are seven and nine years old, very smart in white school shirts and blue school tie. Intelligence and happiness shine from them.

Sinead sits on the arm of the chair and wraps her sheet around Sean and her. She puts an arm lovingly around his shoulders and pulls his head onto her chest. He continues to sob and seems on the point of breakdown. He is no longer the warrior leader but sits exposed as a broken man weighed down with an outrageous, impossible burden. They sit together for a few moments. Sean exhales and then speaks, "I've already lost one son. I couldn't cope with loosing Will, too. He's insisted in being involved with our Operation. I tried to stop him but his mind was made up. He won't take 'No!' for an answer."

Sinead smiled, "He's his father's son. He must strike back, too. He'll also be terrified of any harm coming to you but I'm positive he'll be immensely proud of what you are doing."

Sean looks into Sinead's eyes. He isn't convinced and looks for courage from her, "I'm terrified of harm coming to him and everyone else who has taken up arms with us. I even fear for those who stand in our path."

"You must be strong for everyone, in spite of your doubts. We need you to inspire and lead us. You know I'll help you cope. We both know the loneliness of command," she consoled.

Sean leans back in the chair and stares at the ceiling, "I read somewhere that courage is like an old-fashioned cheque-book. Everyone has a finite amount of cheques they can cash in. I hope I have enough left to see us through."

Sinead gives him a soft lingering kiss on his lips. Her eyes smile. He sighs and responds by taking her in his arms, embracing passionately. He breaks the embrace by kissing her on the fore-head. He gets up, crosses the room and pours a couple of malts into crystal glasses. He gives her a glass. Sean sips and becomes more focussed, "I taught my sons the kind of individualism that I inherited from my country. You know... that refusal to be pushed around. I look around the world and see far too many who no longer subscribe to that ideal and are pushed around by governments and by certain leaders. Today is a very bad time for Scotland's civil liberties. Our freedoms are being blatantly removed and manipulated by stealth in the name of fighting terrorism. This is something that I now recognise. Will and I and every other man and woman who believe in personal freedoms must now protest. We must stand free. The world of today is in many ways a darker place, which makes the spark of democracy in our small corner all the more precious."

"Where is Will now?" Sinead gently enquired.

"Heading to the Castle with the rest of the lads and lassies. He's going to be my runner. I couldn't think of anyone I could rely on more..." he replied.

"Aren't your lads being exploited just like every other soldier?" questioned Sinead.

Sean breathed deeply whilst staring down into his dram, thinking hard. "They're volunteers. They don't have to be there if they don't want to." He extended his right fore-arm to expose an un-officer like tattoo of flowing scroll script, "It is in truth not for glory, nor riches, nor honours that we are fighting, but for Freedom – for that alone, which no honest man gives up but with life itself..."

"And what will you do with that Freedom?" a famous Australian once asked," laughed Sinead in her broad Dublin accent.

Sean laughed with her, "Why should we risk our lives for a fanciful concept? Naw. It's to ensure anyone living in Scotland will never, ever again be exploited by the British state and its corporate masters. Enough is enough. London is taking us down the road of all wealth, and therefore power, being held by a handful of selfish, greedy, fascist bastards. Scotland's got to be a country where competence is more important than background. How can we live in a system that brings about illegal wars in order to sell military hardware which results in obscene profit for those self-serving, avaricious scum? Who don't give a flying fuck for the broken men and women who return from their bloody wars to societies devastated by heart-braking loss? Fucked up veteran communities reliant on food-banks and charities. It stops now. Today. We're giving our political leaders some breathing space to bring about international support in order to make our own way, to start mapping out the kind of community we want to live in. We're doing it to determine our children's future and their children's children."

"You sound like a politician," mused Sinead.

"Listen, I'm no politician nor would ever want to be involved. This is more than that. It's Life. The Universe and Everything", he laughed again.

"War and fascism are what the elites are offering us all across the world. Take one example and ask yourself what options are being offered? For God's sake, the immediate and medium-term future will see automation replacing jobs and work. 'Technological unemployment' they're calling it! If decision making is in the hands of our own communities then there are bright, shining opportunities to use these changes to our advantage. To massively improve the quality of life for us all from cradle to grave. How absolutely fantastic would that be? Tax becomes a joy that redistributes wealth. Let's go mad and have a system that provides every single citizen with a universal income of two thousand Euros per month to do whatever they want to do. London, the BNUP and the neoliberal corporations are saying we couldn't afford such nonsense plus it would encourage people not to work. Oh fuckin' really? Well, do you know what? Self-determination is exactly that. We get to choose, no' them! We fuckin' determine how we look after our young, our infirm and our elderly ourselves!" He looked at Sinead who was smiling broadly.

"What? Are you laughing at me?" he demanded defensively.

"No, Sean. Quite the contrary. I'm loving every word. I need more, please," she smiled.

He smiled back, "OK, then. Try this. We've long been in a situation where 7% of the population owns 84% of wealth. What happens when folk no longer receive cash from non-existent jobs or from 20 hour weeks to spread out the few jobs available? Revolution? Rebellion? The elite recognise this. Their answer? Suppression of dissension. Conformity. Call free-thinking people extremists, separatists and saboteurs. Remove the ballot-box as an option from the electorate. Those who hold power and wealth strive to retain them or have a damascene moment and hand them over to the people?

British Empire 2.0 has absolutely no intention of the latter. Are we to continue to listen to their self-aggrandising bullshit when they can no longer pay our incomes? How will they control peoples and maintain dominance over them when offering us nothing? They offer us racism and imperialistic nationalism. Hate 'Spics if you're American or hate immigrants if you're a Brit. For Fuck's sake! War is good business, invest your sons and daughters? No. Not anymore. We determine a better way for our communities ourselves."

"You've been thinking about this for a long time, haven't you?" said Sinead who has become more serious now. "Your motivation is about your lost son and the sons and daughters your community has lost...and how people are treated, not just veterans."

"Aye. I've always known the truth. But when the so-called great-and-the-good say black it's difficult to argue white, which is on the one hand. On the other hand, the military are well aware that Solomon Asch, the famous psychologist conducted social psychology experiments way back in the 1950's to investigate the extent to which social pressure from a majority group could affect a person to conform. He proved it's very difficult for the normal guy in the street to resist group opinion even when a person actually knows they have the correct answer. Nazi propaganda is a notorious example of warping people's opinions. Add in Stanley Mailgrams psychological experiments in the 1960's and 70's which confirmed a natural obedience in us all to authority figures. As I said, the military and police enhance and use these techniques all over the world but UK mainstream media have also been utilising such twisted practices for decades to browbeat the electorate towards voting as directed and not necessarily what people know to be the truth. Fortunately, social mass media have undermined the news and state corporations by exposing lies and fake-news for what they are.

"But the real truth is since Scotland polarised politically between the minority hard-right Brexit and the majority anti-Brexit self-government electorate there was always going to be a decision point. It happened democratically but the anti-democrats are trying to kill fairness and replace it with hellish tyranny," he paused. "I sound like a fucking drama-queen on a gin fuelled rant...I couldn't do politics..."

Sinead broke the long silence simply by quietly saying, "Please go on...."

Again he let out a long sigh, "Thank you for letting me download. Your ability to listen is one of the massive reasons I love you," he blurted out emotionally.

"Go on," she whispered.

"OK. You asked for it," and smiled, "The people of Scotland, and everywhere else on the planet, cannot risk being trapped in the post-Brexit type nightmares that BNUP and their likes plan. Rightwing politicians in Britain, France, Hungary and the Netherlands are intent on dividing Europe. Actually," he laughed, "The right wing of those countries must be extremely jealous of the size of the right-wing British vote!

"Two World Wars have taught them nothing – unless the motivation is to have other people fight each other whilst they profit. That way ruin truly lies. Scots, in the main, vote against right wing parties like the BNUP because they know how anti-ethical they are to communities. Margaret Thatcher said there is no such thing as society. My God, what a horrendous viewpoint. It's why Scotland rejected Thatcherism because they knew the veracity of such administrations benefit the rich. Always. And not the poor."

He fixed her with a gaze of unbridled, heartfelt passion, "The English NHS is described by the British Red Cross as a humanitarian crisis. The BNUP want to reverse Scottish policies that guarantee free NHS and free university tuition. We want to protect an egalitarian society. They want to eradicate the very concept and replace it with an American system where loyal subjects are required to pay for health, education and pensions. Oh, the back-enamelled irony! We reject this because it's disgusting. Enlightened countries provide allowances to encourage families to have children when London requires mothers to prove they have been raped in order to receive similar allowances. Can you smell the vicious lunacy? Scotland needs more children to look after our society as we all live longer. What's not to like? We need immigrants for the same reason. However, London chooses to pull up the drawbridge at Dover! We need workers' rights but London proposes bans on industrial action. If England wants such a draconian, reactionary environment then crack on! If they prefer to pay billions for nukes instead of using that cash for the benefit of their society, then let them! But we are seceding from such madness! Brexit allows them to do this simply by removing European rights for us all and safeguarding the profits of Westminster's imperial masters. They indulge racism by arguing that any such redistributive welfare state is viable only in an ethnically homogenous state. That viewpoint is truly abhorrent. They promote the militarisation of our society in a manner that makes legitimate criticism of "our boys" seem unpatriotic. Any Scots Defence Force will focus on defence! Not illegal bloody wars with the danger of nukes being used purely for shareholders and corporations profits! I've ranted enough. The right wing press argue social democracy is dead. Is it fuck, because we are going to defend it."

Her eyes were shining brightly, "Aye that's it, Sean. London has had its day with telling Dublin and Edinburgh and an Empires worth of other capital cities what they can and cannot do."

Sheepishly and half-smiling, he murmured, "Have I left anything out?"

"Aye, Sean, you have. You missed naming the right-wing dominated, isolationist, backward-looking, chauvinistic, xenophobia," as she struggled to keep a straight face.

Giggling, "Oh aye...so I have...that and democracy must mean something other than the two wolves that are London and Washington and the Edinburgh sheep voting on what to have for dinner...."

Army HQ, Scotland

In the dark grounds of the Army base, Colonel Margaret Ross and Lieutenant Colonel McCloy are having an intense discussion beneath a majestic and towering oak tree in the gardens. Both are aware they can observe anyone approaching them and being outside makes it very difficult to be overheard by electronic means, or by the human ear, unless close. They have agreed to leave their mobile phones in his office.

She is asserting her military rank over the nominally more junior officer who argues, in return, that her rank is a honourary political expedient."You'll do as you're fucking ordered, McCloy! Don't be in any doubt that I have the full backing of not only Prime Minister Harris but CGS!" she emphasised.

McCloy was visibly shocked, "The Chief of the General Staff?" As a career army officer he was well aware that this was approval from the highest ranking officer. He digested this for a moment as he mulled over the ramifications of a politician being given military authority. He also was beginning to detect very dangerous constitutional territory.

As the authoritarian potential dawned on him though, he realised this could be of use to his intelligence gathering functions. "I take it that you're happy to, shall we say, co-operate on matters of Scottish political interest?"

"Absolutely. I can see you are beginning to understand where the British government wants me to fill in here. I have an excellent network throughout political Scotland, so I aim to provide as much information and intelligence as I can to guarantee Scotland remains a region of Britain," she affirmed.

"Very good, ma'am. I'm glad you've explained your role and I'll look forward to working with you."

CHAPTER 9

SEIGE: STIRLING CASTLE JUNE 2019

Stirling Castle: 0230hrs Sunday 23 June

A MILITARY CONVOY grinds up the main cobbled street, lined by 18th Century buildings, towards the castle. The convoy consists of troop carrying trucks and two huge logistics vehicles. The lead land-rover is suddenly joined, at speed, by the rear vehicle. The two land-rovers halt at the esplanade entrance.

From the castle a wall runs down either side of a broad, wide, cobbled esplanade to narrow 500m away at this bottle-neck entrance. The other side of the esplanade walls are sheer cliff drops into the darkness.

The troop carriers go past the bottleneck entrance and pull in against the west esplanade wall. The two logistics trucks continue to the castle gate and drive into the castle. Armed SLA soldiers jump out from the troop carriers wearing green combat shirts, McKenzie tartan kilts, white belts, brown leather sporrans, green hose and black highland brogues topped off by the world-famous distinctive glengarry headgear and each wearing his/her medals. There are three pipers and three drummers. They congregate talking quietly in groups. Some smoke.

A uniformed camera crew dismount from one of the two land-rovers and begin to arrange their equipment. Andy pulls back the flap at the back of the other land-rover and four soldiers leap out in full-combat gear. Each of them carries a modern RPG 32 anti-tank weapon on their backs, two carry a heavy machine-gun (MG), and the others are burdened by ammunition boxes. Andy points to where he wants each MG team to take up sentry position either side of the esplanade bottle-neck. They jog into their positions, behind cover, facing downhill covering the approach road. Both teams lie down, load the MGs and settle down grimly, ready to fire, at the area to their front.

Each team carries a pre-prepared hessian screen which they erect in front of them which have already been painted to ensure, to an approaching casual observer, that they blend into the stone-work of the castle. They can easily see through the hessian without being observed.

They don't have long to wait. Two soldiers walk up the street towards them, keeping to shadows. Both MG teams cock their weapons and aim at them.

The approaching soldiers, about 100m from a MG position, slowly and deliberately move to the centre of the dark pavement with arms extended with their weapons clearly shown. They kneel down on one knee, their arms still extended. The tense gunner prepares to fire. Hoarsely, he whispers a code-word, "Bon?"

"Accord!" replies Sean.

The gunner motions them forward and exhales loudly as the tension floods from him. Sean and Sinead jog past the MG-team and head up past the others into the castle.

Military Operations Room, HQ, Scotland

McCloy, exhausted and dishevelled, pours himself a black coffee. A knock, the door opens and an officer walks in carrying a large file, "Here's the Reserve training programmes, sir. There's been a bomb-alert at Stirling Castle."

Nodding, McCloy responds, "I'm clutching at straws. We've got no-one else to call on except these bloody Weekend Warriors. Armchair heroes, the lot of them."

The officer raises his eyebrows, "Sir, I worked with a lot of them in Iraq and Afghanistan. We stopped calling them STABs, or Stupid Territorial Army Bastards, a long, long time ago. The majority were excellent, extremely competent. We were always so short of men we were delighted to see them. They're now very experienced soldiers with racks of medals on their chests."

McCloy looks thoughtful as the officer leaves. He settles down with his coffee to study the files.

Stirling Castle: Pre-Dawn 0300hrs Sunday 23 June

The camera crew are now high on a vantage point recording this historic day. A kilted Sergeant Major Andy MacCreadie marches crisply out to the centre of the esplanade. His brogues crash out the Halt on the cobbled esplanade, then carries out a perfect about turn to face the waiting soldiers. He looks every inch an imposing Scots Sergeant Major, ramrod straight, chin raised high causing him to look along his nose to fix every soldier with his piercing gaze.

The first rays of the eastern sunrise dance on the hushed Stirling Castle. The sun begins to illuminate a magnificent statue of King Robert the Bruce on the esplanade on Andy's left. Facing him, in the distance behind the waiting soldiers, the pinnacle of the Sir William Wallace Monument, funded and raised by the people of Scotland in memory of Scotland's greatest hero, imperceptibly begins to emerge from the gloaming, mounted on the towering escarpment of the Abbey Craig. The background to Andy's wonderful vista is the heather clad Ochil Hills which impose their grandeur over the whole area. He was well aware his anti-aircraft platoon on those hills should be dug in, and ready, by this time. The Castle is an extraordinary place and an extraordinary moment to begin this Scots Rebellion. It is the 23rd of June, the 705th anniversary of King Robert the Bruce's victory of deliverance from the English, at the nearby Bannockburn.

He takes a deep breath and roars out an order, "1st Battalion, Scottish Liberation Army, Get on Parade!"

The soldiers immediately jog towards him and quickly right-dress into a formed body in three ranks. The pipers and drummers take post at the end of the soldiers, nearest the castle, on Andy's left. They all stand at Attention. The suns glow slowly radiates on them. Andy barks out the command to "Stand at Ease". They wait.

A soldier mutters to his mate, "Whit did the RSM say? SLA? Why are we wearing medals wae jist green combat shirts – it looks fucking shite, by the way...."

The RSM fixes a death-stare on the chattering mischief maker even though he is only one of many identically dressed soldiers in poor light. The reprobate closes his eyes and grimaces a whispered, "Aw naw...."

After a few moments, Sean, in the same kit, marches smartly out of the Castle Gate towards the soldiers. In his right hand is an officer's Highland broadsword. As he marches down the esplanade, Andy calls the soldiers back to the position of Attention. They move as one, their right thighs immediately raised parallel to the ground then instantaneously and simultaneously, their right brogue crashes loudly on the cobbles. Every Scots soldier braces up ramrod straight, each chin raised, left arm parallel straight to the body and right arm extended at the elbow holding an AK-47 to their right shoulder. Andy executes a left-turn and marches towards Sean. They both halt. Andy cracks off an immaculate salute, "1st Battalion, Scottish Liberation Army on Parade, Sir!"

Sean returns the salute with his broadsword, "Thank you, RSM. Fall in please."

They both take post and stand perfectly still. Sean is front and centre before the Scots soldiers with Andy directly behind them. There is no other movement or sound. A slight breeze causes the tapers which hang from the back of their Glengarries to sway. The pleats on their kilts also ruffle gently in the morning breeze. High on the Castle Esplanade these soldiers look superb as the sky turns from a red-orange glow to expanses of blue. The town of Stirling sleeps below. The hills that surround the area seem to rise to the heavens. The moment is majestic.

Sean gazes along the ranks of his soldiers. He declares loudly, "Sons and daughters of Scotland! Today is the anniversary of the Battle of Bannockburn! On 23rd June 1314 our forefathers, vastly outnumbered, faced the mightiest English invading army of that time. They fought at Bannockburn, for King Robert the Bruce, to free Scotland from English Occupation. They achieved their aims, as we shall surely achieve ours.

"I see before me a body of soldiers with military decorations from every campaign the British Army asked you to serve in. Northern Ireland, Bosnia, Sierra Leone, Kosovo, the Gulf Wars, Afghanistan and Syria. Your medals evidence your fighting prowess and the demands of London government to face the Queens enemies, then, and the Kings enemies now. No longer. Scotland will decide when, where and if her sons and daughters are placed in harm's way. You will no longer be taken for granted, exploited and then forgotten."

Sean pauses. Every Scot hangs on his every word as he continues, "History repeats itself. We again find ourselves subjugated by London. Our democratic right to self-determination has been ripped from us by modern day tyrants and their Scottish Quislings. They have torn the ballot box from our people therefore they force us to choose between meekly accepting their rule or to fight for our freedom."

Sean brandishes his broadsword high above his head. His face aglow with the exhilaration of the occasion, "London has betrayed our trust. They therefore forfeit the right to plunder Scotland's sons and daughters ever again! I ask you now to follow me to secure Scotland's Freedom!"

Each soldiers face shows the intense emotion of the event as Sean resumes with the immortal lines from Scotland's Declaration of Independence written in the year 1320 in the Abbey of Arbroath,

"For as long as but one hundred of
us remain alive, never will we under
any condition be brought under English
rule. It is in truth not for glory,
nor riches, nor honours that we fight,
but for Freedom — for that alone,
which no honest man gives up,
but with life itself."

The excitement and tension is palpable. Andy, his pulse racing, roars out a command, "Battalion will move to the right in three's! Right turn!"

The battalion executes the turn with yet another simultaneous, thunderous crash of brogues in unison. Sean marches to the head of the column and Andy takes post at the rear. They pause.

High on the battlements, his son Will, is a kilted soldier wearing a blue pantone- azure full double breasted, high-collared jacket in the style of the Danish Royal Guard with broad white cross-belts creating a Saltire effect. Will pulls at pristine white cords to raise an immense St Andrews Cross on the flagstaff at the highest point on Stirling Castle, which his uniform clearly replicates. A gust of wind lifts the flag to fill the sky above them.

Spontaneously, every Scots soldier lets out a throaty roar of approval, waving their Glengarries high above their heads. It is an outpouring of utter joy and pride.

Andy shouts a command – instantly causing the soldiers to replace their headgear and regain their composure. Sean bellows an order which commence the pipes and drums to play "Scots Wha Hae" at a spirited march-tempo. The pipe-tune is well known to all of them as a Rabbie Burns song but, according to tradition, the tune was played by Bruce's army at the Battle of Bannockburn. On Sean's next command, they advance in column keeping step in time with the ancient martial rhythm of the great highland bagpipes, towards the castle. As they march, they skirt the statue of King Robert the Bruce. Sean orders, "Eyes right!"

As they pass the statue, every soldier's heads turns sharply to the right as Sean carries out a sword flourish in salute. As Andy passes the statue he roars, "Eyes front!"

They continue on and into the Castle gates, their kilts swaying in time to each pace. Andy is the last soldier in the column to disappear into the Castle as the sounds of the pipes and drums echo from inside and gradually fade as they melt into the ancient fortification.

As the skirl of the pipes dwindles to silence, the drivers of the troop carriers burst into activity, swing their huge vehicles around and block off the esplanade bottle-neck, then run back into the castle. The two MG-teams chew gum as they lie in wait.

Castle Ramparts: 0700hrs 23 June

On the ramparts of the castle, Sean, now wearing combat gear, Sinead and the camera crew discuss TV satellite broadcasts. The crew rig up the cameras via laptops. Sinead checks Sean's appearance. Will enters smiling, "You looked great, Dad... and so did the troops. They looked magnificent. What a buzz!"

Sean looks self-conscious as he hugs his son, "I must confess when you raised the St Andrews Cross, I had a lump in my throat and a wee tear... Seriously embarrassing!"

"Your dad always looks great, Will," says Sinead admiringly, "but it's vital the world sees and hears about the drama of this event, right now. We could have sneaked into the castle in the dark or we could march in wearing our best gear with medals! There is no shame to this action, the world gets to see the theatre of it and it's recorded for posterity. The SLA must maximise the news value or we'll defeat the aim of Operation St Andrew."

A uniformed cameraman gives them the thumbs up, "We're ready. We've sent the piece on the occupation of the castle to every news service, terrestrial and satellite that we know of. We'll do the live broadcast as soon as we have a live link."

A former Territorial Army Press & Information Officer suddenly points at a laptop screen and gives another thumbs-up to Sean, the screen shows "CNN - LIVE", then Sean as a talking-head.

Confidently he begins, "Good morning, my name is Lieutenant Colonel Sean MacAlpin, Commander of the Scottish Liberation Army. We are a force of Scots National resistance. We now hold Stirling Castle in the name of the elected representatives of the Community of Scots to demand immediate recognition of our 18th September 2018 democratic Referendum of self-determination under the UN Charter of 1945. We have been forced into this course of action by London's denial of the democratic process. We call on Scots parliamentarians to immediately make their way here, to free Scots Territory, and establish a provisional government in order to commence negotiation of terms with London, the EU and UN for Scotland's Independence."

Pausing, Sean looks off camera to the crew who indicate 1 hour, "We shall broadcast again in 1 hour. Thank you."

Sean walks to the camera crew and kneels beside them. They all pay rapt attention to a laptop screen as a flustered CNN announcer attempts to clarify the world exclusive they have just been given.

"OK, we're going to have the planet on our doorstep within minutes. It'll be curious to see who reacts first – the media or British Security Forces," jokes Sean.

"Why didn't you give the exclusive to a Scots TV station?" asked Sinead.

"That's very simple," replied Sean, "There isn't one. The BBC is no better than Russia Today. The clue is in the name – British. UKTV bought the majority shares of the only Scottish station last year to ensure Scotland has no TV station. Another example of London democracy in action...Von Ribbentrop would have heartily approved of complete control of the national propaganda machine."

Andy approaches as a man in control, "The support weapons and ammunition have been distributed and everyone is at their posts, fully briefed. As soon as you're ready we'll walk the ground, Boss."

Shouldering his weapon, Sean commands, "I want the dummy communications HQ up here and the alternative comms kit ready within the hour. The first place the Brits will try to take out will be our comms. It's vital we retain the ability to let the world know we are here. Complete internal radio silence from now. Understood? Have all personal cell-phones been handed in?"

They acknowledge and Sean follows Andy along the rampart.

Margo McCrindle's Home

Margo, Scotland's deposed First Minister, has pressed the pause button on her TV remote. She sat blinking furiously, incredulously. She put down the remote and put her hands on her head in aghast disbelief at what she had just heard Sean state in Stirling Castle.

She let out a slow, anguished, "Oh my God, Sean. What the fuck have you done?"

Her phone buzzed on the table beside her which she answered. A familiar voice, which she recognised as one of her political parties Member of the European Parliament (MEP) asked, "I take it you saw that? What are you going to do?" She immediately replied, "I'm going to deny all knowledge and condemn military action. We have campaigned for 80 years for independence on peaceful grounds. That can't change but," she paused, then said, "Perhaps we can exploit this. Someone once mentioned the 'Fog of War' to me, that if we focus on our strategic aim of Independence we can react faster to unfolding events."

"So you want me to book you onto the first flight to Brussels, then?" the MEP asked. "Exactly," she replied, "Meet me at Brussels airport."

Barrack Room, Stirling Castle

A small group of SLA soldiers are deep in quiet conversation, sitting and lying on bunk-beds, in a corner of their barrack room. Most are cleaning and preparing their personal weapons. Auld Bill is holding court, "...you see, this political scenario has been unfolding in my lifetime...in 1955, 98 per cent of the population voted Unionist, Labour or Conservative...the figure for 2015 was just 39 per cent... so what? The evidence is there that the Scots population, thems who for fought for King and Empire in World War Two, was simply dying off being replaced by a younger free-thinking generation... but the Scottish Unionist parties have only ever seen the problems and challenges of the 21st century Scotland through the prism of 20th century Westminster politics. We had found our identity but the Scottish Unionist parties failed to find theirs. Which is why we won that last Independence Referendum whilst they still stand on the side-lines failing to understand what has taken place."

A young intelligent looking soldier asks, "Why couldn't they talk up a narrative for the new Scotland by addressing the issues that are important to us? Surely they must've wanted to escape the suffocating Westminster agenda?"

"You would think, so, young Colin. But these Scottish parties were only ever branch-offices of their London bosses. Brexit is an English phenomenon. By rejecting it Scotland showed our broader humanity, our internationalism and our embrace of difference and diversity. Therein lies our political dichotomy. We, in Scotland, need to express a way to present ourselves to the international community which is different in tone, style, language and is less angry in its outlook and delivery from England. Our Unionist parties didn't get it so they've been rejected."

Colin nods in understanding, "Aye, it's the complete opposite of what my generation perceives of Brexit being founded on a lure of British greatness... did ye see what I did there?" causing a ripple of laughter as response but a more pointed, "Aye, ya fud!" from one of his less impressed comrades. More seriously, Colin continued, "Aye, this false attraction of Great Britain, being a poor European team player immersed in sentiment and nostalgia of days gone by, an historic sense of exceptionalism, and increasingly drifting to the right on a wave of economic nationalism as lavish embrace of the old Empire campaigning in favour of the excesses of neo-liberal market forces instead of promoting the common good."

"For fucks sake, man! Where did ye pick up this pish?" quizzed an incredulous comrade.

"University of St Andrews, old chap. A PhD from the School of International Relations," Colin replied evenly.

Auld Bill tittered, "A Doctor, no less, but a private soldier in a rebel army. Please continue, young sir...."

Indulging in an elaborate, mock theatrical wave Colin continued, "Scotland needs to make ambition and aspiration matter, by building a mood, momentum and a movement that once again captures the imagination of Scots making inequality, which has been poisoning our society, the issue of our time. We can't do that whilst the big economic levers are at Westminster. We've got to represent our working people in parliament to pursue a fair and just society. The Labour party was founded in 1900 with principles like that but have clearly failed to deliver within London's constraints," he paused sadly, "I thought when I voted in that last

Referendum I was exercising my democratic right to change that through the ballot box...until London told me to fuck off...."

"You're not really surprised, are you, ya idiot?" remonstrated one of his more down to earth friends, "It's always only ever been about wealth and power. We're just keech that don't count unless it's tae fight their fucking wars for oil or whatever. That fucking 'Forever War' hingmgy...don't laugh, ya bastards...ah read it somewhere....the state manipulates never-ending combat and we're duped intae daen' the fighting...when we're daen the fightin' we forget about the unemployment, shite wages, our fucking debt tae the bank and credit companies, collapsing NHS innat...they're smart bastards the toffs so they are...wae their bastard newspapers that ah widnae wipe ma erse wae...and then they hav' the fucking brass-neck tae ca' me unpatriotic when ah banged-oot o' the regular army, b' Christ...they elites who decide whether me an' ma likes get tae thrive or no'...well, ah'll tell ye this, boy...we are all created equal and we better win this battle to mak' sure they know it an' we can watch their power crumble into the damned sea and ah get a say in spreadin' the cash aboot mair evenly! Ah had enough of the 'Ye'r bonnie laddies for the fightin' and fall-in when ye hear the rattle of the drum and the skirl o' the pipes...'."

Laughing, Auld Bill interrupted, "You're both right. But we're a' volunteers, here, right? We've been exploited for centuries so we gotta change our country for the better or allow that to continue. It's stand-up-and-be-counted time. I'm absolutely scunnered at the way they've mobilised racial prejudice and terrified social conservatives like our pensioners on behalf of the status quo. It's repulsive. They fuck democracy over and because they've been doing it for so long they don't see it as any reason to be democratic anymore. The far-right are emasculating Scotland first. Many countries are looking on in fear because they ken they might be next."

Finishing off assembling his rifle, Colin cocks it a couple of times and fires off the mechanism with satisfying clicks, when he pulls the trigger, whilst aiming at an imaginary target at the far side of the billet, "We've got to offer something that the people can believe in. The Irish Easter Rising in 1916 was a military disaster but was the key to unlocking the hearts and minds of many Irish people. They didn't turn into a successful European country overnight... but ask any of them if they want to return to London rule. You all know the answer to that one, right? So, we've got to break free from the past and find the way forward. The ballot-box has been denied us," as he loaded a full magazine of 5.56mm short rounds onto his weapon system.

"Listen up, pilgrims," laughed Auld Bill, "Young Colin here is the immediate future and whoever controls the past, controls the future. He who controls the present, controls the past. Now let's go. We're burning daylight."

Military Operations Room, HQ, Scotland

An exhausted McCloy and Harry stare in disbelief at the large, wall-mounted TV screen, as Sean announces the SLA's occupation of Stirling Castle. Harry buries his head in his hands as Justin reaches for the phone. His voice is tremulous, "Get me the General Officer Commanding, Scotland immediately."

He puts the phone down and then re-dials, "Get in here right away."

Within seconds an officer enters, holding a notebook and pen.

McCloy commands, "Get a helicopter equipped with surveillance systems over the Castle right away. I want a fully manned command team in here, ready for the General including a Royal Marine liaison officer from Condor, pronto. Get police armed response teams to seal off the Castle immediately. No one-gets in or out. All military and police units to move to the highest alert state...and everything you have on that bastard MacAlpin!"

The officer finishes his notes and runs from the room. Harry looks as though he's going to throw up and bleats, "They've made us look like fucking idiots. We're completely flat-footed. The PM is going to go absolutely mad."

Harry's mobile rings. He listens and begins to look even more ill. He puts the phone down and is mumbling quietly, "The Prime Minister is flying to Scotland, but first he has been summoned to

Buckingham Palace to explain what's happened. We need to send a briefing immediately."

McCloy looks at the papers on his desk. He lifts a sheet headed ARMY RESERVE, 6TH BATTALION ROYAL SCOTLAND REGIMENT. He winces at the name at the top, Commanding Officer, Lieutenant Colonel Sean MacAlpin. The obvious dawns on him and shakes his head in disbelief. He lifts the 6th Battalion Training Programme and walks to his map boards. He looks at the pin on Stirling Castle and notices it relates to a bomb incident. There is a blank space next to "OUTCOME". He swears loudly in exasperation as he writes SLA/MacAlpin in the blank space.

He flicks through their training programme and reads the units recent focus on weapon training on ex-Soviet equipment, including much live-firing. He closes his eyes and groans.

He calls for another staff officer, "Which Reserve units are based in the Stirling area? I want numbers of available trained soldiers."

Stirling Castle, Approach Road

Two police cars and a van, blue lights flashing and sirens on, roar up the hill towards the castle. An SLA MG team member pulls the pin from a smoke grenade then rolls it into the cobbled street belching red smoke which rapidly billows a fog which obscures the esplanade bottleneck and its two blocking troop carriers.

The leading police driver slams on the breaks, slews across the road and slams into a parked car. The following vehicles screech to a halt narrowly missing each other. Dazed, concussed, heavily armed policemen spill out of the vehicles. Some take up fire positions and commence firing at the castle, blazing away in undisciplined fury. Others pull unconscious bloodied cops from the lead vehicle. As they drag their colleagues to cover the crashed police car and the collided vehicle explodes with an orange-balled roar throwing debris into the air and in all directions.

Stirling Castle Battlements

Sean and Andy, both in camouflage combat gear, are on the castle battlements as they hear the firing and explosion. They both run to the front of the castle.

"And so it begins, Scotland's second War of Independence..." muses Sean. He lifts his handset to his lips and instructs the MG teams to return fire.

They immediately hear the machine-guns rapid double-tapping rhythmic fire in the middle distance.

Stirling Castle, Approach Road

The police return fire increases in volume with rounds impacting all around the SLA MG-teams. The cop's riposte is suddenly drowned out by two explosions as both MG teams each unleash a round from their RPG32 light anti-tank weapons, at the remaining two police vehicles, with direct hits. The MG teams follow up with machine gun fire into the police survivors. The police firing stops.

Thick black smoke billows into the blue sky as flames roar from the wrecked vehicles. Emergency vehicles wail in the distance. Screaming, panic-stricken civilians stream from nearby homes, fleeing the carnage.

The two MG teams prepare and then load belts of ammo and anti-tank weapons. One team fires short bursts at the wounded police officers and police cars forcing them to crawl and scramble into whatever cover they could find as the other team scurries back towards the castle. After some distance, they go firm and commence firing, allowing the first team to extract. The teams continue this professional manoeuvre, one firing, one moving, until they are secure within the castle. There is no response from the battered, armed police in this one-sided opening action.

Leuchars Military Base, Fife

Air-crew run from a low building towards an RAF helicopter. They quickly carry out their pre-flight checks and start up engines. Quickly the aircraft lifts and screams over the base perimeter fence.

Two pre-positioned SLA soldiers rapidly appear from a camouflaged dug-out in a wood-line directly on the flight path outside the military wire. One of the soldiers stands up and arms a Surface to Air Missile (SAM). Within seconds, he fires and watches the missile streak directly towards the chopper. The aircraft attempts to peel away but is caught by the SLA missile resulting in a massive air explosion. The fireball crashes to earth. Within seconds, RAF Emergency appliances race towards the crash scene.

An alert SCOTS DG guard, patrolling within the base, spot the SLA soldiers. He immediately radios a sighting report.

The two SLA men sprint away through the woods to a barely visible wheeled military personnel carrier where they rapidly pull off the camouflage, jump in and then speed off down a muddy farm track.

Two land rovers, full of armed RAF Regiment personnel, scream out of the airbase gates in pursuit. They make only a few meters when they are brought to a shuddering, blazing halt as machine gun green tracer rounds are seen hammering into both ambushed vehicles. Two SLA MG teams, firing from different unseen positions, pour continuous bursts of fire into vehicles and men at the gates. The tracer rounds, fired from different angles, dramatically interlock in the blazing RAF vehicles, caught in a killing ground. Mortar rounds impact in the area of the vehicles and base gates. The tracer rounds continue to hose the area until there is no movement.

The recce helicopter and ground reaction force are perfectly anticipated and eliminated by the SLA.

Wooded Area, Leuchars

The SLA wheeled personnel carrier skids to a halt at a farm track junction, the driver keeps the engine running whilst the co-driver leaps out and opens the back door. Haring through the woods towards the vehicle runs a heavily burdened group of soldiers. They carry heavy machine guns and small mortar tubes.

In a slick drill, a couple of soldiers leap into the back while the others hand-ball the weapons in, followed immediately by the remaining soldiers. The co-driver slams the door shut on them then dashes to the front and has barely time to climb in as the vehicle accelerates away. The Leuchars base-siren wails.

Prime Ministers Aircraft

The pilot leaves the flight deck and approaches one of the PMs team, "A terrorist attack has just been made on Leuchars. A SAM brought down an RAF helicopter. We must advise the PM of this. We have no guarantee of a safe airport in Scotland, because we must assume other attacks are imminent. We recommend diverting to Newcastle and for the Army to organise a road convoy from there into Scotland."

The PMs adviser nods and moves up the aircraft to sit with the PM, who is surrounded by a busy team. He speaks rapidly to him and receives the reply he seeks. He returns to the pilot and agrees the course of action. The pilot returns to the flight deck and radios ahead to Newcastle.

Stirling Castle

In a battlement castle tower Sean and Andy observe the burning vehicles. They scan the surrounding area with binoculars. Smoke still clouds the area. Police vehicle lights can be seen flashing below in the surrounding town as the area is cordoned off and ambulance staff extract the killed and wounded policemen and women. A large media circus can be seen gathering in the vicinity at the foot of the hill. Andy turns to Sean and conversationally asks, "What next, do you reckon?"

"The marines, the army and the RAF will be co-ordinating a plan of assault. They won't use the police again. They'll be pulling things together as rapidly as possible but concurrently they need intelligence. We can expect constant land, air and satellite reconnaissance. We've got to keep our lads on their toes and keep under cover until the time is right. We can also do our best to disrupt the enemy planning – by cutting the head off the snake...."

Andy's mobile phone rings. He listens then switches it off and grins, "SITREP from our Leuchar's team. Scratch one RAF recce eye-in-the-sky. That'll focus the head of your snake...."

He pats Sean on the knee as he squeezes past him on the way down from the tower. Sean remains alone, silent and thoughtful. He looks up to the sky and his mouth sags open as he notices two very high altitude white airliner vapour trails. The vapour trails form a perfect St Andrews Saltire cross streaked across the heavens. Sean shouts down to Andy who is already looking skyward. Unprompted, the Scots begin to cheer.

Military Operations Room, HQ, Scotland: 0800hrs 23 June

General Cumberland, General Officer Commanding Scotland, is rapping out orders to an assembled group of officers. They are rapidly scribbling as he continues, "...and confirmation has been received that the Glasgow Police HQ bomb was a hoax. Now. Summary of Execution! Intelligence gathering is my immediate priority. No dialogue with the rebels. The assault will commence one hour before dawn tomorrow to dislodge them from Stirling Castle. B Company from 1 WESTMINSTER will carry out a diversionary assault on the castle from land, C Company 3 WESTMINSTER will provide a military cordon in the immediate castle area and both 47 COMMANDO Royal Marines Close Combat Company's will carry out a heli-borne assault on my command. Questions?"

An officer is putting his pen in the air to ask a question when the room is abruptly filled with the noise of a succession of explosions. The windows explode inwards showering the General's command team with shards of glass and wood. Screams and shouts fill the room. Thick black acrid smoke chokes the room prompting the fire alarms and sprinklers to go off. The room is in hellish chaos as horribly wounded people shriek with pain in the darkness as the explosions continue.

Dirt Track, River Forth

A large open-top military logistics truck is parked parallel to the river on an isolated track on the northern Fife bank alongside the River. The dramatic world-famous triple Forth rail and road bridges silhouette in the background. A pair of SLA soldiers briskly bob up and down on the reinforced vehicle floor, expertly loading and firing one 82mm mortar tube facing out of the vehicle across the river towards Army HQ, Cragiehall. Three other teams kneel silently at their mortars standing by to adjust fire.

The fire is directed at their objective on the opposite bank approximately four kilometres away where mortar explosions can be seen. The Mortar Fire Controller (MFC) protrudes out of the cab observers' hatch. One hand holds binoculars to his eyes and his other hand scribbles instructions he is receiving in his radio earphone. He shouts Fire Control Orders above the popping of the range-finding mortar, "Drop 200 Meters! Left 100 Meters!"

Army HQ, Scotland

Jill is in her car on a nearby hill overlooking the military buildings of HQ Scotland, which are being bombarded. She calmly gives target adjustment, into a handheld military radio, on the fall of the mortar rounds. As she gives corrections the impacting rounds can be seen to being "walked" towards a large prominent building with a red roof. Two mortar rounds detonate on it. Immediately, she excitedly shouts, "Rounds on target! Fire for Effect!"

The MFC roars delightedly "Fire for Effect!" All mortar crews immediately adjust their sights and commence rapid firing. The vehicle rocks on its suspension. The MFC grins as round after round lands on the HQ Scotland buildings.

Jill observes the structures fold in on themselves and dissolve. Within only a few minutes she calmly reports, "Fire-Mission complete. Target destroyed. Well done. Out."

She starts her car, drives down the hill and stops on a scenic bridge over a small river where she throws the military radio. She drives on towards the HQ.

SLA Mortar Platoon, River Forth

The MFC frantically pulls off his headset and throws his binos, map and note book down into the cab. He is jubilant and punches the air, "Cease fire! Target destroyed! Noo, let's get tae Fuck!"

He disappears into the cab. The mortar-crews behave like football fans whose team has just won a cup final by leaping up and down, cheering, back-slapping, high-fiving and hugging like madmen. The MFC re-appears like a rabbit from a warren, "Get a grip youz bastards! The whole British Army, Air Force and polis will be here in minutes!"

He disappears again to start the vehicle engine. The mortar-crews hurriedly pull the top-cover over the weapon systems and sides of the truck, fastening them. Task complete, the truck speeds out of sight into cover in a nearby wood.

Army HQ, Scotland

Jill motions her pass towards the chaotic guardroom and is waved through. Almost immediately, she pulls over to allow two military ambulances to scream out of the gate.

Soldiers are running everywhere carrying fire equipment and first aid boxes. She gets out of her car and walks towards the ravaged HQ building, avoiding large blackened mortar holes in the grounds. Fire rages from many wooden buildings.

An officer is wearing a luminous yellow jacket and has set up an Incident Control Point near the scene – marked by a large board. His face is streaked with sweat, blood and smoke. It is Rupert. He manfully co-ordinates the arrival of ambulance and fire crews and directs the wounded to a first-aid post set up on a large grass area.

Medics struggle to cope with the bloodied wounded. A number of corpses lie neatly in a row under army blankets, paper ID tags tied to their right boot, except for those with no feet.

Jill throws up at the sights amidst the sound of crackling flames, collapsing buildings and the screams of the wounded and maimed. She barely recognises McCloy staggering from a jagged hole in the HQ wall. He falls onto the grass on all fours, bleeding profusely from a wound in his side.

Dreamlike, she stumbles towards him and gently lies him down. He is in shock, smoke-blackened and coughing blood. Pathetically, all she has available is a hanky from her pocket. She holds it to a head wound and holds his hand. She calls his name and tries vainly to reassure him. McCloy is mad with pain, rambling deliriously,

"...stop the Prime minister... must tell the Prime Minister... don't let Prime Minister come...."

She whispers, "OK Justin, how do I tell him? Where is he?"

He groans, "I know him... can't land in Scotland......he'll insist on driving across the border tonight...from Newcastle airport...turn him back...Scotland unsafe..." he stammers.

McCloy slumps and passes into unconsciousness. Jill shouts for a medic until a stretcher team runs across to help. She stands appalled, hellishly covered in blood. She forces herself to look at her watch and gathers her resolve. She staggers through the chaos back to her car where she puts her head on the steering wheel for a moment. She checks a map, jots details on a prepared notepad, then sends a text message before driving from the base.

Stirling Castle

A signaller sits in a cold underground stone room surrounded by I/T kit. He shows Sean a code-pad, headed with a mobile phone number which Sean recognises. Seemingly meaningless punctuation marks on the left of the pad, decipher into a message format on the right:

FROM	J
FOR	SKULL
RENDEZVOUS	GRID FQ 22573821
DATE/TIME/GROUP	232100Z

"Send this to Skull," commands Sean. The signaller sends the message.

Jill's Apartment, Glasgow: 1500hrs 23 June

Jill steps out of her shower when she hears her mobile receive a text "OK". She dries herself and dresses in a dark shirt and jeans.

Scottish Borders

Skull sits in his land-rover deep in a silent forest. Insects and birds buzz the hidden vehicle dappled in summer sunlight. He feels his mobile vibrate. He reads it and writes in a code-pad deciphering the message:

PERSON	J
RENDEZVOUS	GRID FQ 22573821
DATE/TIME/GROUP	232100Z

He glances at his watch as he takes out a military map-book. He studies it for a few seconds then throws it onto the passenger seat. He tears out the message, takes a cigarette lighter and burns it. He surveys the immediate area, starts his engine and slowly moves off.

RM Condor, Royal Marine Base, Arbroath: 1600hrs 23 June

A RM brigadier is listening intently to a briefing from an RAF officer at a lectern. The room is full of stern-faced officers from the Army, including Rupert, RAF, Marines and police force.

"...in short, Brigadier, we can only supply you with six Chinooks for your assault on Stirling Castle, plus a command helicopter. They are due here tonight. All other aircraft you need for this type of task are on Ops in Syria, I'm afraid. We can launch airstrikes from RAF Lossie and English bases."

The brigadier rubs his face in disbelief. He flicks his hand and the embarrassed RAF officer is replaced by an Army officer.

"Sir, we confirm we have two under-strength infantry battalions, 1st and 3rd WESTMINSTER, on standby. We are on 1hr notice to move."

"Why are your battalions under strength, Colonel, when the Army is now fully manned?"

"Firstly, two hundred men are en route as Battle Casualty Replacements for units in Syria. Secondly, another hundred on career courses and annual leave and thirdly..." he hesitates.

"Spit it out, Colonel – and thirdly?"

"Approximately two hundred soldiers, the equivalent of two rifle companies, are in hospital and jail because of fighting over the Scotland versus England game yesterday...." The colonel pursed his lips in anticipation of the Brigadiers outburst which immediately followed.

"Bloody Hell, man!" exploded the Brigadier. "You should have six rifle companies and you can only deliver me two under strength companies! Make sure your sick, lame and lazy plus all your cooks and bottle-washers are paraded and made available. Oh and get those fucking thick cunts out of jail!" he roared.

"Absolutely, sir" the embarrassed colonel mumbled.

The exasperated Brigadier points at a very weary-looking obese senior policeman. The copper waddles to the lectern. The marine covers his face with his hands in incredulity and mutters to himself.

The policeman's delivery is a high-pitched squeak, "I have every man looking for the terrorists who carried out the attacks on HQ Scotland and Leuchars this morning. We also maintain the cordon at Stirling Castle. Further, we are dealing with sporadic outbreaks of civil disturbance across the country. We are receiving assistance from English constabularies as we have no reserves left. Unfortunately, English constables are becoming part of the problem and not the ideal solution"

The Brigadier stands up and smacks his fist into the palm of his hand. Caustically, he addresses the group, "Any other good news?... No? Does anyone have any intelligence on MacAlpin's people other than they are Jockanese Weekend-warriors? Weapons? Numbers? Have you people been asleep up here?" He pauses for sarcasm, "That'll be a negative-silence then?"

Everyone avoids eye-contact with the Brigadier. He stands with his hands on his hips.

Bullishly, he continues, "Let me summarise then! These porridge-wog terrorists have captured Stirling Castle, wiped out HQ Scotland therefore immobilising the Command structure and have the RAF terrified to fly. We have no more men, equipment or helicopters because they are all away fighting Abdul-Abul-Bul-Emir! We can launch air-strikes which are just as bloody likely to obliterate Stirling as destroy the bloody castle which we would still have to take in a ground assault. Plus we seem to be up against amateurs who are taking the piss! Have I missed anything, gentlemen?!"

The silence is deafening. The brigadier points at the map,

"Gentlemen! The assault goes ahead as planned with what we have available! We shall not allow those bloody terrorists time to consolidate in their lair! Prime Minister Harris has ordered that we remove these scum immediately! Ensure your battle preparation is meticulous. We assault on schedule one hour before dawn."

125

The Brigadier allows the room to clear, then a side door opens and two mean looking soldiers wearing SAS berets enter and approach him.

He commands, "You must insert a surveillance team after last light. I must have eyes on the ground. These people are no amateurs. I know MacAlpin. He's an excellent commander. Choice of entry into the castle is yours. You can have any assets you want. Clear?"

The two SAS troopers look at each other and nod. One of them, "...something else you should know, Boss. We have a Scottish renegade Reserve SAS officer at large with one of our sniper rifles. He's an Olympic silver medallist marksman and one of the best shots I've ever seen. We've got people looking for him...."

"Oh fucking brilliant..." the Brigadier mutters. He is well aware that a top sniper punches well above his weight on the battlefield. He is completely unaware there were two SLA snipers on the ground.

Stirling Castle Battlements

Sean and Tom Stanic tour the soldiers' positions. Tom observes, "Morale is high and your soldiers are happy to chat. The Jocks seem up for the fight."

Sean laughed, "Situation Normal, then. Aye, they are good people. Every single one of them has recent Operational experience in Iraq, 'Stan and Syria. They all know how to battle," acknowledges Sean. He points behind him to a golden-coloured building, the Great Hall, "They know to sell their lives as hard as they can and when the time comes to fall back on that building, we'll make our last stand there and hold out for as long as we can."

"Will the UN and the European Union save you?" asks Tom.

"I honestly hope they will, Tom. They must. If those organisations have no integrity or will-to-act then all freemen must live in fear. Croatia knows that lesson. Brussels and the UN ignore the lesson of the Balkans and also Catalunya at their peril," asserts Sean.

Tom ponders doubtfully, "I hope you are right, my friend."

126

RM Condor, Royal Marine Base: 1900hrs 23 June

RM helicopter handlers in luminous vests stare out to the North Sea. A couple of them point at barely perceptible dots on the horizon. The dots suddenly become huge twin-prop Chinook helicopters. The heli-handlers signal them to land. The noise is deafening and the downwash forces the marines to struggle to remain upright.

Heavily laden marines pour out of the aircraft and head towards military vehicles nearby and climb in. A small armed group peels off and pushes a dozen hand-cuffed uniformed men into squatting positions on the grass. The armed men force the prisoners to put their hands on their heads.

The RM brigadier watches the arrivals with his waiting staff. He stares with concern at the prisoners. When the chopper engines shut down he and his staff approach the small group, "What the fuck is this!?"

A Military Police sergeant salutes, "Sir, they are Scots who refuse to soldier. Marines and two RAF air-crew. They were caught trying to damage the Chinooks before take-off."

The Brigadier is apoplectic, "Jail the bastards! Get them away and out of my sight! This is unbelievable!"

He storms away thundering about treacherous Scots, with his staff in tow. Rupert and another officer peel off to converse, "I don't like the way this is going. Our young men killing and jailing their young men is appalling. I thought we all enlisted together to defend democracy."

Thoughtfully his companion agrees, "It's insane, Rupert. It's as if we've learned nothing from Ireland...I've heard Scots servicemen are being disarmed and jailed wherever they are serving King and country, including Syria." Rupert appeared astonished at this news.

The two officers frown and move to catch up with the Brigadier. As they approach him they are joined by a portly, aged Reserve Lieutenant Colonel who introduces himself as Joseph Plate, Commanding Officer of Forthbank University Officer Training Corps.

Pompously he declares, "I have thirty armed senior officer cadets at Forthbank in Stirling who are available right now to deploy in support of Crown Forces. Where shall I tell them to report to? They'll be under the command of a regular army Guardsman NCO, Permanent Staff Instructor – he knows exactly how to deal with rebel scum."

The two officers stare at each other in disbelief. Rupert askes, "Sir, these cadets are teenage university students, right? With no operational experience? Surely, they'd be a menace to themselves more than the insurgents?"

The pretentious Reservist explodes with anger, "They are bloody good chaps from some of the best public schools in England! They're ideal for bringing down rebel Scots! My eldest son is their Senior Officer Cadet and can't wait to get a crack at them!"

The Marine Brigadier comes over, attracted by the outburst, "... and who are you, exactly?"

The cadet Reservist quickly introduced himself and why he was there. The Brigadier listened and quickly made a decision, "Wait for a written order from my staff then get your people to the cordon commander at Stirling Castle as quickly as possible. Ensure your people complete their Weapon Handling Tests before they move."

The Reservist effusively thanked the Brigadier who waved him away muttering, "We're down to the bottom of the barrel now..."

Scottish Borders

Jill sits in her car at a lay-by on a deserted lane in a heavily wooded area. She is alert, checking her watch constantly. Skull, heavily camouflaged, cradles his sniper rifle. He observes her from a distance. He also scans the surrounding area, particularly the road. Satisfied Jill is alone he leaves his position.

Jill squeals with fright as Skull suddenly emerges from undergrowth against her car door.

"You better have a good reason for bringing me here!" admonishes Skull.

She splutters "...I believe the Prime Minister is arriving in Scotland along this road in a couple of hours... I've confirmed with his staff he'll cross the border at Carter Bar."

Skull stares in disbelief, then grins with excitement, accentuating his skull-like features, "He'll be in a fast-moving convoy, south to north. I'll only get a couple of shots... what a target!"

Jill suddenly starts the engine, "I've got to get back to Glasgow. Good Luck."

Skull, smiling, steps back into cover and climbs to higher ground. He again scans the area like a hunted animal then pulls out a map and GPS, takes a bearing, and then heads off deeper into the woods.

Newcastle Airport, VIP Lounge

The PM remonstrates furiously with his security chief, who appears un-intimidated and stands firm, hands on hips. The PM shouts, "I'm not waiting any bloody longer! You organise whatever means necessary but I want to be on the road into Scotland right away!"

Patiently, the Security Chief replies, "Sir. Taking three vehicles into Scotland is folly. They are un-armoured. We would be driving into Apache country. My role is to protect you. I cannot condone an act of potential suicide. We should wait for a safe air-corridor or until the army can pull together an armoured convoy, as advised."

The PM is seething with rage, "Enough! We're going! Now! You are sacked!"

He turns to one of his staff and thrusts his face into his, "You're second-in-command of my Protection Team! I want the cars ready to move in 10 minutes!"

The man obediently leaves the lounge. The simmering PM and his staff gather their belongings and head for the exit. The security chief stands speechless staring at the ground.

Newcastle Airport, Airside

The PM climbs into the middle vehicle of the convoy. They speed out of the airport to a junction, at the main road. Uniformed police officers halt other traffic at a road sign that indicates SCOTLAND.

The convoy turns, at speed, tyres squealing. The cars quickly disappear from view towards the Scottish border.

Stirling Castle: 1900hrs 23 June

Sean and Andy study a map of the castle. They are calibrating the map and the area in front of them.

Andy points out to the castle grounds, "I've rigged anti-personnel mines on every point they can land choppers on, plus, each of those areas is covered by fire. If any choppers try to touch down we'll annihilate them."

Sean, "What about SAMs?"

"The Surface-to-Air-Missiles are pre-dumped all over the castle. We have air-sentries posted," replied his RSM.

Sean queries, "Chemical attack? Gas?"

"We don't think it would be effective high up here because the almost constant breeze would dissipate it. Plus the risk of drifting onto the civvy population in the town," responds Andy

"What about a night infiltration, either recce or attack?" probes Sean.

"My judgement is that they will try and scale the 300 foot escarpments. Sentries will be doubled after Last Light plus e-cameras and personnel detectors," replies Andy.

Sean nods with grim satisfaction and claps Andy on the shoulder. The sun was setting in the west. They are both tense and alert.

Scottish Borders

Skull is in a long lowland glen. Along one side, a country road has a steep barren slope running up and away. The other side has a gentle grass banking running down to a boulder-filled river. On the river banking is an old stone circular sheep-pen. Skull is busy in the sheep-pen with a combat-shovel. He pulls a large object from his ruck-sack. He goes to work again with the shovel then places the object in the newly dug hole. He covers the area he was working with, carefully replacing the cut turfs to ensure no trace.

He pulls on his ruck-sack, lifts his sniper rifle, checks the area is still deserted then sprints up the banking, crosses the road and grabs a discarded orange plastic bag at the verge. He places a rock to secure it, then scrambles up the barren slope into the tree-line to where he left his sniper ghillie suit, then heads up through the woods. He stops where he has a clear view of the bend in the road, the river and the sheep-pen. He sweats profusely. He takes out two small identical electric gadgets with a switch, a red light and a button and extends the aerials. He flicks the switches and the red-lights glow. He places them carefully on a rock beside him. He pulls on his camouflage ghillie suit, adjusts his cam net with local, fresh camouflage over his fire position then settles underneath it with his rifle, concealed, pointing at the bend. Carefully and deliberately he adjusts the weapons sight to the range of the orange bag. He waits as the gloaming settles on the glen.

CNN Broadcast Wagon, Stirling Castle

A talking-head is doing a piece to camera whilst being over-flown by a clattering military helicopter. She points up at the castle in the background, and then turns to indicate many heavily armed soldiers purposefully patrolling towards the castle. They are form-ing up at the base of the hill.

CNN Announcer, "It looks as though the British Army is taking over securing the area from the police and may even be gather-ing man-power to assault the castle itself. All TV crews have been given five minutes to leave the area."

Helicopter, Stirling Castle

The chopper circles the area without getting too close to the castle. It is festooned with surveillance equipment.

The pilot speaks into his boom-mike. His observer stares into a small TV screen on the aircraft instrument panel which is zoomed-in showing the castle walls.

Pilot, "...I'm keeping away to avoid any SAMs... I like my ass just the way it is. No! I won't be flying any closer! The satellite imagery is booming through!"

Castle Battlements

Sean and Andy are secreted in a battlement tower with binoculars observing the activity on ground and in the air. Sean scribbles notes and Andy marks his map, both totally engrossed in extracting information to be analysed later by their HQ team. The information will rapidly become exploitable intelligence to be distributed to the castle defenders for their lethal use.

Stirling Army Ranges, Rest Hut

School-age Army cadets are play-fighting in their room. A few of the older cadets are watching the large TV screen, enthralled at the CNN coverage of the siege. They shout at the other cadets to be quiet, who quieten and gather around.

CNN Announcer, "...and so the noose tightens around the Scots rebels in the castle. Will they meekly surrender or will they try to hold out against the British Army? No announcement has come from the London government as to the whereabouts of Prime Minister Harris, which is currently unknown...."

The teenage Cadet Sergeant Major suddenly shouts, "We've got to help the Scots in the castle!"

The effect of his cry is like a gun-shot in the room. Cadets stare at him. Most light up at the prospect while others look appalled.

A very young cadet murmurs, "My mum's expecting me home."

This attracts derision and abuse. Tears of hurt appear in the small boys eyes. He bites his lip. The rest all speak at once, inducing chaos. The 16-year old sergeant major, known to his contemporaries as Big Man, stands up on a chair and shouts for quiet.

Big Man, "We can do this! Sanjeev! You can drive the minibus can't you? We've got weapons and ammunition! We'd be doing it for Scotland!"

They cheer to the rafters. They brim with naivety and youthful enthusiasm. A few cadets still look frightened and doubtful. The sergeant major appeals for quiet.

Big Man, "Senga! Take the doubters and say to Sergeant McClafferty that they're no' well. That'll keep him busy. The rest of you...we'll volunteer to load the minibus with the weapons and

132

ammunition now we've finished our range week-end...then we'll jump in and go and help the lads in the castle!"

They gleefully run outside and head towards their adult instructor who emerges from the range administration hut. Unsuspecting, he agrees to the requests.

The cadets work frenziedly. They secure the boxes containing the weapons and ammo in the vehicle within minutes. Sanjeev, a Glaswegian-Asian urchin in uniform, approaches Big Man proudly holding a set of vehicles keys aloft.

Sanjeev, "Nae bother, Big Man! It's a dawdle, so it is...."

Big Man, "Right, get behind the wheel. Everybody else into the minibus!"

Excitedly, they swarm in, male and female cadets. Sanjeev is behind the wheel and Big Man in the front beside him. He slaps Sanjeev on the shoulder and gives him the thumbs up so they drive off. Big Man turns around to the rest.

Big Man, "Every cadet takes a weapon, prepare it for live firing and divide up the ammo! Bomb up the mags! Give me two rifles up here!"

Frantic activity immediately takes place in the back of the minibus as the young Scots split the tasks into small teams. They expertly and rapidly strip the weapons down to check and lubricate the working parts in preparation for firing as the other half frenetically, and just as expertly, load 15 rifle rounds into each of the weapon magazines. Their parents would be quite amazed, and some quite horrified, at the weapon-handling skills and drills of their children.

Range Admin Hut

McClafferty looks up at the sound of the minibus engine driving away. He stops what he's doing with a First Aid kit and runs outside. He is just in time to see the minibus disappear. He turns back and looks suspiciously at Senga.

McClafferty, "What's going on, Senga?" Senga stares at her inelegant brown combat boots. The other cadets do like-wise, except the wee boy who mumbles, "Big Man's gone to the castle to fight for Scotland and kill the English, Sgt. McClafferty...."

He is incredulous as he grabs his phone from his pocket and dials rapidly.

Stirling Castle, Approach Road

The minibus drives erratically at speed. Cadets are hanging out of windows. They are howling with laughter. Scots folk-music blares from the minibus. They fail to notice an Army roadblock in the distance.

Westminster Regiment soldiers and Forthbank University Officer Training Corps at the road-block spot the minibus weaving up the street towards them. A soldier, with binos, shouts a warning, "Armed men in the minibus! Prepare to fire!"

An NCO grabs the binos and stares at the fast approaching vehicle. He sees the rifles and swears. He lifts a megaphone to his lips, "Halt! Army! Halt or we fire!"

Big Man and Sanjeev, and the other cadets, are singing the Scots folk-song, "Flower of Scotland" at the tops of their voices along with a CD. Some of the cadets are laughing hysterically in a way that only high-as-kites teenagers can. They can't hear the mega-phone.

Army Road Block

Soldiers and Forthbank military students crouch and take aim. The NCO shouts again into his megaphone. The minibus doesn't slow down and is speeding towards them. The NCO raises his arm. Cadets hanging out of the minibus windows stare in alarm at the sudden realisation at what they confront. As those cadets shout in panic, before the Westminsters' NCO can drop his arm firing commences from three of the uniformed, armed UOTC students. He immediately drops his arm as he sprints cursing towards the undisciplined teenagers. His own soldiers immediately interpret his arm signal as authorisation to fire and all let rip.

He stops in his tracks as he realises he has lost control of events. Torrents of automatic fire are poured into the minibus. In a dream-like state, he speaks into his radio to send a calm, trained, almost automatic "Contact Report" to his superiors.

Rifle and machine-gun rounds slam into the minibus shattering the windscreen and windows causing the vehicle to swerve wildly. They tea-bag the vehicle with a thousand perforations. Rounds continue to hammer the minibus that ricochet furiously inside. Screams come from wounded and bloody cadets. The minibus smashes into a car, crosses the road and slams into another. Rounds continue to pound the vehicle incessantly. Big Man and Sanjeev, held upright by their seat-belts, slump forwards, bloody and lifeless.

The back doors open and an unarmed girl and boy stumble into the road. The boy, holding his bloodied face tries to get up, screaming and blind before he is cut down in a hail of machine-gun fire. The wounded girl is on her knees screaming hysterically. The English NCO, appalled, screams to cease fire. When silence returns, the only sound heard is the scream.

The Forthbank University Officer Cadets cheer wildly as they high-five and backslap each other. Their cut-glass public-school accents yahoo in exultation.

The soldiers remain in cover with their weapons in the aim position. The NCO sends some of his men to secure the vehicle, ignoring the girl. They open a side door revealing the stomach-turning carnage of smashed, mutilated, juvenile bodies. There is no movement from the slaughtered children.

A soldier vomits as two combat-hardened but visibly stricken soldiers attempt to calm the maimed girl whilst administering practised battlefield first aid in a Stirling suburb. They both manfully go about their business, themselves lapsing into blood-covered shock. One of them began mumbling continuously and uncontrollably, "I'm so sorry, love, I'm so, so sorry...."

A convoy of TV vehicles appear at a junction behind them. Military Policemen on motorbikes, at the head of the convoy, are escorting them away from the castle and are focusing on getting their charges across the road and out of the area.

The military cops, encased in their restrictive, shaded helmets, fail to see the scene in the road behind them, but the TV crew do. Within seconds, cameramen and reporters are sprinting up the street towards the massacre of innocents. The soldiers make futile attempts to prevent the baying pack of newshounds reach the scene. Within seconds photos and footage are being taken and reports are sent from mobiles across the world.

Soon, the unbearable images are being broadcast across the world's media provoking immediate massive popular and official condemnation.

Stirling Castle

Sean, Andy, Sinead, Tyson and Sgt. Hussein stare, shocked, at a TV screen in their communications room.

TV Screen

A CNN reporter is simultaneously trying to avoid the shoves of soldiers and file her report. Pandemonium is evident as squaddies square off against newsmen as they attempt to physically prevent the reporting of the incident. The scene is more Aleppo than Stirling.

CNN Reporter, "...this is unbelievable. A vehicle full of Scots adolescents has been shot dead, effectively executed by soldiers from the Westminster Regiment! The massacre is dreadful to behold. There are reports that the soldiers are claiming they were returning fire after being shot from inside the vehicle. Whatever the causes of this massacre, this is Scotland's Bloody Sunday."

Sgt. Hussein falls back against the room wall with a hideous shriek as though he's having a fit. He stares at the screen and rams his fist into his own mouth and slides down the wall. Tyson is the first to him and immediately cradles his head with one hand and takes Naveed's fist from his mouth. Naveed emits a bloodcurdling keening sound....

The screen shows Sanjeev. His head is at a completely unnatural, lifeless angle and his body is pock-marked with bloody gunshot wounds. Andy recognises Naveed's son. His reaction is one of horror as he turns to Naveed.

Andy, "Oh God help you, mate...." He kneels beside Naveed and cradles him with Tyson. They merely muffle Naveed's sobs.

Andy turns to those in the room, "It's his only son...."

Sean looks furiously back at the screen. Sinead is taken aback at the look of savagery. He snarls at Sinead.

Sean, "Get Naveed a doctor! Now!" as he crashes open the door and storms furiously from the unfolding tragedy in the full knowledge that he had unleashed war with all of its uncontrollable atrocities and butchery.

Scottish Borders, Deserted Road: 2130hrs 23 June

Through the sight of his rifle, Skull observes a three-car convoy speeding from the opposite end of the Lowland glen. The powerful vehicles have blacked out windows. In the fading light, he glances at his watch and two buttons, still with their red lights on. He presses one as the first vehicle draws level with the innocuous orange plastic bag which is, in effect his range-marker, at the roadside. A tremendous explosion catches all three vehicles broadside, sending them spinning in different directions.

Skull observes the scene through his 'scope. The first car is burnt out turtle-like on its roof whilst the rear vehicle has crashed off the road and is nose deep in a small gurgling stream. The middle car's front and rear doors are sluggishly pushed open. The driver comes around the car and takes up a fire-position, behind the passenger door with his pistol, scanning for targets. His co-driver pulls an injured man from the rear of the car. Skull recognises the man as Harris. Skull fires a single shot into the driver's upper chest, throwing him backwards onto the crouching co-driver and Prime Minister who both stare wildly around themselves in blind panic, searching for cover and escape. Their instinct is to sprint downhill to the stone sheep pen and they set off with the desperation of terrified men.

The co-driver hangs back slightly, as they race towards the sheep pen with his pistol in hand as he attempts to cover the PM from the unseen threat. Harris vaults the wall head-first into the shelter of the sheep-pen as Skull delivers a single shot into the co-driver's torso that sends him headlong onto the sheep-pen. His lifeless body slithers down the drystone wall. Skull reloads. Like a game of cat and mouse, he waits for the PM to show himself. Above, one of the cars on the road explodes sending orange-black flame and black smoke into the evening sky. Still there is still no movement from the sheep-pen.

Skull slowly reaches for the second button, savouring the moment. He quietly hums an old song:

Lay the proud usurpers low,
Tyrants fall in every foe,
Liberty's in every blow,
Let us do or – die!

He squeezes the button and the sheep-pen disappears in a massive explosion. Stones and rock hurl through the air. Skull patiently waits until the grey-black cloud disappears. A huge darkened hole lies in place of a long-departed shepherd's sheep-pen. Skull methodically packs his kit, cleanses the area of spent rounds and any other traces of his presence. He scans the area of the ambush one last time with the 'scope from his rifle. The last location of the British Prime Minister is marked only by a scarlet, blackened, limbless mess. Where his face used to be, is only a black, charred, hideous lump of flesh. Satisfied, Skull strides up the slope and recedes into the woods.

The last light fades in the western sky.

RAF Lossiemouth

In the aircrew rest area adjacent to the Operations Room a young Flight Lieutenant sat alone watching the live TV news from Stirling Castle. This pilot sat forward incredulously at the carnage of the adolescent Scots whose innocence of war had led them to their suicidal approach on the army road-block.

An Ops Officer briefly pops his head into the room, gave a thumbs-up and said, "Good to go."

The pilot pulled on the flying-helmet lying on the next chair and walked trancelike to the waiting aircraft on the panier. The Typhoon FGR4 aircraft was "loaded for bear" – live rocket systems used in ground attack Army Co-operation roles. Paveway IV bunker-busters.

The pilot taxis the aircraft onto the runway having been cleared for its bombing runs at the military ranges in Cape Wrath in the far north-west of Scotland.

The aircraft roared into the clouds above Moray but instead of heading north towards the ranges pulled south towards Edinburgh and the River Forth and was overhead in minutes as the aircraft approached Mach 2. Unnoticed from the ground however, the air traffic control staff immediately attempted to contact the pilot on their communications systems. Their attempts were ignored.

At 50,000 feet, the Typhoon was below maximum operational altitude but high enough to be above commercial aircraft in the area. This did not prevent immediate consternation at the Prestwick airport NATS air traffic centre. Frantic calls took place between civilian and RAF controllers. The aircraft showed as "friendly" on radar systems, but was it?

Above the River Forth the pilot scanned the area and identified the new target: *HMS Queen Elizabeth*. The Typhoon descended towards the three Forth bridges and lined up on Britain's newest aircraft carrier. The 70,000 tonne as-yet unarmed vessel was sailing out of the port of Rosyth on sea-trails heading out into the North Sea. Rapidly, the pilot armed the aircraft weapon systems and adjusted them to the target. Unsuspecting Royal Navy ships crew watched and waved at the RAF Typhoon as it thundered past it out to sea.

The aircraft disappeared rapidly but hard turned again back towards the aircraft carrier. The pilot selected the weapon impact angle, attack direction and fusing to post-impact delay mode.

Two laser guided bunker-busting weapons boomed from the aircraft and flashed towards the helpless aircraft carrier. Seconds later, the weapons smashed through the flight deck and into the bowels of the ship to the fuel pods of ship and aircraft.

As fuels and power systems exploded within the stricken vessel it immediately began to list to starboard.

One of Americas' two British proxy aircraft carriers was heading to the bottom of the cold, bitter depths of the North Sea. The US president, on hearing the news that one of his aircraft carriers had been sunk was apoplectic with furious rage.

As the Typhoon soared past the aircraft carrier it climbed then pulled hard right which gave the pilot a perfect view of the massive vessel below. At this moment, the post-impact delay mode detonated. The multi-billion Royal Navy aircraft carrier erupted in flame, explosions and grey-black smoke.

The pilot did not look back as the aircraft dived to low-level and made for southern Norway. It did not take long before the aircraft was able to contact Norwegian air-traffic control in order to obtain permission to make an emergency landing at Stavanger airport.

The aircraft landed and taxied to the far-end of a runway and remained there as instructed until emergency services reached it. The pilot climbed out and walked towards two Royal Norwegian Air Force officers waiting at their vehicle. As the pilot neared them the helmet was removed allowing beautiful long red hair to be released with an elegant turn of her gorgeous head.

Unsmiling the pilot extended her hand to shake the hands of the two stunned Norwegians, "I am Flight Lieutenant Viccy McSween and I claim political asylum from the Norwegian government as a Scots insurgent."

Across Scotland: 24 June

The country woke with incredible sadness over the killing of the children. In many places, the sorrow had provoked furious responses as evidenced by Flt Lt McSween's spontaneous Typhoon attack and sinking, of the pride of the Royal Navy, the aircraft-carrier *HMS Queen Elizabeth*.

A group of Glaswegian campers sat drinking late afternoon beer in a pub on Lochranza, Isle of Arran, watching the unfolding drama on TV. There was no animation from them as they sat shocked. The door of the pub opened revealing two of their group who immediately walked to the bar to order drinks.

Having secured their beers, they sat down with their five friends. "What the fuck is gaun oan?" one asked, "It's like a war, man. Those poor bloody kids, eh?" No-one responded as they were glued to the continuous live TV reporting.

Another item shows a distance-shot of Stirling Castle with its massive Saltire flying defiantly above it. At which point, Heid-the-Ba', as he was known to his muckers blurted, "Let's take Lochranaza Castle!"

"Shut it ya daftie!...and talk quieter or you'll get us lifted!", remonstrated a small, skinny guy in his early 50's. He was typical of the passing generation of inner-city Glaswegian poison dwarves. One minute he is your very best new found pal and the next he is slashing a kitchen knife across your face because of an imagined, Buckfast-induced insult.

Mikey leant forward to Heid-the-Ba' and whispered, "How the fuck would we get haud o' a castle? You a king or something?" to which, equally conspiratorially Heid-the-Ba' opened his hand to reveal a large key and in a mock stage-whisper, "Naw, man. Ahm jist the durty wee rascal," and cackled delightedly at his own humour, "It's the key tae the Castle! Me and Big Davie were across the village havin' a swatch aboot and saw a sign on the castle door. It said, 'Visitors can pick up the key at Post Office between the hours of' blah and blah."

It was Mikey's turn to laugh and reach over to close his friend's hand, "Get the motor, get yersel' doon tae Brodick, get a copy made and get the biggest St Andrews Cross you can find plus empty the supermarket of two-week's worth of messages," and winked as he rolled off a number of £20 notes from a large wad, "mind and get whisky and take Big Davie tae help ye." His companion knew far better than to enquire as to where the massive amount of cash had come from.

Heid-the-Ba' and Big Davie left immediately which caused the other lads to question what was happening. Mikey held up a yellow, nicotine-stained finger to his chapped lips to silence them. He drained his glass and indicated to the others they should do the same which they reluctantly did.

They followed him the short distance to the camp-site over-looked by the L-plan tower house of the abandoned 13th century castle. They sat down outside their tents and sparked open cans of beer and lit cigarettes or vaped. Looking at his watch, Mikey rasped, "It'll be dark at 10 o'clock. We've got to have all of our kit packed ready for Davie and Heid-the-Ba' getting' back fae Brodick. As soon it's dark we're gaunnae occupy the Castle."

A few of the guys started to choke on mouthfuls of beer as the others stared open-mouthed with one of them laughing, "We're gaunnae whit?"

Drawing a long breath of cigarette smoke deep into his already damaged lungs Mikey asked, "What else have you lined up for the next couple of weeks? Queuing up for your Giro, ya fud? Listen. We can make history by barricading ourselves in there like the guys in Stirling. How many cops are there on Arran, two, four, six, mibbes, if they haven't already been taken onto the mainland?"

By now, some of the guys were giggling incredulously. One said, "Mikey, you've pulled some fucking strokes in your time but steal-ing a castle? That's tops, man. Ahm in, man! Stealing a castle, man! 'Mon the rebels, man!" which induced them all into parox-ysms of laughter.

A few hours later the conspirators were very drunk, sleeping and lying on their packed tents and ruck-sacks when their confederates arrived back at the camp-site with a car full of tinned food, toilet roll, water, beer and whisky plus a huge flag. Big Davie, shook his head in unsurprised amusement, but took charge as he could see his muckers were wasted, "Take the key back tae the Post Office, and say nothin', and then let's work out how we're gaunnae get the gear and them intae the castle."

A few hours more and the two friends had been joined by Womble, the most sober. "Listen, me and you, Womble, get the motor up tae the Castle entrance, open up and we hand-ball the gear inside the hallway. You," pointing at Heid-the-Ba', "Round up this posse and get them intae castle. Clear?"

"Nae bother, Davie," replied Womble, "I've seen there's huge logs washed up at the shore so we can grab them after we're in tae secure the door. A JCB will be needed to open it up once we're sorted. We shall not be moved, boy!"

Incredibly, the occupation of Lochranza castle went off smoothly. Complete silence was maintained from the moment Mikey threatened to stab anyone who made a noise. They marched the short distance in darkness onto the small peninsula and entered the castle which was grandly outlined by the gold-red rays of the setting sun behind it.

The following morning, the bemused English matronly Post Office manager saw a massive Saltire draped from the battlements of the tower also lined by seven bare arses receiving slaps from their owners. Appalled, she immediately rang the police who advised her it would be some hours before they could react because the country was in melt-down. The manager did the only thing she could do in the circumstances which was to dig out her high-powered binoculars and observe the lads – particularly, to her, their interesting variety of private parts. Indeed, she found it necessary to give a running commentary, by phone, to her southern friends.

Similar reactions saw the overwhelmed police force dealing with many other types of impulsive rebellions including traditional Scots Fiery Crosses being set up and lit across numerous prominent points throughout the land. The fire-brigade soon gave up chasing such incidents as one was put out another was lit in an incessant show of public defiance.

Many more castles from North to South and East to West across Scotland, were occupied with the one constant thread of each occupation identified by massive, sometimes obviously homemade, St Andrews flags.

One of the first mainland castles that "fell" to the rebels was Dean Castle in Kilmarnock, Ayrshire by the simple expedient of a tour-guide inviting her local friends to join her with enough provisions to last a siege when she opened up. The ruined mediaeval fortress of Dunottar, Kincardineshire "fell" similarly as did Urquhart Castle, Drumnadrochit on the beautiful banks of Loch Ness. That evening bemused police who arrived at the scene could clearly hear bagpipes, singing and revellers indulging in a full-blown ceilidh.

A decision was taken at Police HQ level to leave the rebels alone unless it was obvious they were armed and dangerous which the vast majority were not. Fortunately, the police had learned their lesson from their non-cerebral behaviour at Stirling. Unlike, the death and destruction visited on that area, these other acts of defiance were barely tolerated but unchallenged simply because of lack of manpower and resources, and not least, jail-space.

More concerning, attacks on the meeting halls of the Unionist Loyal Orange Order and the association clubs and offices of the BNUP were multiplying. The police had to deploy their thinly-stretched resources to separate vigilante Loyalists as they battled with arsonists intent on burning and stoning halls.

Scotland was becoming ungovernable which was entirely in keeping with the SLA strategy and causing great disquiet in London.

More worrying for the English leadership were the constant and sustained cyber-attacks from Scots post-graduate cyber specialists that undermined their ability to govern, as evidenced by shut-down of basic power and water in London. This was causing regular public protests throughout the metropolitan area fuelled by the strong public suspicion that more National Cyber Agency resources were devoted to protecting the cash generating City of London stockbrokers and banking systems of the few from attack than there were on life essentials for the many.

This manifested in a spike of anti-Scottish race hate crimes across England such as the murder of a young kilted Scots piper who was playing at a wedding in West Yorkshire, stabbed to death in a frenzied assault. An appalling police shooting took place in London of a drunk Scot who had been carrying a repaired table leg, in a plastic bag, home from his local pub. A racist local phoned the police to report, "A Scotsman with a gun wrapped in a bag." Close to his home, an Inspector and a PC, the crew of a Metropolitan Armed Response Vehicle, challenged the drunk from behind. As he turned to face them, they shot him dead at a distance of 15 feet. The English High Court recorded an "Open Verdict", the policemen walking free.

Stirling Castle: Night

Four lightly-armed British Special Forces silently ascend the castle escarpment. A sentry patrols the battlements above them, unaware of their presence.

Jill's Apartment

Jill, frightened, meticulously gathers incriminating paperwork into a bin-bag to sanitise her apartment before making a rapid escape.

Hospital Room

McCloy is recovering, sitting up in bed watching TV. Impassive, he watches an interview of some thugs posturing outside a Glasgow pub called the 'Bridgeton 1690'. They are very drunk, antagonistic and predominately wear the red, white and blue of the Union Jack plus an assortment of Orange Order sashes and cheap Burberry baseball caps. Two of them wear British Army combat jackets. They are an extraordinary collection of inner-city Glaswegian neanderthals.

A tattooed fuckwit with teeth like a row of condemned buildings screeches,"...ye cannae have any sympathy with those rebels that got shot in the minibus the day. They pure deserved everything that happened tae them, Man! We are the people, Man! We pure love the King and the Union Jack! These rebel scum in Stirling Castle better stay there for their ain safety 'cos we'd sort them out, Man!"

His brutish and obnoxious friends belligerently begin to roar offensive anti-independence chants. The TV interviewer uncomfortably winds up the piece, quickly withdrawing from the baying sub-humans.

Harry, his arm in a sling and with bloody scars on his face, enters the room with a sadistic-looking man. Harry is shaking his head in disbelief, "They've murdered the Prime Minister. There's a news black-out for now. He was ambushed in a road convoy just after crossing the border into Scotland."

McCloy lies back stunned on his pillow, thinking furiously. He suddenly pushes himself out of the bed, tries to walk and crashes onto a chair and shouts in pain as he hits the floor, "That fucking bitch! That traitorous fucking bitch!"

The man and Harry gets the infuriated McCloy onto the re-righted chair.

McCloy snarls, "I was concussed and rambling after the mortar attack this morning. I told her to save the Prime Minister by stopping him cross the border! She's the only person I told! The whore set me up!"

McCloy suddenly recognises the man with Harry, and grimaced "Sergeant Billy Campbell. Last time we worked together was in South Armagh. A long time ago, but we got results, didn't we, Billy?"

Pleased that McCloy remembers him, Billy responds with a very soft, menacing Glasgow accent, "That's right sir. Do you have a wee job in mind with this rebel bitch? Harry said you might be needing me."

"Get a car to the front, Billy." McCloy was regaining his composure and looked focussed. "I'll meet you outside in five minutes... Harry – find my clothes!"

Smirking, Campbell leaves whilst Harry nods affirmatively and helps McCloy get dressed.

"GCHQ also picked up a coded text message from Jill's mobile this morning from the site of the HQ Scotland mortar attack," says Harry, "We think you're right about her being an SLA agent."

McCloy looks murderous.

Balmoral Castle, Royal Deeside

Margo McCrindle steps out of the chauffeur-driven limousine and crunches across the gravel driveway towards the resplendent arched doorway of the main entrance. She is visibly strained and exhausted after her two hour drive from Aberdeen airport having just landed from an EU Summit meeting in Brussels. The London government attempted to stop her attending the summit but Margo, and her ministers, were being very active on the international stage after her suspension. She swats at swarms of highland midges which are no respecters of royalty or world leaders.

Minutes later she is seated outside the royal chamber. The royal family and her government are aware of the assassination of the Prime Minister and so she has been called to this private meeting in an attempt to resolve, somehow, the increasing unrest in the country.

The young King ascended the British throne after the recent deaths of his grandmother, Queen Elizabeth II, and the immediate heir to the throne, the 70-year old Prince Charles, who unexpectedly died soon after broken hearted – devastated by his mother's death but also the impending break-up of their United Kingdom.

Inside the chamber an agitated monarch is being counselled by a royal adviser, "Your Majesty, you will achieve more from this discussion if you try to win over Miss McCrindle rather than antagonise her. Please listen to her first."

The angry King dismissed this advice with a belligerent stare, "Her and her type bloody well killed my father! She needs to understand her place."

Exasperated, the advisor requests, "Shall I show her in, Sir?"

"Yes. Show in the bloody First Minion!" the monarch commanded.

Margo, impatient at being kept waiting for over an hour, entered the palatial room and stood before the King. Pointedly, she did not bow or curtsy, she extended her hand, "Your Grace." The King gasped at the intentional point the First Minister had just made and the additional, obvious Jacobite white rose in her suit-jacket lapel.

The adviser coughed politely, "The normal greeting is "Your Majesty."

Margo replied evenly, "Not any more...in my independent country. The King of Scots has always been addressed as "Your Grace." Furious, the Sovereign invites her to be seated at a highly-polished Chesterfield sofa. His ingrained manners insisted that he offer her tea which she refused with a shake of her head. The atmosphere could have been cut with a knife.

A deafening silence followed which was eventually interrupted by the King, "Miss McCrindle, I shall come straight to the point. Any control you have over the rebels in Stirling castle must compel them to lay down their arms and surrender immediately. Additionally, my government requires you to obey their lawful command that you are suspended from duties and that all activity towards self-government is suspended for the period advised. You are therefore ordered to refrain from any further meetings with the EU, UN or any other heads of state. Do you understand?"

Breathing deeply Margo attempted to retain her composure, "Your Grace, I have zero contact with those at Stirling. I do not condone their actions. I strongly advise, however, that Crown forces should be restrained from further action in order that these circumstances are resolved peacefully through the political process. As for my Edinburgh government ceasing diplomatic contact with world-bodies who are also actively involved in establishing peaceful resolution to our legal right to self-determination then that won't happen. The days of royal divine rights are long gone," she defiantly added.

"Listen! At the 2014 Referendum my grandmother, the Queen, advised the Scots to, "Think very carefully about the future." You clearly did not heed that counsel. Your people are indulging in treason! I shall show no mercy when decisions are made on punishment for such traitors," he seethed.

"Indeed," replied Margo evenly, "I hear your commands clearly. I must advise you, however, that the EU summit I have just returned from will decide in the next few days whether to recognise Scotland's independence and if we are to be immediately accepted as an EU member state in protection of our existing rights as EU citizens. The political landscape is changing rapidly and, frankly, outwith London's control. I repeat my request that all Crown forces, in Scotland, cease military action immediately."

"You bloody woman! How dare you! Enough! You don't tell me what I can and cannot do! I shall ensure your bloody rebellion is crushed and that Prisoner-of-War status is denied those rebels. They'll be treated as the criminals they are! This audience is finished, "and stood up having had the final word, he thought.

Slowly, Margo stood, "How are we traitors, when England is foreign to us?" and goes to leave the room but turns as she reaches the door, "You want a close relationship with Europe but come out of the EU? Scotland is trapped in this endless board-game we never get to win. The dice has always been loaded. We get it, now. We reject your ultra-right-wing coup. Goodbye...Your Grace."

Stirling Castle, Battlement Tower

An SLA observation post watches a night-vision monitor which gives a view of the castle escarpment. They spot movement climbing up and so toggle their hidden camera onto four armed men.

Battlement

The four men on the escarpment wait just below the parapet rim above them, listening intently. Satisfied, they briskly hoist themselves over into the jet black darkness of the esplanade. Immediately rounds fired from unseen positions slam into the four killing them instantaneously. SLA men skirmish from the shadows and professionally search the bodies.

SLA Communications Room

Sean, Andy and Naveed study maps. They look up as a panting sentry enters the room.

Sentry, "Sir, an enemy recce team has just been taken out entering the castle."

Sean, unsurprised, responds, "Well done. Thanks. Return to your post. Andy, I want you to put the whole Battalion into their Stand-To positions. The enemy assault won't be long behind the recce. Good Luck, Gentlemen."

The boss shakes their hands and the two then leave. They pass Sinead, Tom and Tyson as they leave and exchange grins and backslaps. Sean looks relaxed and in control.

"Good timing! In Scotland, at this time of year we have only a few hours darkness. I suggest you, as our honoured guests, choose where you want to fight," said Sean.

The three look relieved, like the veterans they are. Tom speaks first, "We'll set up in the Great Hall. We can make sure that it is in safe hands until you need it, and then... we'll just go with the flow...."

Tyson and Tom stand forward and hug Sean. They smile at Sinead and leave the room. A signaller is busy watching his screens on his electronic kit and is oblivious to the pair.

Sinead and Sean exchange a long passionate kiss and embrace. They hold each other for an extended moment then stand apart. Sinead smiles lovingly.

"Destiny has brought you here, Sean," smiles Sinead, "Every part of my being, tells me you won't fail yourself, Cammy, Will or Scotland. It's the enemy who needs luck!"

She turns and leaves. The signaller gets Sean's attention and shakily hands him a code-pad:

PM KILLED BY IED
GRID FQ 22573821
242145A

Sean elatedly punches the air. A score has been settled. He takes out a lighter and ignites the message he holds out in front of him, then drops it to watch the burning paper float slowly to the floor. He grinds his boot forcefully onto the embers to leave a dark stain. The signaller waits expectantly.

"Set up a satellite broadcast," orders Sean.

The signaller jogs from the room and returns with the camera-team and helps set up their equipment. The team rapidly connects leads to camera paraphernalia. Alexander, the television specialist, receives the thumbs-up from the crew then gives the same signal to Sean. A flapping CNN anchor appears immediately on a TV screen in the room, direct from Washington DC, accompanied by a "Live from Stirling" label.

CNN Anchor, "...we interrupt to go live to the siege in Stirling Castle, Scatlan' I believe we have Lootenant Colonel Sean MacAlpin...."

Sean, "Good Evening. The Scottish Liberation Army continue to hold Stirling Castle and will do so until we receive recognition of our independence from either or both the United Nations and the European Union...."

The CNN anchor is beside himself with excitement at this new world exclusive, "Yes, sir! We have earlier reported talks between the London government, Washington and Brussels on the best way to resolve this crisis but the unknown whereabouts of Prime Minister Harris has hindered these talks...."

Sean interrupts, "Harris will be unable to attend the talks. An Active Service Unit of the SLA assassinated that lying warmonger this evening as he crossed into Scotla...." The broadcast was interrupted by deafening white noise from the TV equipment in the room. The SLA communication team immediately began to shut down as one shouted the obvious, "We're being jammed!"

The CNN anchor, meanwhile, turns off camera with a furious look at his crew as his TV screen goes blank.

In the castle the camera-crew, Alexander and Sean throw off earphones and grimace in pain at the horrendous noise. The team rapidly complete switching off all the kit and laughs uproariously.

"The Brits were too slow, Boss! We got the message off before they jammed the signal to CNN!" exults Alexander.

The camera sound-man, shouting in pain, "I'm glad some bastard's happy...I'll be deaf for months!"

Sean lifts his rifle and chambers a round into the weapon, his mind already in another place, "I suggest, gentlemen that you look to your personal weapons. Get yourselves to the Great Hall and check alternative means and frequencies to ensure we retain the option to broadcast for as long as possible. Good luck."

Sean leaves, checking his rifle magazines from his belt-kit as he goes.

Bundestag, Berlin

Margo McCrindle is sitting alone in the private chamber of the Chancellor of Germany. Margo is a fluent German speaker as a result of her father's long military service in that beautiful country. She smiled to herself as she reminisced of her love of Osnabruck in Nether-Saxony and Munster in North Rhein-Westfalen and many happy summer days spent sailing on the wonderful Dummersee and beautiful evenings in nearby Diepholz.

Her recollections were interrupted as the German Chancellor entered her chamber, accompanied by one of her aides. Margo and the Chancellor embraced warmly as they had met, secretly, a number of times before and during Scotland's Independence Referendum campaigns and during the Brexit shambles. They sat together in intimate fashion in expensive, classy chairs.

The Chancellor, as was her way, got straight to the point, "Margo, the assassination of Prime Minister Harris is appalling. Clearly, Germany will do it all it can to provide diplomatic support to bring the rebellion in Scotland to a halt as soon as possible as the instability this is bringing to Europe is extremely unwelcome. We had only just persuaded the Madrid government not to militarily attack Barcelona last year and accept the Catalonian Independence Referendum result. But in this matter of Scotland, and of Brexit, we may have a potential solution. London is extremely unpopular in Europe because of Brexit and now the military suppression of a democratic vote. Berlin cannot stop England leaving the EU. However, we can support Scotland staying, as we did with Catalonia. What do you think of this?"

Margo's eyes flashed with excitement, "It's what the people of Scotland have voted for. Twice. Can you persuade the EU to agree?"

"We already have. The Parliament will have an emergency vote tomorrow to ratify this. London will be furious but England have already decided on their path. We understand Scotland must be democratically allowed, and supported, to choose theirs. There is one further question. Are you willing to accept unarmed EU military observers to oversee the necessary ceasefire?" she smiled.

Immediately, Margo recognised the offer as one which would place London in a very difficult position as they should not interfere with EU military observers on, effectively, what would be EU soil. English military forces would be compelled to de-escalate the situation and withdraw from EU territory. "I agree," replied Margo, "I anticipate immediate EU and UN recognition of my government?"

"You already have it," replied the Chancellor, "We must stop the fighting immediately and bring permanence and strength back to Europe. Go back to Edinburgh and respond to the EU parliament after the emergency vote."

They hugged again and Margo left instantly.

RM Condor, Helipads

The Royal Marine Brigadier shakes each burdened Marines hand as they shuffle out onto the helipad to the choppers. The noise of six huge Chinooks is thunderous, the down-blast forces everyone to lean into its power. The loading is slick and the first of the Chinooks powerfully lifts and heads inland. All are extremely conscious they are embarking on a heli-borne assault onto a likely "hot" Landing Zone without "friendly" Apache ground attack helicopter support – because none is available because of over stretch. Nevertheless, they are going.

Fishing Trawler

A bearded trawler skipper, aboard his blacked-out fishing boat from the small village of Johnshaven, watches the shore in the middle distance. Lying off Arbroath, his boat rolls in the swell. He observes six massive twin-propped helicopters lift from the darkness, their silhouettes sharp against the sky. He speaks into a radio mike.

Skipper, "Hullo, Malky, this is Fergus. A flock of six shite-filled seagulls flying towards you now. Good luck...."

Stirling Castle, Approach Road

Brit soldiers advance up the street, keeping to the shadows of the houses. They halt near the abandoned SLA trucks which block the esplanade. A team slither to the vehicles and begin searching them. Watching soldiers stare anxiously at their task and up to the castle. Unseen, an experienced, specialist Royal Marine team in civilian clothes are concealed in the rafters of the nearest house overlooking the esplanade. Their communications gear is tuned into the approaching chinooks in order to give "eyes-on" up to the last minute to the heli-borne assault. Their laser guidance systems also ensured pin point navigational accuracy to the helicopter crews.

Castle Battlements

SLA observation-post teams briskly toggle their remote hidden cameras in the trucks. They watch the searching Brits.

High on a battlement Sean and Andy observe the area. Will creeps towards them and crouches. He cups a hand over Sean's ear and whispers a message. Sean nods then grabs his upper-arm which he squeezes in thanks and pushes him away. Will bustles down into a courtyard where a few SLA wait and gives a member of the team a thumbs up. One of the team pushes a button on his mobile phone in his hand.

Instantaneously, the vehicles being searched detonate in one thunderous, gigantic explosion. Houses nearby suffer massive damage and immediately ignite. Two screaming soldiers on fire spin drunkenly from the inferno. Soldiers run forward and roll the pair on the cobbles, extinguishing their flames but not the horrendous screams. Medics sprint forward to their aid.

Rupert commands the main body forward towards the castle onto the esplanade on either side of the blazing inferno, silhouetting themselves. SLA MG fire, from the Castle, mows them down. Castle rocket propelled grenades and mortar fire add to the mayhem. The slaughter is atrocious. The combined machine gun, RPG and mortar fire is expertly co-ordinated onto the tight killing-area eviscerating any British movement into a disgusting red mist.

From the town of Stirling, the castle appears to be in the grip of a monstrous fire-works display.

Chinook Helicopter

A marine officer checks his expensive luminous watch in the dim glow as his men sit back to back down the centre of the cavernous interior of the throbbing aircraft. They are all lost in their private thoughts, but grimly determined. Some check their weapons, most are bathed in sweating fear.

Jill's Apartment

Billy Campbell drives his car into a lane, hidden by shadow, opposite the silent apartments. McCloy and Billy quickly cross the street and enter the brightly lit foyer where they move straight to a lift.

After a few moments, they leave the lift and walk slowly along a dim corridor towards apartment door numbered 3. Silently, McCloy produces a small key and, extremely slowly, opens the door. Campbell produces a huge, evil-looking knife, which flashes lethally, from inside his jacket. McCloy ghosts inside, followed by Campbell.

Jill switches off the living room light plunging her flat into darkness. She pulls on her ruck-sack and leaves the room.

She enters the dark hall and is instantly pinned to a wall by Campbell's knife pressed savagely against her throat. She is unable to scream because of the force of the blade on her windpipe. McCloy appears from the darkness, pins her hands to her sides and savagely whispers into her ear, "Off on our holidays, are we? You fucking bitch!"

Jill is terrified. Tears and sweat mingle on her top-lip and chin as she gulps painfully as Campbell slowly forces the blade into her throat, drawing blood. Both men are panting cruelly as they enjoy the sadistic moment. Jill makes animal-like whimpers.

McCloy, "You conned me big-style, didn't you? You fucking Scotch whore! Every move we made was anticipated by your rebel comrades because of you. Well.....not any longer, darling."

Campbell suddenly leans ferociously onto the end of his knife with both hands and smiles as the blade disappears into Jill's throat drawing frothy blood from the wound and her mouth. Her hands automatically attempt to come up but are instantly held tight by McCloy. The murderers hold her until her eyes lose their lustre and sparkle as they end her life.

They release their grip and allow the dead girl to slump down the bloodstained wall onto the floor at their feet. Campbell wipes his knife clean on her clothes. They leave the flat, pulling the door closed behind them.

Stirling Castle: 0200Hrs 25 June

The trucks continue to blaze. The battle rages as the Westminsters continue the assault. The noise crashes around the castle. Dead, in macabre positions, litter the area.

Sean and Andy, high on their vantage point, watch wounded defenders being dragged back as their casualties mount as a result of accurate supporting fire from the assaulting Brits. Will, crawling behind cover, approaches Sean and shouts above the din, "Six Chinooks full of Royal Marines left Condor five minutes ago heading towards us! We've alerted the teams in the Ochil Hills!"

Sean gives a thumbs up. Will stays with the two as tracer rounds ricochet around them.

Chinook Flight Deck

The pilot concentrates on the horizon in the vibrating, instrument filled cockpit. They fly low, heading south-west, towards the Stirling battle. The horizon is rapidly dominated by a long range of hills high in front of them, running east to west. The other five Chinooks fly in line abreast alongside them.

Ochil Hills

A long dark wooded ridge of hills, running for miles, masks off the Castle from approach from the North. Just below the ridge line, along its length, camouflaged roofs are silently pushed off hidden trenches. Pairs of SLA soldiers emerge hauling long tubes. One member of each pair hoists a tube onto his shoulder and they both begin to arm the Surface-to-Air-Missiles (SAMs). They all have a perfect view of the open northern sky in front of them containing the approaching Chinooks.

Chinook Flight Deck

The co-pilot flashes five fingers to his pilot, who speaks into his helmet, "ETA target five minutes. Split now. Out." Immediately, two Chinooks veer off to the west into the darkness. The other four continue flying low and fast towards the looming ridge-line on the horizon.

SLA Trenches, Ochil Hills

The SAM teams can see and hear four rapidly approaching Chinooks. They accelerate the arming process to bring the SAMs to whirring LED-flashing life. As each team is ready the No.2 slaps the firer on his helmet, who brings his sights to bear on a Chinook and locks-on.

Immediately, the Chinooks take evasive action as their electronic defence systems detect a ground threat which immediately causes a furious eruption of chaff and flares spewing in a spectacular light-show which arc in multi-directions to divert any missile attack.

The SAM teams fire sending missiles hurtling towards the choppers as the anti-aircraft assassins are instantly illuminated surreally on the pitch dark hillsides as they fire. Simultaneously, deafening blasts shatter the ghostly silence on the hillsides.

Chinook Flight Deck

Taking evasive action by throwing the heavy machines at 160 knots through the night sky, the pilot and his co-pilot frantically grapple with the controls of their aircraft. Alarms and flashing warning signs reverberate in the cockpit. The flashing indicator stating SAM LOCK-ON is superfluous as they both stare intensely at glowing missiles hurtling towards them.

Behind them, Marines in the aircraft are hurled around as if on a monster roller-coaster. Unsecured weapons and military kit flash through the air causing devastating injuries to the hapless men. Utter panic erupts. A massive explosion detonates at the rear of the leading aircraft causing a ferocious orange fire-ball to surge through the aircraft fuselage engulfing the screaming marines. Almost instantaneously, the fireball blasts into the cockpit incinerating the aircrew.

SLA Trenches

The teams arm and fire more SAMs, sending missiles streaking towards the Chinooks. A massive flash and bang overhead sends SAM teams diving for cover as burning fuel and debris spew from a stricken aircraft onto the hillsides causing trees to ignite. In the distance, two further Chinooks disintegrate in huge orange fireballs as the barrage of missiles find their targets.

Eventually, the anti-aircraft teams which had expended their deadly ordnance peek cautiously from their trenches when they could no longer hear any helicopter rotors.

Burning trees roar around them, but they are jubilant as they identify three clusters of orange, red flames of three aircraft wreckages impacted around the countryside in the northern middle-distance in front of them in addition to the fourth which crashed onto the hillside amongst them.

Chinook Cockpit

Inside the cockpit of the two westward-bound remaining Chinooks, shocked crew members listen on their radio systems to the dying screams of their comrades. Dawn's first rays are a backdrop to the rapidly approaching Stirling Castle which continues to be engulfed in a devilish flashing battle.

Stirling Castle

Assault soldiers have reached the main castle walls and they deploy rope ladders to attempt to enter the SLA bastion. A ferocious gun battle continues around them as the defenders swop death with their attackers.

Rupert, concealed in a mortar-bomb culvert on the esplanade, receives a radio message saying a heliborne assault is imminent. His bloodshot eyes, streaming with sweat and almost blinded by acrid smoke, can barely make out the statue of King Robert which lies smashed nearby. The cacophony and flashing, blinding light of battle rip at his nerve-strained senses.

The two remaining Chinooks suddenly roar up from ground-level in the western darkness, blind-side to the defenders who are focussed on the battle on the esplanade, achieving complete surprise.

Both are manoeuvred into an aft position at the silent, dark rear of the castle. They are held in the hover – the majority of the aircraft jutting out into thin air, only the rear wheels in contact with two flat roofs identified for the purpose from earlier photographic reconnaissance. The rear doors lower allowing a Troop of thirty heavily armed marines to disgorge from each. They descend from the buildings, and rapidly disperse into the castle. The task complete in a very few minutes, the Chinooks lift off with a roar and drop their noses in an accelerating movement towards the ground to rapidly pick up speed to escape. SLA anti-aircraft teams eventually respond by unsuccessfully sending a flurry of SAMs towards both swiftly diminishing targets hurtling from the battle.

Battlements

Sean spins around as he detects the noise of chopper rotors over the din of battle. He, Andy and Will scramble to the end of the battlement and sight the retreating choppers.

Sean commands, "Andy! Direct the battle against the Westminster assault. I'll see what the Chinooks offloaded." They quickly move to their tasks.

Sean and Will are astounded to see an equally stunned-looking marine appear around the corner of a building. They all fire but the marine is hit in the face and drops dead. Sean and Will dive into a doorway.

Sean uses his radio handset to summon Naveed to him. When he arrives Sean points to the dead marine, "Take your men to the rear of the castle. Marines have been landed by two Chinooks. I estimate a Troop from each so 60 to 70 of them! You must hold them off until I can get more men to you."

Naveed retorts, "Nae bother, Boss." Then to his men lying in whatever cover then can find, "We've got enemy at the back of the castle! We've got to hold them off here!"

Turning to Will, Sean cries, "Get to the Great Hall and tell Tyson to bring me the Reserve, then tell Andy what's happening."

Will dashes off and Sean peers around a corner but immediately pulls back as he attracts a stream of automatic fire. He leads a team of his men up and onto the battlements where a vicious fire fight erupts.

Eventually, Will and Tyson make it back to Sean where the din of battle is overpowering. Will shouts into Sean's ear, "I've got the Reserve you asked for!"

Pulling out a Fablon covered map of the castle Sean lifts a bullet from the ground and uses it to point on his map at a crenulated line running from one side of the castle to the other.

"OK! We've pinned marines down at the back of the castle on the other side of this line which is the internal battlements we're on now," articulates Sean, "Naveed won't be able to hold them much longer. You must form a cordon on this battlement to ensure the marines get no further and to allow Naveed's boys to withdraw back to your line. Clear? OK! Get cracking!"

Everyone shakes out to their tasks. While Tyson positions his people on the battlements Sean dodges to Naveed's positions. The volume of fire is intense. He pulls out his map again and quickly explains what he wants them to do. The Scots-Asian understands immediately. The marines fire suddenly wounds two men, one of whom is Sean. Both suffering men writhe painfully on the stone battlements. They are grabbed unceremoniously and dragged away.

Sean has been wounded in his arm and is in agony as a bandage is rapidly tied over the wound.

A tearful, exasperated Will screams, "Dad! Stop getting wounded!"

"Thanks for the advice, son!" grimaces a nauseous, pale-looking Sean.

Naveed shrieks in nervous laughter, "I think you'll be answering to the name of 'Lucky' from now on Boss!"

Sean, clearly in considerable pain, "Very funny! Now tie in with Tyson and make sure those bloody marines don't go anywhere! I'm going to find out how the rest of our war is doing...."

Hauling himself to his feet, Sean is aided by Will and makes for Andy who is directing the SLA freedom-fighters against the Westminster assaults from the esplanade. Weapons fire can be heard from the rapidly, escalating ongoing fire-fight between the marines against Naveed and Tysons men as the rebel commander painfully leaves them to their tasks.

Esplanade

The wreckage of the trucks is strewn across the entrance to the esplanade. Sean and Andy are observing wounded and maimed soldiers being led downhill. Their scattered positions around the esplanade and foot of the castle are scenes of consolidation and defence. The bright, June morning sun made any movement suicide as the whole area was covered by Andy's men.

Briefly conferring with Andy his boss has 100% confidence in his abilities to hold his positions, "They'll be back tonight for sure," says Andy quietly. "Your political pals better be making good use of the time we're buying them with the lives of our lads." He didn't look at all convinced and spoke with the bitter contempt all professional soldiers have for politicians.

Sean didn't go there and merely nodded and headed back into the intestines of Stirling Castle. He stopped at the Great Hall where Tom and Sinead were standing in the doorway, "How's it going with you?" he enquired.

Sinead replied, "We've put all the reserve ammo and supplies in there plus set up a communications link. You should try to get another satellite broadcast done, if you can... the Brits will certainly be putting out lots of their own propaganda."

She notices blood seeping through the bandage on Sean's arm. She moves to him and tenderly touches his cheek. He kisses her hand in a return gesture.

"Thanks, you guys. I'll be back as soon as I've dealt with our uninvited Royal Marine guests. Let me know what the world is saying about our efforts!" as Sean turned purposefully and jogged off.

CHAPTER 10

BATTLE: STIRLING CASTLE
JUNE 2019

Stirling Castle: 25 June

Later in the afternoon, during a continued lull in the fighting, Sean and Andy study the map of the castle. They are high on the battlements with a clear view of the whole area.

Effectively thinking aloud Sean muses, "Underneath in the Castle rock there is a warren of tunnels. We must make sure that the marines don't get into them and behind our positions. We must exploit the tunnels and secure them first."

Peering at the map, he stabs a pencil at a building, "There's a tunnel entrance here that can bring me out within the marines' position. When our assault begins, we'll pop red smoke."

Andy nods, "How long will it take you to get into position?"

"Ten minutes," replies Sean, "My guys have already been re-supplied and briefed. Be ready to nail any Marine movement when we kick off!" The laconic Andy merely replies, "Roger," and Sean leaves him to lead his assault team and disappears into a nearby castle building.

Castle Tunnel

Slimy water runs noisily down the walls of the dark tunnel. Splashing through the mire, Sean leads his men with a red torch in hand. He stops at the bottom of worn ancient stairway leading up from the tunnel. He checks his map then motions forward a couple of his men and points to the stairs. The soldiers creep up to an old wooden door, followed by Sean and his son. They gather at the door and listen intently. There is no sound. As they open the door, it lets out a violent creak. Horrified, Sean and Will crouch in the doorway as the other two men push inside to a dark room. One of his men looks back to Sean and gives a thumbs-up. He nods and brings up the rest of the Scots.

Immediately, about twenty SLA fighters cram into the dark room with Sean. The first two peer out through a window then signal to Sean to look. The rattle of small arms fire can be heard and Sean sees the backs of firing marines. They have achieved complete surprise and so the colonel pulls a smoke grenade from his combat belt and moves to the outside door.

The spearhead group opens the door slowly as he pulls the pin on the smoke-grenade and softly rolls it into the yard where it suddenly belches red-smoke. All hell breaks loose as, at the sight of the red smoke, SLA men unleash devastating fire at the marines as they dash right and left out from the room, joined immediately by the sound of smashing glass from the room windows as a few SLA pour supporting fire into the marines' rear.

Sean dashes out, firing, after his men who are spreading out as they mow down the ambushed marines. Battle noises and screams are accentuated by the closeness and height of the castle walls. Savage hand-to-hand combat erupts everywhere. Sean is ferociously attacked by a huge marine. They beat at each other mercilessly until Sean frees his kukri, attached to his belt. He makes a killer slash against the unprotected carotid artery on the marine's neck with his Gurkha weapon. The lethal arterial wound immediately produced a gushing fountain of life-blood which engulfs both of them in its sickly scarlet mess.

As they both fall together, Sean is bayoneted in the thigh by another marine who thrusts at him in fury. He crashes back against a wall with the impact of the lunge and slumps unconscious to the ground.

Will sees the next impending death blow which he manages to prevent by dispatching the marine with a close range shot to the back of his neck, as he is about to stick his father again. In abject horror, Will grabs his slumped gore-drenched father and hoists him over his shoulder. They both lurch back to the door they had entered the courtyard from as the savage, vicious close quarter combat bedlam continues.

Tunnel

Will staggers as he carries Sean along the tunnel and eventually emerges into the sunlight within the inner walls where the pair are spotted by some SLA men and assisted into the Great Hall.

Great Hall

Wounded men from SLA, Marines and Westminsters, lie together on army cots along one wall as a SLA doctor and medics tend to them. Sinead, Will and Tom stand over Sean, unfocussed and in pain, who lies on one of the cots, slowly regaining consciousness.

Sinead orders him, "You had better take it easy... the international news is fantastic. Listen! The EU and the UN have both demanded an immediate cease-fire and full recognition of the referendum by London within 30 days. Both organisations have said they recognise Scotland as a sovereign nation whatever London demands. It's brilliant isn't it? And what's even better there is an EU military peacekeeping task-force being assembled to act as peacekeepers in order to protect EU citizens – which includes every Scot with a current EU passport! Margo has done brilliantly."

Sean tries to sit up and is firmly pushed back by Tom. The anguished SLA head doesn't resist but chokes a reply, "Yes, but what about the SLA? Will London agree to a cease-fire?"

The Croat frowns, "That's the bad news. London wants our unconditional surrender. They insist we will not be awarded Prisoner-Of-War status and says we are traitors who have rebelled against the Crown," he paused before continuing, "And remind us the death penalty still exists in Britain... for treason."

Sean begins to laugh but only induces a coughing fit and pulls Sinead's arm bringing her down to his side where he manages a smile in spite of his agony, "This must sound too familiar, colleen!

164

So we fight on until London agrees to a cease-fire. They'll be back... in greater numbers. Bring Andy and Naveed to me."

"I'll get them," assures Tom, "Now you get some rest."

Sean drifts into exhaustion whilst Sinead remains beside him, busily loading rifle magazines.

RM Condor

The Marine commander is in a video-conference link with the Acting Prime Minister, Margaret Ross, in London, "We continue to have a foothold in the castle. I have two Troops in a bridgehead in the northern corner. They have beaten off repeated rebel attacks to dislodge them. I need your permission to mount an all-out assault on the castle tonight to bring this little matter to a successful conclusion. We have reinforcements, we have the capacity, we can settle this."

Margaret Ross had placed herself perfectly within the BNUP hierarchy to exploit the assassination of Harris. She had not hesitated to grab the role of Acting Prime Minister.

She looks determined and consults with her advisers, who are off camera and responds, "You have my permission for the assault. But understand this, Brigadier. None of the rebels must be allowed to escape. Crush the saboteurs. This issue must be ended tonight. The Scots can have as many martyrs as they like but there will be none left from Stirling Castle to negotiate with or lead future insurgencies. Do I make myself clear? We cannot withstand the intolerable pressure the international community is bringing on us. It's playing hell with The City. The British Commonwealth, with their bloody expatriate Scots, are causing us as many problems as the EU and the UN put together. You have until dawn. Don't worry about collateral damage to the town of Stirling... just get the job done."

Her face is contorted with fury that the "issue" hadn't already been resolved, "We must put on hold our plans to occupy the Scottish Borders, Shetland and Aberdeen until the SLA are eliminated. However, we will trigger the Conscription Act. Ensure that you instigate plans to conscript 5,000 military-aged men and women followed by logistic plans to bring them to England. Manual labour jobs will follow for the males and food production work, of national importance, on our farms for the females to replace the EU agricultural workers. Convert Berwick Castle into an internment camp immediately to detain political prisoners. Finally, every secondary school in Scotland will have a military cadet force unit in order that we can ensure every pupil, male and female, embrace British military values, keeping them in line, so to speak."

A staff officer switches the conferencing monitor off. The Brigadier turns to the long table at which his staff wait, "OK, Gentlemen. The gloves are off. Let's smash these rebels and teach Scotland a lesson they'll never forget! We shall ensure maximum metal meets their flesh. It'll concentrate the minds of the Scots with those 5,000 hostages. Re-enforcements?"

An RAF staff officer replied, "1st and 2nd Battalions, Parachute Regiment, will arrive here from Colchester at 2200 hours local, Sir. Both of their 105mm artillery batteries arrived within 10 kms firing range, south of the castle one hour ago. US Army Aviation Units from the 101st Combat Aviation Brigade, from Germany, will supply sufficient lift for the Paras plus Apache and Black-Hawk support. Additionally, Sir, we have two companies of Royal Guards, totalling 178 Guardsmen, being flown up from public duties in London to RAF Kinloss. They'll be held there as a mobile reserve."

The Brigadier, stood up slamming the table, "I'll have that bastard McAlpin's heart on a plate!"

His staff breaks into huddles to plan and prepare for the assault. McCloy approaches the Brigadier and they step out of earshot of the rest. McCloy still carries facial scars from his wounds, and looks utterly malicious, "I'd like to volunteer to bring you McAlpin's heart, Sir. It would give me great pleasure to join the assault with the Paras tonight." The Brigadier maintains full eye contact, "No mistakes, McCloy. Do whatever you have to do...."

McCloy leaves the room where Billy Campbell waits for him.

10 Downing Street, London

Margaret Ross turned from the video-conference camera to her staff, "Everyone out, except '6'." As soon as everyone else had left, she hissed, "Have you found out where that fucking cretin McCrindle is yet? We can mallet the rebels but I also want the head of the bitch. I don't believe her denials of non-involvement for a second. She bloody knows what's going on. We know they were at school together in a butt-fuck shanty town in Ayrshire and my people established they met together nearby a few months ago...."

"We believe she is in Berlin, Ma'am. Do you want surveillance increased?"

"No! I want her fucking dead! They killed Harris and she is the head of the Scottish snake! I want her gone! Do it!"

The head of MI6 did not reply but remained stony-faced as he considered his response.

"Well! What are you waiting for?" she roared.

"Ma'am, with all due respect, murder is not always the first option. Murder of a political leader is definitely not the first option," he repeated.

"Listen, you bastard! Forget the diplomatic niceties! Have her exact location on my desk in 10 minutes and I'll find someone who does not question orders! We're finished here! Get out!"

Great Hall, Stirling Castle

Occasional shots can be heard outside in the background. His torso heavily strapped with bandages Sean sits in a great ancient chair holding a Council of War, "We hold out for as long as we can. Politically, we have already achieved our aim but they must be able to consolidate their UN and EU gains... but the Brits will come looking for revenge tonight. Do not expect any quarter."

Pausing to hold eye-contact with everyone to satisfy himself that they understand his words, Sean continues, "My original plan stands. We make them pay dearly for every inch. We retire to this Hall until I gave the command to break out."

Naveed laughs, "Will you be issuing the troops wings to fly off this here rock, Boss?" The others, including Sean, laugh with him.

"Not at all, buddy," Andy replies, "All will be revealed when the time is right. Just leave it to your Uncle Andy!" The laughter reflected that their group morale is still very high.

Sean salutes them, "Be very proud of what you have achieved. When we break out we do not rest until the last London lackey leaves Scotland. We shall visit their worst nightmares upon them by making Scotland ungovernable to them... Gur math a thèid leat![5]"

They respond in kind then purposefully gather up their weapons and disperse, except Andy who sits casually sits on the arm of Sean's chair and speaks quietly, "Skull will lead the teams which will break the cordon when we need to breakout. He says the Westminsters are undermanned and he is confident his lads can make sure we get away."

His boss smiles wistfully causing Andy to immediately look concerned, "I don't like that mad look you've got on you! You better no' be thinking about the least bit heroic martyr bollocks!"

Smiling again Sean lifts a bottle of whisky from the table and looks at it,

"...and catch the moments, as they fly,
and use them as ye ought, man.
Believe me, Happiness is shy,
and comes not aye when sought, man."

Andy calls Tom, Will and Naveed over causing Tom to grin at the scene as their commander pours some whiskies, "Have a dram with me."

"Dae you huv' ony watter fur me? Ye know fine well it's haram" the Glaswegian Mohammedan sighs. They all laugh and down the whiskies. Teasingly, Andy ribs Will, "You're no' doing a very good job, Will. You've let your Da' get shot and bayoneted...keep the mad bastard alive, eh?!"

In response, Will groans deeply and shakes his head, which provokes more laughter. Andy walks over to Sean, "We've got resupply of ammunition, food, water and med kit coming in tonight by drone from our cache. The American kit that Tyson obtained arrived from Barbados last week and was secured, no problem."

Grinning, Sean raised his glass, "Here's to America's gun laws."

---

5   Good Luck. (guh NIGH-rhee LAT)

Stirling Castle: Monday 0300hrs 26 June

The SLA re-supply drones climbed to their maximum height and flew, unnoticed, back towards their West Highland supply base.

Separately, four British artillery guns sit at the base of the castle hill. One fires. An Observer officer calls range and direction adjustments. This happens twice until the Artillery Officer shouts, "Fire for effect!"

The gunners adjust the guns which then fire simultaneously, the vast majority impacting on the castle but some overshoot into Stirling homes. The guns keep up the incessant barrage. Simultaneously, Javelin anti-tank missile systems fire over open sights into the castle gates. Designed for anti-armour they are also highly effective bunker-busters. All available weapon systems are deployed to ensure successful break-in.

The first artillery rounds cause many casualties as the surprise effect catches the SLA as Brit assault teams storm into the castle and immediately engage in hand-to-hand combat. An invading Brit fires a green flare into the sky signalling a number of simultaneous events.

Artillery Officer, "Cease Fire!"

The guns fall silent as helicopters roar towards the castle. The first choppers hover over large open gardens, just inside the castle then ropes appear and instantaneously Paras abseil down. Some helicopters are instantly hit by SLA fire and hurtle and crump into the castle-grounds. Fire-fights and hand-to-hand combat engulfs the castle as the Paras spread out.

Casualties mount on both sides as the battle rages. Booby-trapped obstacles obstruct internal pathways and lanes forcing the Brits into SLA killing grounds. Cohesion breaks down amongst both sides as commanders become casualties, command and control becomes almost impossible. Sean, Will, Tom, Naveed, and Andy are all fighting now, shoulder-to-shoulder alongside their men against frenzied assaults. They encourage the Scots fighting alongside them as they are all involved in the worst type of gutter fighting. No quarter is asked or given.

High above the battlefield inside the roof of the tallest building Tyson moves one roof-slate to the side giving him a small aperture onto the battle raging below. The gap is completely imperceptible to those below – exactly how a trained sniper would want to set up such a shoot.

Lovingly, he takes out his Barrett M82A1 sniper rifle from its carrying case. He speaks to it in affectionate terms addressing it repeatedly as Ol' Jack Hinson. This bizarre behaviour is nothing new for a Southern boy to be on intimate terms with such a world-famous Tennessee sniper rifle.

He laid his 0.50 calibre BMG ammunition in their 10 round box magazines carefully on a hessian sack beside him. He adjusts the bi-pod legs and positions the weapon just far enough away from the slate aperture that it would not be seen from outside but close enough that he had maximum view of events below and in the sky in front of him.

Lying behind Ol' Jack, Tyson carefully examines then places a 10 round mag into the weapon, operates the bolt mechanism placing a round into the chamber. He takes his time to position and aim the weapon and himself for maximum effect whilst consciously controlling his breathing. Finally, he looks through the sniper scope adjusting it onto targets below in the fight. Satisfied, he picked out a Westminster commander identified by his soundless encouraging gestures and direction to his men, 500 meters away on the esplanade. He released the safety catch, holds his breath then squeezes off the trigger action. The high-velocity weapon cracks sharply and pushes back into his shoulder. Way below the round smashes through the officer's face and bursts a much larger hole through the back of his skull killing him instantly. Slowly and methodically Ol' Jack sends slow, regular beats of death to Brit soldiers below.

The rifle is well named. Ol' Jack Hinson was a Tennessee Confederate sniper of Scots ancestry. During the War for Southern Independence Union soldiers executed two of his civilian sons and placed their severed heads on Ol' Jacks home gateposts. In cold-blooded revenge Hinson carried out more than 100 successful sniper attacks on Unionists. He was never captured.

Great Hall

Battle sounds echo around the Great Hall which has become a slaughter floor, decked with the dying and wounded. A harassed doctor and medics work ceaselessly. Sinead, dismayed, quickly counts the SLA casualties. She looks over to where a handful of exhausted freedom-fighters constitute their Reserve then stares at the bodies covered by blankets, immobile in the corner. She recognises the situation is unsustainable, she makes up her mind, picks up and cocks her rifle and leaves the Hall to find Sean.

The Castle is an inferno of hellish noise and light. Sinead darts from the Great Hall into the shadows as she hears the battle-cries of the Scots, the sound of their courage and sacrifice gives her wings, propelling her up the nearest stairs.

Dodging a hail of bullets, Sinead soon finds Sean but is taken aback. He is bleeding again from both of his wounds but is exultantly shouting encouragement and orders to those around him. He seems to be more alive than she has ever known him, glowing with the aura of battle. The warrior king within him shone through. His mentors at the Royal Military Academy at Sandhurst were paying a heavy price for what they had created.

She gets to his side and pulls him down, telling him of the mounting casualties. Listening intently to her then to the noise of battle around him the combat veteran senses that all his fighters are engaged and defying constant assaults. He recognises what Sinead has told him.

He pulls a flare-gun from a holster. He aims the weapon straight up and fires a blue flare. He loads again and then fires a white flare. The Scots recognise the signal to withdraw to the Great Hall.

Stirling Town

Skull sits in a vehicle in a darkened, deserted street watching the pyrotechnics high on the castle through night-vision binos. He spots a blue then white flare soar high above the mayhem. He starts the car and slowly drives off.

Stirling Castle

The SLA make a fighting withdrawal, dragging and carrying their wounded with them. As Will, Sinead, Tom and Sean near the Hall Sinead screams as she is shot in the back and thrown forward. Visibly appalled, Tom and Sean grab her and carry her inside.

"We've got to buy time!" Sean scowls at Tom and Will inside the darkness of the Hall. Tom stares at Sean, "You're already in tatters and you gotta make sure Sinead is OK. If Will is up for it we can make up a section of eight men each and drive the Paras back for a while?" he says looking at Will, who nods in agreement.

Tom and Will leave the injured to be tended and round up fit SLA men and women and, in desperation, a few lightly wounded.

Explaining intently, Tom gives Quick Battle Orders to the two sections using his index finger on the dust strewn floor to draw a map of the Great Hall and the vast courtyard outside, "You guys with Will, are gonna be One Section. The rest with me will be Two Section. We leave here fast. One Section break left and my guys break right. Understood?" to which he receives a combination of thumbs-up, nods and "roger" as acknowledgement. "Good. Make sure you all have full mags and grenades. When we form-up outside, Will, I want you to give me a wave that your guys are good to go and I'll do the same. We're gonna have seconds to do this. "

Tom goes back to his floor dust-map and draws an arrow from the line marked, "One – we sprint first towards the end of the courtyard, 10 meters maximum, and find cover. Your Number Two Section, Will, must, must, must supress with fire any enemy as we move. You blast them with rapid automatic, OK? As soon as you see us on our belt-buckles, you sprint pass us by another 10 meters, gottit? We'll be winning the fire-fight by pouring fire onto the enemy to support your move. We repeat this by fighting forward until we clear the courtyard. We're gonna clear the courtyard of all enemy using this 'pepper-pot' movement. Questions?"

Looking around, Will replies, "We've got a couple of heavy machine-guns and ammo in here. I can also place a couple of MG teams at the windows to fire over our heads at the enemy in support of our attack." Tom slaps Will's shoulder in agreement, "Let's go. Moving in 10!"

Going around the teams, Will and Tom ensure the soldiers have as much ammunition as they can carry whilst encouraging and motivating them. They form up inside the hall and Tom gives a final confirmation to the grimly determined Sections, "Move fast and slick. Bring down your targets. Kill them all! Don't stop until we clear the 'yard and we hold there for as long as we can. When the time comes we 'pepper-pot' back on my command, or Will's if I'm down! OK?" No questions resulted in Tom signalling to the two MGs to commence rapid-fire from their window positions as he launched two smoke grenades from the main door as far into the courtyard as he could throw.

The two teams dashed out right and left and took cover behind whatever rubble, bodies and battlefield detritus they could find. Within seconds, Will signalled Tom as his Section opened rapid-fire on the fire-flashes of the Paras who were dotted, in cover, around the courtyard walls and doorways. The Paras dived, heads-down onto the cobbles under the devastating combined automatic fire-power of Will's Section and the tracer-firing MGs from the Great Hall windows.

Immediately, Tom's Section tore forward, to their fronts, exposing themselves for only the few seconds it took to cover a few meters then crawled forward in adrenalin pumping motion. Tom screamed, "Fire!" which induced another torrent of automatic rounds towards the few foolhardy Paras who were attempting to return fire.

Instantaneously, Will's Section were up and had darted forward overtaking Tom's team and began to pour down fire the instant they were on the deck. The MGs fired constantly over them as they fought their way to the end of the courtyard.

This rapid, spectacular movement continued until, within minutes, the sheer surprise, aggression, firepower and momentum of the Scots had cleared the yard. Those Paras who had not been able to extract themselves fast enough lay bloody and dead where they lay.

Exhausted, gasping for breath and twitching madly from near-death shock the SLA soldiers rapidly consolidated themselves in a defensive position with their backs to the Great Hall. Debris, wreckage and rubble were pulled and hauled into whatever cover they could rapidly construct. The wounded were immediately sent back for treatment with instructions to have more ammo sent up.

Crawling along the cobbles Tom found Will, "We hold here for as long as we can. They'll throw everything they can at us. Get back to the Hall and control the MG's fire when we have to retreat," Will started to protest, "You've gotta give us a chance! See to our wounded and our ammo re-supply – and water! I'm relying on you, dude! Go! Go now!" and pushed Will away, hard, who needed no second invitation.

Great Hall

A few hours later the Scots survivors are all in the Hall including Tom and the survivors of his heroic assault. The scene is grim. Brit fire has died down but ricochets continue from random rounds. Scots double bar the huge doors. The able-bodied and walking wounded congregate around Sean in the centre. They are all extremely defiant, no hint of despair as they look expectantly towards their chief.

Sean explains, "We don't have much time. I shall parley for a surrender of the wounded. The rest of you follow Andy to the exit point he has prepared. He has abseil ropes to get you down the side of the rock. A diversionary attack from the town below will ensure you get through the cordon. Do it now and get into our country and make life hell for the invaders! We make Scotland unmanageable for them. Make them want to go home in the face of impossible victory."

There is no protest. Will tearfully hugs his father. Sean kisses his sons forehead, and in obvious agony whispers, "You must go. Make sure your mum is OK. I'll always love you both."

Will, pleading, "Love you too, Dad. Please stay safe...."

His father, contorting painfully responds laconically, "Nae bother, son...."

Casting a glance over his shoulder to his father Will leaves whilst giving him a smile and boyish wave which belong to a doting wee boy from long ago – not the young warrior he is now. Involuntary, Sean wells ups with the very deep emotion only a father can have for his sons.

They follow Andy to the door, discipline maintained. Sean accepts a white flag from the doctor who says, "You're doing the right thing, Sean. Your lads and lassies have given everything. Save their lives."

He climbs up on a pile of debris and pokes the flag out of a window then looks back at the un-glorious carnage inside. High on the walls, ancient Scots battle-flags and tattered pipe-banners look down on the scene. A distinctive white-over-black flag is somehow unharmed. He swallows hard to prevent his own tears. Gradually, the firing outside ceases. He sees Sinead being tended by Naveed.

Hearing a voice of authority shouting from outside Sean pulls himself up to better hear.

An English voice shouts, "...throw out your weapons! I want everyone outside with their hands on their heads. You have two minutes to comply or we shall assault the building!

"OK! We'll throw out our weapons first! Hold your fire! Don't shoot!" responds Sean.

Sean, Naveed and some of the wounded, remove the bars at the door. Sean speaks to his remaining men, "We must buy time for Andy and the rest of the lads! Throw out the weapons a few at a time."

The fighters comply. Sean climbs the debris again then suddenly stares down at Naveed and points to the rear door. Naveed merely smiles causing Sean to shake his head angrily at this sole act of indiscipline. He reluctantly returns to the window, "Hold your fire! Weapons then wounded first!"

Stirling

Skull, in civilian clothes, briefs a small group of armed SLA soldiers in a wooded area of a public park. They listen intently then disperse into the darkness. Skull walks quickly from the park into the legendary Raploch area of town. A group of menacing youths stand around under a street-light. As Skull approaches them a shrill whistle pulls in others, hidden in the shadows, to listen. Within a few moments they are jogging as a large intimidating and threatening gang down the street and back into the park.

Stirling Castle

Andy, Will, Tyson and Tom throw black ropes from a barely visible tunnel entrance to the ground from a ledge in the castle rock-face. Six ropes are belayed on the rock ledge floor. SLA fighters queue up in a tunnel which comes out on the ledge where they can see the twinkling lights of a motorway and its traffic in the middle distance. The far horizon holds dark hills and escape. Andy tugs ropes ensuring they are secure whilst Tyson and Tom attach abseiling hooks to the waiting fighters kit. They wait. Andy breaks the silence, "As soon as the diversion begins... we go."

Shortly, sounds of rioting drift up from town nearest the foot of the castle escarpment. Instantaneously police sirens are heard as simultaneously blue flashing lights appear in the distance below. Rifle shots are heard. Andy uses binos to spot rifle-flashes in the area of the rioting where he picks out a small Army patrol being attacked by a mob. Two army vehicles suddenly put their lights on in the area immediately below them and head to the scene. Andy, "The diversion's working! Let's go."

Without hesitation the SLA men hook up and lean out horizontally from the cliffs. Andy gives thumbs-up and they throw themselves backwards, out and into the darkness. In seconds, the first men are on the ground, un-hook themselves and dash forward into the nearest cover. Almost immediately, they are joined by more SLA. In relays, the SLA men are all on the ground. Tyson, Will and Tom hook up and balance themselves ready for the abseil. Andy is motionless but spears them with commands, "Lead the lads to the

Grid Reference I've given you to meet with Skull. He'll lead you into the hills. I'll make sure Sean joins us...now go!"

They stare at Andy disbelievingly. Tyson begins to protest but Tom reaches out an arm to cut him off and flicks his head at the ground below. Tom grabs Tyson who grabs Will, "Let's go... the men are waiting for us!"

They leap off backwards and into the darkness below. Andy picks up his binos and watches the dark shapes scuttle away from the castle and join the others. Together they all head off towards the main road in the middle distance.

Country Lane

Skull hooks up with the SLA escapees in the darkness and brings them at a run to a few battered old vans parked in a sunken, tree-lined lane. He encourages them to get quickly into the vans. Lamps out, the small convoy crawls off along the lane. Undetected, they soon put distance between themselves and the Castle rock.

Great Hall

A large pile of weapons are in front of the main door. A medic waving a white bandage comes out first. Rupert orders him to cross the courtyard towards them. He is ordered to the ground, face down. Badly wounded SLA men and women trickle out of the Hall. Rupert orders forward Brit medics to aid the wounded. Sean and Naveed delay the flow of the wounded to use up time.

Andy joins them from the abseil, telling Sean the break-out was successful.

Foot Of Castle Escarpment

A Brit patrol identifies ropes on the cliff-face. The commander sends a brief radio report causing Brit heads to suddenly appear high above them over the battlements. One speaks rapidly into a radio.

Great Hall Cordon

Rupert is handed a radio hand-set. McCloy and Campbell stand in the shadows near him, watching. Rupert curses horribly, returns the hand-set, then speaks to a sergeant, "It looks as though there's been a break-out from the Hall using a hidden cave system! Get some men, silently, up into some windows and confirm if there are any able-bodied rebels in there."

The sergeant grabs the nearest men, quickly explains, and then watches as they disappear as wounded SLA trickle out of the Hall to where the others lie where the Brits are still very watchful.

Quickly, soldiers return with collapsible ladders. The sergeant leads them to the side of the Hall then quietly extends the ladders up to some windows. Cautiously, soldiers ascend them.

Great Hall

There are only a few stretcher cases left. Andy and Naveed stand guard at the door. Sean limps over to the doctor who tends the barely conscious Sinead. He tenderly takes her hand, "We've got to go now, Sinead. The Doctor will make sure you get to hospital...We have to go...."

The doctor puts his hand on his shoulder and nods in agreement. Sinead sees the gesture and attempts to smile, coughing painfully, "Grand so, sure I'll be smashin'...even the Brits don't shoot wounded colleens...."

The doctor wipes blood from her lips. Sean leans close to her ear and whispers intimately. Her eyes are closed but she smiles again and grips his hand a bit tighter. He tearfully kisses her forehead and stands up.

Brits, discreetly peering through the high windows, observe the scene, un-noticed by the SLA men.

Sean, Naveed and Andy grimly head towards their exit door. The last medic stands in the main doorway to cause a few seconds more delay. As he turns his head to look over his shoulder into the Hall he is suddenly machine-gunned. His bloody body is thrown back into the hall by the force of the impact.

Sean, Andy and Naveed drop into the nearest cover. Grenades appear through the windows and main door. Deafening explosions, shrapnel and smoke fill the Hall. At once, a small group of Brits storm in. The three SLA men, still unhurt, dispatch the attackers. The doctor throws himself over Sinead.

"Get out you two! Get out now!" commands Sean.

Naveed holds up a hand covered in blood from a wound in his side, then laughs. More Brits charge through the door and windows. Sean pulls himself up against a wall. He has no ammo left. In pain-induced desperation, he pulls a highland broadsword from a display above his head and charges the Brits with an ancient battle-cry, "A Beauséant!"

Sean cuts down two soldiers as Andy curses and kneels up on one knee and fires at the same time as Naveed.

Brits fire from the windows above. Sean, Naveed and Andy are thrown screaming to the floor as shots hit them. The firing finally ceases.

McCloy charges into the smoke-filled room with Campbell. Sean, still conscious, sees McCloy slowly approach. He also sees Campbell, with a pistol, walk along the stretcher cases checking for life. He can hear Andy and Naveed choking and moaning with pain. Sean can't move and seems on the verge of insanity in a private nightmare.

McCloy continues towards him as Campbell pulls the dead doctor off Sinead. Campbell grins evilly in recognition and he aims his pistol at Sinead's head. Sinead, in silent agony, weakly tries to lift her arm as if to ward off the shot.

Campbell sneers, "Sinead O'Clare...Ye Irish feckin hoor, ye...."

As Campbell is about to pull the trigger, Sean vainly attempts to reach a rifle. McCloy sadistically stands on Sean's bloody arm causing him to scream in animal pain and leans his scarred face into Sean's whilst grinning like the madman he is.

Rupert enters with a squad of medics. With horror, he is powerless to prevent the barbarism being perpetrated.

Sean's screams of pain and Campbell's pistol shot merge. A single gun-shot wound appears on Sinead's forehead. Simultaneously, blood and brain-matter ooze from the back of her head exit wound dripping onto the floor.

Rupert runs at the laughing Campbell, and barges him to the blood stained deck and disarms him. McCloy shouts at Rupert, "Release that man! We've got work to do!"

McCloy and Rupert angrily square up to each other, sanctimoniously McCloy growls, "Wind your neck in, Mother Theresa, and don't interfere!"

Rupert, furious, "We're not bloody animals! This is not the English way!"

McCloy pushes him out of the way, joining Campbell at the door and leaves. Grime and sweat stained Para NCO's order their men to clear out the remaining rebels to form up the prisoners outside.

About 15 bedraggled Scots prisoners, mostly wounded, are battered into a column and are pushed off to captivity by Paras who have now removed their combat helmets to reveal their famous, but occasionally notorious, red berets.

As they are leaving the vast courtyard down a cobbled and narrow gateway full of watchful and suspicious Paras, a badly-wounded prisoner stumbles and inadvertently kicks a discarded Para helmet lying on the ground.

The helmet spins and skids across the cobbles coming to a stop in front of a group of victorious Airborne soldiers. The helmet tumbled over revealing a macabre, bloody grinning head still inside. A roar of collective outrage spontaneously bellows from the Para captors and within seconds they surge forward to mercilessly batter the Scots rebels with fists, boots, weapons and anything that lay to hand. The Para officers matched the savagery of their men as any possible thoughts of Geneva Conventions disappeared in the frenzied, brutal attack.

The pitiless, callous reality of men who are at the mental and physical edge of screaming fear and terror over a sustained period of combat unleashes the demons and devils of primeval cave-dwelling viciousness and barbarity. Men who are constantly trained in controlled aggression within the Laws of Armed Conflict are, in truth, mere mortals who are DNA'ed to react to insane combat stresses by a natural savagery.

Bloody bayonets flashed in the night sky and stabbed from scarlet fists as the Paras finished their gory paroxysms on the silent blood-spattered corpses of the prisoners to satisfy their death lust.

Gore seeped between the cobbles, in the eventual silence, down the covered ancient Castle tunnel. A grunting, blood-soaked giant of a Para laughs maniacally as he saws an ear from a dead prisoner which he proudly holds up as a disgusting trophy.

Some comrades grinned and began to mutilate more prisoners until a young Scots Para screamed, "Enough you fucking bastards! Enough!" His face contorted with horror turned to his Platoon Commander, "Stop them, Sir! You know this is so fucking wrong!"

"Shut the fuck up, you whinging Jock cunt," was the heartfelt response from the recently minted product of the Royal Military Academy Sandhurst. The lieutenant stared with wide-open yellowing insane eyes at his terrified youthful soldier and grinned, "We are all suffering from recognised mental illnesses, matey. It's a tried and tested legal defence" and laughed. "Embrace this. This is war. This is what we do. It's what you must do to the Kings enemies or fuck off! No English court will convict any of these heroes for smashing this fucking Jock rebellion, you dicksplash!" He turned his back on the quaking Scot and walked away as the insane laughter of his men echoed around the castle walls.

CHAPTER 11

RESISTANCE: SCOTLAND
JUNE 2019

RAF Kinloss: Dawn 0330hrs 30 June

A FARM TRACTOR, towing a very long slurry tanker, chunters towards the main gate protected by alert, armed RAF Regiment airmen. The air is very warm and still, below a cloudless blue sky. Perfect conditions for an effective lethal chemical attack.

The sentries step forward to halt the vehicle which begins to slow down as it swings into the manned check-point. An airmen climbs up to look into the cab and smiles warmly, "Jeezo, lads. Muck-spreading this morning? You two really keep this Station's fields and greens looking fantastic. My father's fields in Cornwall don't look as good as you keep them here!" he laughed in a broad Southern twang, "I won't be searching your flower-wagon, if that's OK?"

Perspiring, the familiar farmers forced a smile in return. The gates opened and the tractor is waved through and heads towards the open expanse of green fields beyond the runways. After a few moments, they stopped which gave both an immediate opportunity to swig some water they had with them in the cab. Noticeably, their hands shook furiously as they drank. Sweat poured down their faces in spite of it being so early in the morning.

The older farmer spoke, "I don't know if I can do this, son. I know we've discussed the how and the why but my Speyside-Malt whisky bravery is wearing off. It'll be a wilful act of mass murder."

"It's no' murder, Dad. It's a war! Just get me up behind the accommodation block where the Guardsmen have been put and I'll do the rest. You're just the get-away driver, OK?" and smiled weakly at his poor joke. His father's ruddy farmers face topped with a tousled grey mop of hair stared back with wretched fear. However, in spite of himself, he put the tractor in gear and headed up to a modern, low, single-storey accommodation block at the rear of the administrative buildings.

As one-time sub-contractors, they had been involved in providing plant and machinery when the accommodation was built a few years ago therefore knew the layout intimately. The farmer drew level with the air-conditioning plant housed in a unit next to the structure and shut down the vehicle engine. The plant was mounted on a banking above ground level which looked down on the accommodation.

His son strongly grasped his father's forearm and said, "You know we have to do this, dad. We can't just let our children be slaughtered like beasts and do nothing." His father looks away, so his son takes the opportunity to slide from the cab and immediately pull an extended hose from the back of the tanker into the gently buzzing air condition unit.

Toxic gases such as Hydrogen Sulphide (H_2S), Carbon Dioxide (CO_2), Ammonia and Methane are produced by bacteria during the decomposition of farm manure slurry. Hydrogen Sulphide gas is poisonous to humans and animals. It is fatal in seconds, one breath is enough. Heavier than air and found at ground level in confined areas particularly on calm days. Normally, it smells like rotten eggs, but high concentrations cannot be smelled. Gas release is greatest when the slurry crust is broken, in the first 30 minutes of agitation, after silage effluent has already been added and stored for several months.

The young farmer and his father were well used to the lethal dangers of their extremely dangerous farm product but were confident in their day-to-day work by preventing harm to themselves and those on their farm. Their cargo had been readied for their own fields in the last few days but whisky fuelled fury at the recent events of the rebellion had caused young Seb to come up with an alternative, deadly, assassin's use.

He concentrates hard as he pulls the extended hose from the tanker to the housed aircon system. His young farmers strength ensured this task was completed quickly without fuss. He then worked away silently during the warm, still summer morning and within a few moments the tanker hose was firmly attached to the accommodation aircon. Using pre-prepared cladding he double-checks there is no escape of the deadly fumes between the tanker and the sleeping soldiers' air circulation system.

He walks back to the rear of the tanker and simply pulled a lever which caused quiet, slow-churning metal arms within the tanker to break the crust of the slurry and slowly agitate the prepared contents. His father did not move from the cab. Thirty minutes later Seb closes off the action. There was complete silence from the accommodation.

During that half-hour, the equivalent of a military lethal persistent chemical weapons agent had seeped invisibly, silently and odourlessly downwards into the Guards accommodation. Heavier than air, it trickled through the ground floor where it was contained within the fire-door systems. Heavy and unmoving, it waited in this killing ground to ambush unsuspecting rescuers. In a deadly few moments, all 89 Guardsman were executed as they slept.

Some rebels would see it as a shitty end, at five o'clock on a beautiful Moray summer morning. Unionists would see it as a dirty way to fight.

Seb climbs up into the cab and his father started the tractor engine. They both held their nerve by spreading the manure over the field as they very slowly head to the main gate which opens for them. They don't stop or acknowledge the cheery wave from the Cornish airman who holds up the mug of tea he was drinking at the guard-room window.

A few miles later they stopped at their farm. Both their cars were parked and packed by their respective wives who were delighted at the surprise Mediterranean holidays their spouses had booked. Changed and showered rapidly they headed off in different directions to Aberdeen and Inverness airports just in time to catch their respective flights. Both wives still interrogated their individual husbands on their car journeys about who would be working the farm whilst they jetted off but eventually gave up, easily. Airside, at the airports, the farmers attacked the malts in their gantry bars rather too aggressively for their wives liking. Typically, being men of few words the wives indulged their coarse farming ways. They would have been less pleased if they had known how much money had been transferred to various European bank accounts by their mass-killer partners and that they would not see Scotland for some considerable time.

All over Scotland rebels fought. Ingenuous lone wolf sniper actions concurrent with well-armed, determined, small groups who employed "shoot-and-scoot" ambushes and IED's battered at Crown forces. Whilst large vicious street gangs from notorious urban housing schemes inflicted continuous heavy losses on the occupiers. Police could only operate with military support. The Army re-learned counter-insurgency lessons the hard way and stopped putting foot patrols on the ground and retreated into their modern armoured vehicles. An officer was quoted by international media as saying, "It's like being incessantly attacked by swarms of highland midges."

The army considered using Apache helicopter gunship tank-destroyers, which had been effective in bailing troops out of similar trouble in recent campaigns.

Fortunately, this has not happened, so far, in spite of embattled, surrounded units screaming for such support. It was only a matter of time before such an iron fist was used.

Scotland had become ungovernable as troops alone cannot re-establish governance. London had only limited, temporary control wherever overstretched demoralized military concentrated. They had many tactical victories but at no stage looked like achieving the strategic effect of total subjugation of insurgents that the BNUP demanded.

It proved very difficult, if not impossible, for the normally successful shows of force, whether patrolling or jet fly-bys, information campaigns, low level diplomacy and hearts and minds improvement of local services and infrastructure to gain any traction with the seething, hatred of a population who had, in effect done nothing wrong.

Scots were astounded at how hard their fellow EU citizens, who lived and worked in Scotland, fought alongside them. No-one, on either side of the Independence debate, had foreseen their fury at being lied to when Brit propaganda told them to vote "No" in the 2014 Independence Referendum in order to retain their EU citizenship. This rage had now been savagely exacerbated further by right-wing military force subjugating their 2018 vote to remain EU citizens in Scotland. Poles, Czechs, Irish, French and Germans became embroiled in the fighting along with many other EU countrymen.

They had all only exercised a democratic right to vote for freedom.

Young, and old, of Scots descent appeared in increasing numbers from Australia, Canada, New Zealand and America to take part, in civilian support roles such as medical, in this democratic struggle. Many had military training and were eagerly welcomed into the SLA.

Stock piling, pre-insurgency, of readily available American and Eastern European weapons through virtually non-existent UK "Customs" controls ensured the SLA were very well armed. IRA smuggling expertise was invaluable.

From the beginning, British Army planning and operations Staff understood the cultural and political environment. The subjugation effect London ordered them to achieve, through body-count attrition, flew in the face of every democratic principle many held which constrained many such fair minded professionals. Their surveillance capabilities, information networks combined with an unrestrainedly, belligerent approach to Special Forces operations were effective, as in Afghanistan, but doubly productive at alienation the population of a modern northern European nation. Indeed a senior British G2 officer, in his Intelligence Analysis report stated, "Had London allowed a Scottish Referendum during the insurgency the Yes vote would now be in the 75%–85% spectrum. It may be anticipated the same figure would be replicated in any similar post-insurgency event."

Drone-strikes and midnight rendition raids provoked a flurry of Edinburgh and Brussels legal challenges that successfully attacked the concept of death and kidnapping being administered by the British state with zero regard to law and citizens' rights on a Scottish level but, momentously, as EU citizens. The British state had no such qualms in Iraq and Afghanistan.

Operational command and tactical conduct of the war continuously understood the underlying political dynamics of the insurgency. They had endless data to feed their campaign metrics which failed to produce even the illusion of progress. Even practitioners and proponents of counter-insurgency, who claim to belong to an expert elite, stopped trying to plough on as they sought to create the conditions for strategic success which continued to elude them. They concluded only a Nazi occupation of Scotland would be success. However, they knew how that would be regarded by the international community as they sought to establish trading deals for British Empire 2.0 post Brexit.

Crucially, the huge cost of the war in British body-bags and Brexit-crushing financial constraints began to wear down the war-mongering appetite of the British public and political classes.

British Ministry of Defence and PJHQ repeated their overstretch errors of Iraq and Afghanistan by fighting two wars at the same time in Syria and Scotland. The British military was again left to its own devices. There was no recognisable London strategy other than to crush the Brexit saboteurs. Political expediency is not strategy. Equally, fighting an insurgency in Scotland, in the manner they had done in Afghanistan and Iraq, was to fail to understand the chameleon like qualities of war. It changes. It is a skilled game of chance.

In contrast, Lt Col Sean McAlpin and the SLA extensively focused and executed the teachings of Prussian master-strategist Claus Von Clausewitz. Many in their citizen ranks were military experts and historians in a manner that they absolutely understood and disseminated the national defence holy-trinity of, firstly, violent emotion through hatred and enmity. Secondly, friction coupled with the play of chance and probability, the "fog of war". Finally, as an instrument of policy. This maelstrom was successfully controlled and directed by Margo McCrindle and Sean through their mutual emphatic understanding of their focus on Independence. The strategy from first and last was always Independence. Anything that did not support their mission was not done. Every method that would achieve this aim was aggressively utilized. Through their leadership teams they effectively and cohesively led the citizenry, Scots government and military. They magnificently pulled together in common national cause in "total war" involvement of the whole country. Scotland's people (civilian and military), wealth and assets were mobilised and directed by government, in defence. They did not have to be in the same room or even acknowledge each other even if the "fog of war" allowed them to. The maintenance of the Aim was all. Scotland, by refusing to be governed by usurpers, used war as an act of force to compel their London enemy to do their will. Recognise Scotland's right to self-determination.

However, there is always cost.

CHAPTER 12

AFTERMATH: DIEGO GARCIA
JULY 2019

Diego Garcia, Indian Ocean: 26 July

A USAF C130 transport plane taxis to dimly-lit military buildings at the end of the runway and stops. The propellers are powering down as the aircraft lowers its rear ramp. Three stretchers carrying wounded men are brought out under armed escort and are taken straight into one of the buildings.

McCloy and Campbell walk down the ramp and are met by an American Army Officer. They salute and shake hands.

The American drawls, "Welcome to the island of Diego Garcia. I've been briefed on what you want to achieve with your three prisoners..."

The American waits for an answer and receives only malevolent stares. They all walk to the building with the American continuing, "You have a free hand. This is not Guantanamo Bay. Guantanamo is for world public consumption. No-one knows the prisoners or you are here."

McCloy responds conversationally, "Quite. The Nazi SS had a concentration camp called Theresianstadt which was purely for international busy-bodies like the Red Cross to inspect... the SS did their real work in secret, remote locations...."

The smiling American agrees, "a brutal but accurate analogy."

They enter a spartan office. Campbell is sitting on the desk.

The American continues, "Your accommodation is in the next building. The prisoners are in separate cells at the end of this block. A doctor will be co-located with you, he's former East German... ex-Stasi. We find him...useful."

McCloy merely nods. The American takes his cue and leaves.

Campbell, chuckles, "Just like the auld days, eh, Boss?... ye remember those Provos we played with in in our romper-room in South Armagh in '89... Feck... those boys could scream."

McCloy is impassive. He puts a leather briefcase on the table beside Campbell.

"Check the prisoners are secure then meet me to discuss how we go about our, em, work. We need as much Intelligence from them as we can. I want to start early in the morning."

Prison Corridor

Campbell looks through iron bars into the prison cells. Sean, Andy and Naveed are sedated and are still strapped in their stretchers. They, their bandages and uniforms are filthy rags. Pleased, he ambles to a heavy metal door which he opens. He switches on a bare light-bulb hanging from the ceiling. A metal bed-frame, with leather straps, occupies the centre of the room. An electrical flex hangs from the ceiling directly over the frame. Buckets of water, a table and chair are the only other furniture. He walks, smirking, along the corridor looking into the SLA men's cells. He leaves the building happily whistling 'The Sash' an infamous Unionist sectarian anthem.

Prison Cells: 27 July

Sean is curled in a foetal position on his stretcher with his hands over his ears. His battered, bloodied face is screwed up with the effort of trying to prevent tortured screams fill his cell.

Andy, catatonic, lies face down on a stretcher in the cell opposite. Appalling burns scars, in the shape of bed springs, run from his neck down to his feet. His bleeding, swollen face is barely recognisable.

Sean's body spasms as he hears a new wave of screams. He pushes fingers into his mouth to unsuccessfully prevent himself from screaming. His mind is breaking. His own screams merge with those of the tortured Naveed.

Unseen by Sean and Andy is Colonel Margaret Ross in the corner of Naveed's torture chamber. She is taking noticeable delight in directing the questioning and noting the answers.

Prison Cell, Night

Silence. Sean cowers in the corner on the floor, filthy, naked, and battered with his wrists and ankles bound – coughing up blood. His body is covered in burns. A very young US soldier enters the cell carrying a plastic bottle, "Water!"

Sean tries to focus on the soldier's voice but continues coughing up blood. The soldier puts down the water, looking sickened. He attempts to give Sean some water from the bottle. Sean drinks deeply and nods his thanks. Sean composes himself. Blood and phlegm run from the corner of his mouth. He tries to speak but only manages to croak which makes him smile, "Do you... like Westerns?"

The soldier recovers his bravado and stands up and away from him, "Yeah – but I don' wanna talk to fuckin' terrorists like you, man."

Sean simultaneously laughs and twists lifting his bound wrists, "How can I hurt you?"

The soldier leans against the opposite white-washed wall and stares at him.

Barely audible, Sean continues, "Have you seen all those Westerns when the Good Guy, starts to doubt the murder of the Indians? Do you ever have doubts, son?"

The soldier responds, "Shut the fuck up – don't try and make me think that you are anything other than a fuckin' terrorist, man!"

Sean stares at the soldiers name tag, O'Reilly. Eventually he says, "Your people didn't take the soup – did they?"

O'Reilly, surprised, "Soup? What are you talking about, man?"

Sean, attempts and fails to smile, "Don't you know the story that during The Irish Famine the Brits would only give starving Irish people scraps of food if they would give up the O' of their name... to Anglicise it?... to Reilly?"

O'Reilly, cautiously and suspicious, "Yeah, my folks said our family refused to change their name. They moved to the States to get away from Brit bullshit like that...."

Sean holds eye contact with the soldier, "Some Brits would consider your people Irish rebels, or terrorists, just for such opinions."

O'Reilly nervously agrees, "S'pose. Hey, quit talking, quit messing with my head! You want me to help you – that it?"

Quietly Sean replies, "No. I'd expect you to do your duty, but there'll come a time, like every other Good Guy, when you will doubt whether you are truly serving freedoms cause."

The cell door crashes open and Campbell storms up to Sean and kicks him viciously in the head, then spins furiously to O'Reilly, "What the fuck do ye think you're doing?! You were told to deliver the water and then fuck off! What's this rebel bastard been sayin' tae ye?"

O'Reilly is intimidated, nervous and now at attention, "Nuthin, sir. I just gave some water."

Apoplectic with rage, Campbell roars into O'Reilly's face, "He's fuckin' terrorist scum! Have nothin' to do with him!"

The young soldier attempts to stand his ground, "You're a fellow Scot! How can you treat him like an animal?"

The comment infuriates his adversary further and he points to Sean, "Don't ever compare me with that piece of rebel shite!"

Spraying spittle with rage, the sadist holds up a tattooed forearm and stabs his finger at a Union Jack flag, "See this, sonny! This is my British Union Jack! That rebel bastard," pointing at Sean, "Rejects my flag and our British crown! He's just like any traitorous Irish rebel bastard and will die for it!"

O'Reilly looks perplexed but recognises the insanity and madness in Campbells eyes. He looks fearfully at Sean's battered, tortured filthy body, "Can I go now... please?"

The crazed Campbell, savagely prods O'Reilly's name tag, and laughs provocatively into his face, "Aye. Fuck off ya wee paddy bastard!"

Prison Cells: Night 28 July

The three rebels, in appalling condition, slump against the bars of their respective cells in order that they can communicate.

Andy, sarcastically, "Is this the part when we all sing a rousing chorus of Flower of Scotland...."

Sean wistfully whispers, "I'm more of a 'Bonnie Banks of Loch Lomond' man...written by another rebel prisoner from the '45...."

Naveeds heads is rolling from side to side. His mind has gone. An inane grin appears on his face as he begins to sing tunelessly at the top of his voice, "Scotland shall be Free". Sean and Andy bow their heads at the horrendous self-inflicted lunacy of their situation.

Prison Courtyard: Dawn 31 July

Three empty graves lie side by side at the end of a small courtyard. Sean and Andy, manacled, are led to stand in front of a grave each. Naveed is dragged because his legs are so badly crippled. A chair is produced and he's strapped to it in front of his grave. They are left alone. They do their best to hold up their heads. A US firing squad, including O'Reilly, marches in and takes post at the opposite end of the yard and faces the three freedom fighters. McCloy and Campbell enter the yard beside the squad.

Whispering, "Nae habeus corpus here, Boss," Campbell snickers.

Sean, on seeing McCloy shouts at him, "Have you no shame you Unionist Quisling bastard?"

Campbell mimics a pistol to his own head. McCloy, grinning, raises his arm, "Present!...Take Aim!...Fire!"

A volley of shots sends the three men sprawling. McCloy undoes his holster, takes out his pistol and walks up to the three bodies. He administers the coup-de-grace to Naveed, then Andy. He shouts laughingly to Campbell, "This is so much easier than I thought!"

McCloy points his pistol at Sean's head.

O'Reilly screams, "No!" and pulls his rifle into his shoulder as the furious McCloy again takes aim at Sean. O'Reilly fires one round between McCloy's eyes. His shocked comrades scatter for cover leaving O'Reilly aiming at Campbell who reacts by trying to pull a weapon from under his jacket. The rifle fires a burst throwing Campbell bloodily to the ground. An American soldier behind O'Reilly crashes his rifle-butt into his head knocking him unconscious.

Tegel Airport, Berlin

Margo McCrindle stepped out of a taxi and walked through the pouring rain into the Departure Halls. Her arrival was noticed by a pair of clandestine German Nazi assassins who had been hired by Margret Ross' fascist financial London City backers.

The pair were plotted up separately in order to cover both possible Security- check gates after McCrindle had checked in to her Glasgow flight. They were both armed with poisonous ricin-filled pellets administered from a hidden pneumatic mechanism within a "Bulgarian" umbrella. This weapon is normally employed by Russian operatives which, in this situation, suited the fascist agenda by potentially diverting the finger of blame to Moscow.

As Margo collected her boarding card and unsuspectingly moved to one of the Security gates a Nazi killer made their move from the coffee bar to intercept her and surreptitiously inject Margo with the fatal ricin in an innocuous walk past.

As the fascist executioner covered the final few metres to his prey, he was intercepted by two huge German counter-intelligence operatives who had posed as undercover security guards and immediately barred his path. Very quickly, silently and without any noticeable fuss the contract killer's arms were pinned to his sides and he was briskly escorted through a nearby airport side-door, disarmed and arrested.

His murderous accomplice, on the other side of the Departures Hall, calmly moved to the exit on seeing the slaying attempt unravel. As she stepped outside the terminal she was similarly accosted and bundled away.

Margo continued airside, blissfully unaware of the actions of officers of the German Bundesnachrichtendienst. Given Germany's notorious history of the Third Reich it is now very aggressively anti-fascist and keeps a very close watch on their activities. In this instance they were assisted by a short communication by the Inverness born head of MI6.

As Margo entered the Duty-Free area, her phone rang and she answered. Surprised at the instructions from the caller, she nevertheless coolly replaced her phone in her pocket and headed to a nearby door marked "Zoll" which she knew to be the German Customs service, where a stern, Customs officer was waiting for her.

She was escorted by him to an interview room where two plain clothes Bundesnachrichtendienst waited for her. "What's going on?" she asked in colloquial German.

"Please do not worry, Miss McCrindle. We are acting on behalf of our Chancellor who has reason to believe the British State does not want your return to Scotland. To that end, we have a private aircraft standing by which will get you directly to where we can ensure you are delivered into safe hands. Are you comfortable with this plan?"

Margo stammered, "Yes. Thank you but I'm sure the London government would wish me no harm," and followed the two agents who imperceptibly winked at each other.

A few hours later the Lufthansa luxury jet landed, as cleared, at Prestwick Airport as a flight for German diplomatic golfing enthusiasts. No UK immigration officials attended the late night flight as the blacked out luxury coach waited on the runway to collect its passengers and headed to a nearby opulent Troon hotel. Waiting to receive Margo were her ministerial team and copious amounts of vintage champagne.

Cabinet Office Briefing Room A (COBRA)

Operation MOSHTARAK. The Inverness lad who had become head of MI6 stood silently beside the large screen, gazing in considered contemplation at these two words, in the unremarkable Whitehall room known as COBRA.

Margaret Ross, the Prime Minister, sat scowling at this former Royal Marine and master strategist. She was surrounded by her hand-chosen political Cabinet sycophants who felt equally uncomfortable and awkward in the presence of this intellectual policymaker.

The military and police officers sat in stony silence as they waited for this briefing to unfold.

The Scot spoke firmly and confidently in very clear Kings English, "Prime Minister, Operation Moshtarak took place in Helmand province, Afghanistan in February 2010. The word Moshtarak means "together" in Dari. I was closely involved in the planning and execution of this Operation. I am using it in order to evidence the advice I am about to give you regarding the insurgency in Scotland.

Before battle had been joined we eviscerated the Taliban tactical command by killing or capturing around thirty insurgent commanders. We went on to achieve demonstrable tactical success but, ultimately, strategic disappointment. Why? Because we consistently achieved military victories but concurrently intimidated, maimed and killed local populace. The Area of Operations became a bleeding ulcer. We were the Taliban's best recruiting sergeant. We couldn't defeat a concept, which for the local population, equated to fighting back against murderous invading foreign troops in their homeland. They saw themselves as Freedom Fighters, not terrorists.

From this Operation we created a faster "targeting cycle" based on rapid exploitation of intelligence from multiple sources. Special operations forces reacted to data gathered on one raid which then fed another team who'd rapidly move on to the next target to gather further intel and eliminate or capture more insurgents. This stopped insurgents being tipped off and going to ground. It massively increased tempo resulting in a monster kill/capture ratio. These techniques originated in Iraq during 2006-8 and were brought to Afghanistan where insurgents were relentlessly pursued. So what?

In the ninety days to 23 September 2010 we killed/captured 285 insurgent leaders and almost 3,000 Taliban troops. The Taliban lost its entire middle layer of management but continued to function. Why? Because you can't militarily defeat a concept called Freedom."

The Prime Minister scoffed at this comment, "Get to the bloody point!"

"The point is, Ma'am. The insurgency in Scotland is unwinnable. As it was in Afghanistan. In Iraq. In Northern Ireland. In Vietnam." This evidence provoked a furious, contemptuous glare from her.

He reached for a large manila envelope and poured a large number of A3 colour photographs from it directly onto the table in front of her and this woman's minions. They showed vast amounts of boxes of ammunition, weapons and supplies in a large number of 20 foot shipping containers. In the corner of each photo was an edition of a Scottish newspaper dated a few days earlier.

"I was sent this. With an Inverness postal stamp to my office in King Charles Street. The SLA want me...and you...to understand they are well supplied with war materiel. Yes, we can analyse these photos and find some, maybe most of this kit, but not all. They are making a statement, Ma'am. They'll fight on as long as there's a Scot to pull one bloody trigger. I suspect they have no problems accessing these small arms given their world-wide proliferation and our open borders. There are also two A4 sheets each with one word. UNGOVERNABLE. MIDGES. Their strategy is plain. They will attack Crown Forces in merciless swarms incessantly until we understand we cannot govern."

"Ma'am, we are both Scots..." which provoked a furious response from her as she leapt to her feet, "Don't you ever ! Ever! Class me with these bloody people. I am British first and always will be!"

He held his ground, allowing the words to wash over him. Calmly, he stated to the Prime Minister and those present, "I consider myself to be British too and proud to have served my country for forty years. But in that time I have seen this same insanity go on and on and on. Victory is no longer possible. To say that we are closer to victory today is to believe, in the face of the evidence, the optimists who have been wrong in the past. To suggest we are on the edge of defeat is to yield to unreasonable pessimism. To say that we are mired in stalemate seems the only realistic, yet unsatisfactory, conclusion. But it is increasingly clear to me that the only rational way out will be to negotiate, not as victors, but as an honorable people who live up to their pledge to defend democracy. Scotland voted democratically for independence."

The senior military and police officers all coolly got to their feet. The chief of the General Staff spoke, "We concur with this analysis. We know the Scots. This insurgency won't stop so we must negotiate immediately and bring this to an end. The army is bleeding profusely both literally and figuratively. It is heart-breaking to see so many of our Scots soldiers joining the insurgency. They are not our enemies. They are friends and comrades who have loyally served their monarch. We must stop now!"

Ross was apoplectic with fury, "You bastards will do as you're fucking ordered! Kill them all! Whatever you have to do! No Surrender!"

"I should also add, Ma'am," the general continued unintimidated," that the Scots Battalion that Lt Cammy McAlpin served with in Syria has now refused to soldier. They serve in NATO Multi-National-Brigade South West" as he indicated MNB SW on a nearby map of Syria. "We hesitate to brand this situation as mutiny as this will undoubtedly exacerbate an already volatile situation... as they...ahem...severely battered the Royal Military Police who were sent to arrest their ring-leaders. Additionally, the other two Battalions within the Brigade are Canadian and Dutch. The Hague has categorically refused to have their Dutch troops even remotely involved whilst the Canadian Battalion happen to be a composite unit based on the Royal Highland Fusiliers of Canada and the Black Watch of Canada. These lads have made clear in no uncertain terms to their Chain of Command that they will resist being ordered to arrest their Scots brother regiment. We are in real danger of having an international incident with Ottowa. It is believed many of them have been involved with the Jocks against the RMP!"

"Ma'am," stated the First Sea Lord. "Your orders are also illegal under the Geneva Conventions. My sailors and marines will not kill any more Scots. Our fleet and Commando Units are 22% Scots. Even if Scotland becomes independent we must continue to recruit in their country in order to sustain the Fleet. As with the Army we are losing manpower overnight. We must negotiate and build our respective societies to live and work in mutual harmony for future generations of sailors and marines."

The military officers left the room to the screeching vehemence of the Prime Minister. Her pathetic acolytes winced and attempted to avoid provoking her wrath by looking away with a couple mumbling ludicrously from the room about needing to visit the rest-room.

The head of MI6 simply said, "It's over. No more killing. I'm going home to my family and friends in Scotland. But know this;

Ye Hypocrites. Are these your pranks? To murder men and gie

God thanks. Desist for shame, proceed no further. God won't accept your thanks for murder[6],"

and left COBRA.

The Hague International Court: 2019

O'Reilly, in civilian clothes, is in the witness stand. UN and EU flags hang in the court. Sean, Tyson, Will, Tom and Skull listen intently. The court is packed with International media.

O'Reilly, points at Tyson, "He was my buddy in Afghanistan. Somebody must've contacted him when I was arrested for shooting McCloy and Campbell. He spoke to people and that's why I'm here... I guess."

The Judge replies, "I understand that you are here against the wishes of the American government?

---

6   Robert Burns, http://www.robertburns.org/works/405.shtml

The American dissident replies, "Yes, sir. Washington doesn't allow US servicemen to appear in international Courts in case the verdict may embarrass them. Like today. The Scottish government offered me honourary citizenship which I'm proud to accept. Everyone should be answerable to war crimes...even the London and Washington governments.... "

Holyrood Palace, Edinburgh: 2020

The sun beats down on the Palace and gardens. Arthur's Seat shimmers behind the stately buildings.

In front of a dais rowed with chairs is a kilted Honour Guard wearing glengarries and sky-blue tunics with white cross belts. A huge crowd looks on, filling the gardens around them.

From the Palace, ornate glass doors open and a group of dignitaries exit and walk to the dais. Pipers skirl and the crowd cheers wildly. The Guard Commander barks a command, flourishes a salute with his broadsword bringing the guard to attention.

Sean, dressed as an Honour Guard, limps awkwardly to his seat beside the other dignitaries, who include Will, Tom, Skull, Tyson and O'Reilly. It is clear from one side of Sean's collapsed face and his withered left arm the broken man has suffered a stroke. He accepts the help offered by his son. They stand as a confident, elegant woman takes her place at the array of microphones in front of the world's media.

Reserve Army Centre, Glasgow

Scots soldiers noisily fill a bar-room. Someone turns up the volume on a huge TV screen hanging on a wall. The volume drowns out the babble and quietens everyone. A title at the bottom of the screen says: Scots Independent TV – SCOTS PRESIDENTS SPEECH, HOLYROOD CASTLE, EDINBURGH.

Margo, Scotland's President, declares, "Scotland stands firmly against the suppression of democracy. Let us be under no illusion, arms are abhorrent to us but they were not taken up by the heroes of the Scottish Liberation Army as a matter of choice – our hand was forced. The ballot box was taken from them by London. I, and my government, are desperately sorry for the families of casualties, both Scots and English, and have put in place measures of compensation. The Scots wounded, both mentally and physically, will be given every support they require from this day, to their last. We owe them for their sacrifice. Abandoning them to their fates is not an option."

When the cheering had died down, she puts down her speaking notes and looks directly at the camera. Her tone changes to one of deep emotion, "It is desperately sad that the Stirling Castle campaign took place. But when any nation is violently subjugated, they have the right to fight back!"

Reserve Army Bar

The Scots soldiers, some of them wounded at the Castle, cheer madly – as does the crowd at Holyrood.

TV SCREEN: the President continues, "Scotland, as a free democratic sovereign nation, upholds the 1945 UN Charter which enshrines the right to self-determination of all peoples of the world! Freedom and democracy must always win out! Totalitarian, reactionary fascism, that the UN Charter sought to ensure would be consigned to the history books, must be resisted everywhere. If we fail to learn from the lessons of history, we are in grave danger of reliving it!"

As the crowd cheers, she turns and invites Sean to speak. He refuses. Nevertheless, he struggles to stand, and the President immediately steps forward to take his arm with a warm smile. He whispers something in her ear, then turns to his son, Will, who becomes extremely embarrassed as she escorts him to the mikes. Will, scarlet with embarrassment, coughs and clears his throat. The crowd is going wild at this massively emotional moment. Those on the stage are beaming.

The Scot stares out at the crowd. His earnest, rugged, scarred, youthful face is projected onto large screens within the Palace grounds, and throughout the world. The crowd falls silent in anticipation. Simply and confidently he states, "Scotland is Free!"

The audience goes wild with the police having trouble in restraining the ecstatic crowds.

The screen switches to public gatherings in city and town centres all over Scotland showing the same rapturous acclaim at Will's words. The next screen shows brief glimpses of the Scots flag, together with many others, outside the UN building in New York and the EU building in Brussels. The screen switches back to Will, who is trembling, "I must pay tribute to the men and women, these Scots martyrs, who gave their lives for our freedom...anyone calling them terrorists will be answerable to this country!" The crowd becomes frenzied.

In the reserve army bar many, many champagne corks pop as the soldiers start to party.

10 Downing Street, London

Margaret Ross is beside herself with rage as she watches the live coverage of McCrindle's speech. She can only endure the first few moments of the Edinburgh celebrations before she switches off the television and then hurls the remote at a wall, causing it to smash and splinter, sending batteries and plastic in all directions.

Her cowed staff observe in silent terror. She goes to the open window of the media room and glowers out to the massive Union Jack flags that drape every lamp-post. Seething with rage, she discerns a beautiful white butterfly resting on her sun-drenched windowsill. Gently, she cups her hand over it then lightning-fast sweeps it into her palm. She views the wonderful, exquisite imprisoned creature through her fingers. Very slowly and deliberately she closes her fingers on it crushing its life.

Lamlash, Isle of Arran: 30 November 2020

The winter sun is setting gloriously in the western sky over the Arran hills, a sea breeze mercifully keeping the air fresh and invigorating.

Three UK nuclear submarines sail south, down the Firth of Clyde, accompanied by a flotilla of noisy flag covered boats.

A small group of mourners stands in a graveyard. Sean, Tom, Tyson, Skull, Rupert and some Scots soldiers accompany two St Andrews flag-draped coffins to gravesides. Fergie, the piper, plays the auld Scots lament, "The Flo'ers o' the Forest", as the coffins are placed on the graveside. Will, his mother weeping by his side, accepts the flag from an officer followed by Sean, who with two walking sticks, awkwardly receives the other. The minister says a few words, then the coffins are lowered slowly into the earth. Sean hirples to Will and his mother and they hug tightly.

Mrs MacAlpin, weeping, "thank you for bringing Cammy and the rest of the boys home, Sean. I'm so sorry about Jill... was it all worth it?"

"Are the people of Scotland worth it?" sighed Sean, "We may as well go to Hell in our own wheelbarrow rather than being pushed there by London."

The group leave the family to grieve as the sun disappears.

POSTSCRIPT

IN 1707 SCOTLAND LOST HER FREEDOM TO AN UNDEMOCRATIC UNION IMPOSED BY A UNPRINCIPLED ROYAL CABAL OF SELF-SERVING ARISTOCRATS.

JUST OVER 300 YEARS LATER, THE PEOPLE OF SCOTLAND ARE RETURNING AS A PEACELOVING FREE NATION INTO THE INTERNATIONAL COMMUNITY.

WOULD LONDON AND WASHINGTON DENY THEM, OR ANY COUNTRY, THEIR DEMOCRATIC RIGHT TO DO SO?

WE ARE ALL SCOTLAND'S STORY.

Lightning Source UK Ltd.
Milton Keynes UK
UKHW01f2052040718
325243UK00002B/48/P